"I'D LIKE YOU TO COME BACK TO NEW YORK," ANDREW TOLD HER.

"And move back to my prison?" Lorna inquired dryly. "With no one around but a pack of watchdogs at my door?"

"Lorna, you were under protective custody, and besides, you're the one who said you didn't want company."

"I wanted only yours," she admitted softly.

"That's funny. I could swear I was distinctly told that I was not welcome on a few occasions."

Her temper rose. "You used me, Andrew; you used the entire situation. I witnessed a murder and you knew I was frightened and alone. How could you? You were supposed to be protecting me!"

"I did protect you."

"Is that what you call protection? That's a nice job you have, Lieutenant Trudeau. Very accommodating."

Andrew felt the urge to shake her, to force her to admit that she had wanted him as badly as he had wanted her, that she still did.

CANDLELIGHT ECSTASY SUPREMES

AN ANGEL'S SHARE

Heather Graham

A CANDLELIGHT ECSTASY SUPREME

Published by
Dell Publishing Co., Inc.
1 Dag Hammarskjold Plaza
New York, New York 10017

For Lori Durso Winke

To Our Readers:

Candlelight Ecstasy is delighted to announce the start of a brand-new series—Ecstasy Supremes! Now you can enjoy a romance series unlike all the others— longer and more exciting, filled with more passion, adventure, and intrigue—the stories you've been waiting for.

In months to come we look forward to presenting books by many of your favorite authors and the very finest work from new authors of romantic fiction as well. As always, we are striving to present the unique, absorbing love stories that you enjoy most—the very best love has to offer.

Breathtaking and unforgettable, Ecstasy Supremes will follow in the great romantic tradition you've come to expect *only* from Candlelight Ecstasy.

Your suggestions and comments are always welcome. Please let us hear from you.

Sincerely,

The Editors
Candlelight Romances
1 Dag Hammarskjold Plaza
New York, New York 10017

PROLOGUE

The strangest thing was that she knew it was a dream. She always knew that she was dreaming when she saw the old lady, and yet she was helpless to stop the onslaught of events.

She saw it all as one might see an old photograph. The center was clear, but the edges were blurred, framed by a gray mist.

She knew exactly what was going to happen, like a scene in a play that was acted over and over again, except that this was no play. In the theater of her mind, the story unfolded in the netherlands of memory. The events had been a nightmare; experiencing them again was doubly so. Not even from the cocoon of sleep could she escape the details. She recalled every sight and sensation, what she had heard, seen, and felt, the fear and the anger. And she knew, as always, that Andrew would come into the dream to comfort her with images of the time they had spent together. Magic would caress the canvas with the touch of a sable brush, but then magic would combine in a swell of emotion that was as painful as the initial fear.

She saw herself walking down the street. Wearing a small black hat with a feather plume, a black jacket and blue knit dress, she sauntered through the center of the picture. She had been in no great hurry. She had been absorbing the pulse and the glow of the city. She knew the streets of New York and loved them. Broadway, Times Square, street vendors, and street people. An area where mink and denim could mingle easily.

She had come to New York for life, and New York had not failed her. It had taken her a long time to get over the shock of her husband's death, probably because it had been so stunning. Jerod Doria had been a fit and healthy thirty-three, a man in his prime. Even after the automobile accident, he had been fine, impatient with suggestions that he should take it easy. Then, exactly one week after the accident, he had given her a peculiar little smile over the rim of his coffee cup and pitched to the floor. He thought he'd done no more than bruise his temple in the accident; the doctors told her that the slight bruise had brought on a cerebral hemorrhage.

He'd gone into a coma and his eyes had never opened again. He had just slipped, day by day, until the nurse had taken his hand from hers and told her that he was dead.

For a long time she had needed to be alone. Then she had needed to work. And then, about a year after the accident, she knew that she needed to get away. She chose New York, and New York had chosen to give her the magic that she needed. She was still mourning for Jerod, but in New York she had learned that she was still alive, she was young, and the threads of her existence could be picked up. She had longed for a cure, and the cure was hers. It had come with the hot dog vendors and the neon lights and the eternal, bustling pulse of the city. She was happy to be alive, exhilarated by the night.

She walked for the simple enjoyment of walking, of listening and feeling. It was a Sunday evening and the lovely, melodious church bells had been chiming. The sky had remained an unusual azure blue throughout the day; the night still carried something of its darkened beauty. It was beautiful, and the woman who walked had little on her mind except the night, a newfound joy in her independence, and the resignation that had at last set her free.

The sleeping Lorna knew what was about to happen. She tossed and turned, but there was no way to warn the woman in the mist-framed dream. She remained oblivious to the encroaching danger.

The Lorna who walked noticed the car with mild interest. It was a dark sedan, just like the others cruising along the street, honking and chaffing in traffic like a team of horses worrying their bits. This car pulled to the curb and parked. She gave it little notice. The sedan was just part of the street scene.

Then she noticed uneasily that she was alone on the sidewalk. People thronged the block ahead of her and she could hear the laughter of a crowd of teenagers behind her. But there was no one on her block. Not in the immediate area. In the distance, Times Square loomed in neon splendor, but here . . . here she was alone. Or almost alone. Someone was moving toward her, close to the fence that enclosed the rubble of a demolished building. The Lorna in the dream felt a little shiver of apprehension. Nothing major. Just a little chill. Unknowingly, she caught her breath, but soon released it.

It was just an old lady, a short, wrinkled woman with bright, velvety brown eyes. She wore an old-fashioned pillbox hat, but there was something so lovely about her that Lorna had to smile. The tiny old lady had a spritely walk. She was an endearing creature. Lorna thought she looked as if she had just come from church, and that thought made her smile deepen because the woman looked liked such a staunch pillar of society and yet she was so tiny! Lorna opened her mouth to say hello.

The word became a horrified scream.

Suddenly there was movement on the street. A flash, a streak, a whirl of dark color that came at her so quickly she didn't fully comprehend what was happening.

The whirl was a man dressed in black, his features hidden by a ski mask. He didn't see Lorna; she was in the shadow of the fence. He rushed past her, not coming toward her at all, but racing for the lovely old woman.

For a moment Lorna saw him very clearly—for what little good it did her. He was of medium stature, heavily built but quick. She saw the clothing and the ski mask—ridiculous for the New York streets. Then it seemed as if the film of the dream had been speeded up and distorted. Things came in a jumble. Lorna kept screaming as the man in black raised his arm. He carried something that looked like a heavy flashlight. His arm came down. The old woman with the beautiful eyes was lying on the sidewalk. The man in the ski mask turned and looked at Lorna. From a distance she heard shouts. Whistles started to shrill and horns were blaring. Heavy footsteps were pounding on the sidewalk.

The masked attacker took a step toward her. Dimly she heard church bells still chiming. The sound seemed incongruous, coming as it did along with the ruthless stare of the figure in black.

Both the woman sleeping in the bed and the woman in the unfolding scenario saw his eyes. Not the color or the shape, but the ruthless and lethal gleam directed at her.

She turned to run, but something struck her on the head. She felt a blinding pain and saw the sidewalk

12

rushing up to meet her. The pavement caught her knee, ripping her stocking and scraping her flesh. She was stunned, and yet she lay in horror and fear, wondering if he would strike again.

Then a voice called out from the car. *"Let's go!"*

Instinctively she looked at the car. The door to the sedan opened and Lorna saw the driver. He shouted something to the black-clad assailant, and the man gazed at Lorna one last time. Instinct again took over and she closed her eyes, an inner mechanism warning her that she shouldn't let these men know she had seen anything.

The attacker ran to the car and the door was slammed shut. The driver gunned the engine, then the car screeched into the traffic.

Sirens kept wailing and the footsteps kept coming closer. Against the pain in her skull she opened her eyes.

Fear coiled in her stomach once again. There was another man coming toward her, one with long, unkempt hair, dark hair that fell to his shoulders. A dark, tangled beard covered his lower face. He wore tattered jeans and scruffy boots. The heels of his boots caught at the hems of the jeans, adding to their ragged appearance. His flannel shirt was worn and wrinkled, his denim jacket was patched and missing buttons.

She closed her eyes as a shudder rippled through her. She could hear the sirens and knew help was coming through the night, but not soon enough. The man would reach her first. The man who looked like the type of down-and-out bum one would find sleeping on a park bench at night, or curled up over a heat vent, an empty wine bottle in a brown paper bag at his side.

He was moving toward her, like a vulture coming to finish off the kill after a lion had taken its fill and gone on its way. A bum . . . no, not a bum. Bums were not built like this man, tall and lean, yet well muscled, rugged, and agile.

She opened her mouth to scream, but the cry died in her throat when she saw his eyes. They were warm and green, filled with tension and concern. And beneath his ragged and tattered beard, she saw the structure of his face. Lean features, defined and powerful: a high forehead, dark arching brows, sharp, wideset eyes, a straight nose, and high cheekbones. His lower face was covered by the fringe of his beard, but she could see beyond that to a strong, square chin. And she shivered when she saw his mouth. It was grim now, frightening. But she could imagine it twisting into a grin, full of laughter and sensuality . . .

In a matter of moments she had gone insane, she thought, nearing a state of hysteria. He was getting ready to kill her or rob her or both—and she was thinking that his features were strikingly handsome, that he was the most arresting man she had ever seen. A Skid-Row bum who looked like he had been pulled out of the nearest gutter!

She stared into his eyes. The moment of time encapsulated her; it was the strangest feeling, the most absurd sensation. But it was there, holding her mute. Her past didn't matter at all, not the pain, not the laughter. This moment mattered. All that had come before in her life meant little, it had been nothing more than a waiting period. Life for her had not been meant to begin until this moment, until this man.

He reached into his jacket and the moment disappeared as if it had never been. Lorna gasped as sanity returned. Once again she was staring at a man who appeared to be reaching into his pocket—to secure a knife or a gun?

She opened her mouth to scream again.

All that came out was a little whimper. He had

14

reached for a handkerchief, snow white and clean. He dabbed at her forehead and asked, "Are you all right?" His voice was low and cultured. She nodded.

"Well," he drawled, and she saw that she had been right. His mouth was sensual when it curled into a wry half grin. "Not meaning to be rude, but you really don't look all right. They'll take you into emergency. And there'll be questions, of course."

Lorna realized that there were men all around them then. Men in blue with shining badges. Red lights were flashing in abundance from the street. Some policemen were running to the other woman, others were grouping around Lorna.

"Oh, God!" someone exclaimed. "It's Mrs. Simson. And she's—"

Lorna didn't hear the rest. Someone had shushed the man. But with a horrible chill, she knew. The woman who had been walking toward her, with the lovely sharp eyes was dead.

"Simson!" the ragged man rasped out.

Lorna didn't understand it at all, but apparently a vast mystery had just been solved for this stranger.

"Who are you?" she asked hoarsely.

He looked at her and smiled. "Andrew. Andrew . . . McKennon. You'll be all right now. These men will see to you." As he stood one of the officers lowered himself to his knees at her side. Lorna blinked, then saw that the rag-tag bum was disappearing into the crowd.

The picture distorted suddenly. She was no longer lying on the sidewalk; she was being helped into an ambulance. Another skip in time, natural in the dream, and she was in a hospital room. A detective was talking to her, a kindly, middle-aged man in a blue suit.

"We've been after this man for a long, long time,"

he told her, and she realized he was pleading. "He's been robbing women around the churches for months." He hesitated. "His first victim died. And now . . . well, Mrs. Simson is dead too. We need your help."

There was a police artist at her bedside. She described the man who had attacked her and the man in the car.

The men were silent when they saw the likeness—dead silent.

"Do you know who this is?" someone asked her harshly. Innocently she shook her head, and they let her go to sleep.

When she woke up, there was a priest beside her. A tall, devastating man with extremely dark, compelling hazel eyes. Her heart did a little flutter.

"Hi," he said.

"Hi."

He looked familiar. How? If she had ever met him, she wouldn't have forgotten him. She noted that his eyes were warm, but also sorrowful. He smiled at her gently. "My name is Lucien," he told her, "or Father Trudeau. Or Luke. Whichever you prefer."

"Father?" Lorna lifted a skeptical brow, and then she smiled too. "I didn't know I was hurt that badly. Am I dying?"

"No. You're fine."

"Oh, I see." Lorna laughed. "You're really an undercover cop."

His smile deepened as he shook his head a little ruefully. "No, I'm really a priest." He hesitated. "Mrs. Doria, you witnessed a murder last night and your descriptions helped solve the mystery to a rash of crimes. Your testimony may not be enough, but it may help to put away a cold-blooded murderer." He hesitated again. "It isn't easy to be a witness, Mrs. Doria."

16

Lorna watched him uneasily. He had spoken softly, but with an underlying passion that was both frightening and puzzling.

"I intend to testify," she murmured.

"Good. Thank you," he said. Then he stood, touching a lock of her hair that had fallen over her forehead. "If I can ever be of any assistance . . ." His voice faded, and he smiled again. He was very attractive. She felt again as if she knew him.

The woman in the bed in Paxton, Massachusetts, tossed as the dream moved onward. Night passed to day in a single picture and she was leaving the hospital. Suddenly there were scores of reporters all around her.

"We hear, Mrs. Doria, that you're accusing Mrs. Simson's grandson of conspiracy in her murder."

"You're attacking one of the biggest men in the state—"

The middle-aged detective was there, swearing furiously. "Who leaked this information?" He was raging. "Damn, if everything isn't ruined before we can even get started!"

It was then that the shot rang out. It might have come from anywhere—the street was full of many-storied buildings with scores of windows.

"Get down!"

The reporters were screaming, running for cover. The police were scrambling around. Lorna stood in a daze.

A second shot rang out. "Hey! Down, come on!"

Someone was pulling her arm, tugging her down. She turned to see the rag-tag bum. Andrew McKennon. Except that he didn't look like a bum anymore. He was in a business suit. He wore it well; the shoulders were wide, and his waist appeared very narrow. He still sported his beard, but his too-long hair was

17

clean and neatly groomed. Today he might have been a poet left over from the turbulent sixties. He pulled her along into the backseat of a blue sedan.

"Go, Gary. Let's get out of here!" he ordered to the driver.

The car shifted smoothly into gear and sped down the street. McKennon pulled back his jacket and Lorna saw his gun holster.

Oh, my God! What now? she wondered. Had he dragged her into the car only to kill her himself? Had she been a fool to follow him?

She swallowed convulsively as he stared at her. And then he grinned reassuringly, as if he had read her mind.

"I'm a cop, Mrs. Doria. I should have introduced myself better last night. It's just that I was trying to hold on to a cover."

"Oh," she murmured, still not understanding.

And then he began to explain.

Months before, a series of robberies had begun. "Church robberies," the police were calling them. Single women were being mugged all over the city on their way home from services. One, he told her very stiffly, had died after the mugging. And now Mrs. Simson was also dead.

Mrs. Simson had been very wealthy, the director of a large, affluent corporation. It appeared now that her grandson had carefully planned all the muggings to make the murder of his grandmother appear to be a chance tragedy. The grandson inherited everything.

"But if you know who he is—" Lorna began.

"The D.A. says we haven't got enough yet," Andrew McKennon told her briefly. "Mrs. Doria, that's extremely bad news for you."

"I don't understand."

"I think it's rather obvious. Simson knows that you

18

saw him and can identify him. He's going to try to kill you. He did try to kill you just now."

Terror descended upon her, swirling and settling with a terrible freeze. She realized then the scope of what she had innocently walked into. Simson was ruthless. And reckless. It seemed he was determined to kill her.

"The picture isn't quite as bleak as it looks, Mrs. Doria. We intend to see that you stay alive."

"Thanks," Lorna muttered tersely. She looked him straight in the eyes. "So that I can testify for you, I take it."

His smile faded. "No—because it's our job to keep the innocent alive."

"Well, then, what do I do? Buy a large German shepherd? Install a security—"

"You don't have to do anything. We'll do it." He hesitated. "I'm afraid I'm going to have to take you into protective custody."

"Protective custody? I don't really understand."

She was about to.

Andrew McKennon took her to a small apartment. While she sat on the couch, he started to ask if she wanted a beer. He stared at her a long time and then changed his mind. "A glass of wine?"

She was puzzled by his obvious change. Did the fact that he assumed she would like wine mean anything? He was very businesslike, supplying her with a drink before excusing himself to make a few calls. Lorna took the opportunity to write a note to her friend, Donna Miro. She stared at the note, realized it didn't really say anything, and then shrugged. She felt that she had to say something to someone. Donna was her best friend and the closest thing she had to family in the world. There was a mail chute out in the hall—she had seen it coming in. Lorna decided she would slip

19

out quickly while McKennon was still on the phone. She had barely watched the letter slide down before a hand clamped down on her shoulder.

"What the hell are you doing?"

McKennon was furious.

So was Lorna. She was willing to help the police, but she'd be damned if she was going to be pushed around by them. "I was just taking a look—"

"Well, don't! Don't step out of my sight until I've got you settled."

"Mr. McKennon, I don't think—"

"Right, Mrs. Doria. *Don't think!* Just sit tight—in my full view. Lady, I really don't want to see you splattered on the streets."

The dream flipped pictures again, and she was standing in a different apartment that contained a bedroom, a kitchenette, and a den.

It would become a prison. She sensed it the minute she stepped into it. She knew that she needed to be protected, but she also knew that protection would exact a price.

Lorna wanted to help nail Simson, to testify against him, but they wanted her to live in three small rooms. To make matters worse, she heard Andrew McKennon talking to the officers in the hall. He sounded weary, which made his words all the more irritating.

"Seems we have a socialite on our hands. You've got your work cut out for you. It's going to be a hell of a job watching her!"

Let's trade places, Lorna had thought furiously. I'll roam the streets and stop by occasionally while they lock *you* up in a den.

Andrew did come by—occasionally—and she was polite. She wasn't about to give him any excuses to call her a socialite again.

But she couldn't remain polite as the days became

weeks. The walls seemed to close in on her. Eventually she began to wonder how much longer she would stay sane. She started fighting with Andrew McKennon. Apparently he felt a responsibility to report to her, but all he could ever say was that they were "close" to Simson.

The Lorna on the bed in Paxton shifted uneasily in her sleep. It was coming. The night they had the terrible fight . . .

The night they made love.

He was furious when he arrived with a pizza and a bottle of burgundy. Donna Miro had appeared in the city, alarmed by Lorna's note and determined to find her. Thanks to Lorna's idiocy, Donna had almost been mugged. And what was worse, Donna had been so determined to find Lorna that she had left a trail across half the city. Donna was driving the police insane—and drawing danger down upon herself.

Lorna was horrified; she loved Donna like a sister and wouldn't have hurt her for the world. But damn it, didn't this idiot cop realize that she already felt bad enough? Did he have to rub it in?

Lorna had never seen Andrew so mad. He was shouting at her.

"Airhead! Lorna, what the hell do you think this is, cops and robbers? Oh, my God, what an airhead!"

Airhead!

"You're the airhead, Andrew McKennon. How long have you had? My life has been threatened and the city of New York wants to help me, but what do I get? A real-life Inspector Clouseau with brawn for brains that he sits on! Don't you come in here and rip into me for mailing a letter!"

He stared at her as if he were going to explode. She backed away from him, suddenly remembering that he was a New York cop who worked the streets. Rough streets.

"Inspector Clouseau?" he repeated. His eyes narrowed sharply, a telltale pulse ticking away in his neck. "And I sit on my brains, do I?" Suddenly he laughed. He turned away from Lorna and opened the burgundy, poured himself a glass and sipped it. "Inspector Clouseau?" he said once again, looking at her, perplexed, over the rim of the wine glass. "That's really a low blow, Lorna."

She started to laugh too. It was laugh or cry, and the pizza was getting cold. So they ate the pizza. They argued over politics, then religion. They even argued over the weather. And yet, through all the arguing, Lorna realized that she wanted him to stay. She felt more alive, more exhilarated, more attuned to life, arguing with him than she had felt at any time in her life. They drank the whole bottle of burgundy. Its potency had been like fuel to a fire.

The hour grew late. Andrew started glancing at his watch and she realized she didn't want to be left alone again.

She started to shiver. Andrew told her that he had to leave, but if she would feel more secure, he would wait until she was in bed. She hurried into the bath to change. And suddenly she heard a loud rumbling noise. She screamed and raced out of the bathroom right into his arms, forgetting all their arguments, forgetting completely that he considered her an airheaded socialite and that she had convinced herself that he was nothing more than brainless muscle.

His arms wound around her. His voice was gentle, the most soothing sound she had ever heard. "It was just a truck, Lorna, just a truck. Don't you realize I'm just trying to save your life?"

She hadn't answered him; she had just stared into

his eyes, and that feeling of having waited her whole life for him to come to her was with her again.

The dream played out the next scene with distressing clarity.

She was naked; he was naked. The heated passion of all their arguments transferred to their kisses, breaking out like a storm that had threatened and simmered too long. She could see him so clearly as he had come to her that night, more beautiful naked than he could ever be clothed because he was taut and bronze and lean and excitingly male in the dim light of the bedroom. She could feel the soft brush of his beard against her flesh, the touch of his lips. Hot and thrilling, exploring her, knowing her. She could breathe his scent, simple and clean, revel in the slightly rough, slightly tender touch of his hands over her, all over her.

She had made love before, she had been married. She had loved her husband, but Andrew made her feel as if it were the very first time, as if she had been awakened from innocence. She reached peaks she had never known existed and found a complete, new intimacy.

When it was over, she was ready to curl into his arms, but he turned away from her. She saw his naked back, his head bending away from her. And then he stood, slipping silently back into his clothing.

"Damn you!" he hissed.

But the worst of it was that he looked at his watch. "I'll talk to you soon," he told her, his voice blunt. He was gazing at her, but she couldn't see his eyes. His voice softened. "No letters, no nothing, Lorna. You'll blow the whole thing."

Her flesh still carried the sheen from their lovemaking. She thought that she would burst into tears. He was going to walk out on her. It was as if—as if it was all false. There was nothing between them. She was a feminine body and she had thrown herself at him and he hadn't done anything but follow his male instinct.

She wanted to die. To fade into the covers and die the slow, agonizing death of mortification. Undercover cops didn't fall in love with their wards. But she had been foolish enough to fall in love with an undercover cop.

She rolled over. "Get the hell out of here, Andrew. I won't do anything else to blow your case. I can't go anywhere—the boys in blue are always at the front door. But don't you dare come back."

He left.

The priest came back a few days later and Lorna was glad to see him. He was dressed in jeans and a pullover. He wasn't just handsome, he was nice. And he didn't come to question her or bolster her up as a witness. He just came to play cards or share a little wine; to entertain her and to keep her from being so terribly lonely.

She thanked him for coming, grateful for his company. If she'd had a little more company, she might not have made such a fool of herself with Andrew. Or was that true? If she were honest with herself, Lorna would admit that she would have fallen into Andrew's flame no matter what. She didn't choose to be honest with herself.

Father Luke Trudeau watched her, hesitating. "Lorna, I'm not a disinterested party. My wife was the first victim," he said softly.

"Oh!" She gasped. "I'm so terribly sorry."

"Do you still want me to stay?"

"Yes."

He smiled and redealt the cards. As he bowed his head, she stared at him again, something uneasy growing within her.

24

"Why do you remind me so much of that cop?" she asked sharply.

He glanced up, frowning quizzically. "Andrew?"

"Yes, Andrew McKennon."

He laughed out loud, tossing the cards on the table. "I guess we should look a little alike. We're brothers."

"Brothers? His name is McKennon."

"Just a street name, Lorna. Drew works undercover and he, uh, well, he's really trying to keep a cover for this case because my wife's name was Trudeau, of course. It was in all the papers."

"I see."

Lucien Trudeau looked down then up. He smiled at her, and she felt her heart warm to him. He was a strong man, able to quickly hide his own feelings for her benefit. He didn't want her to feel alone, or threatened, or unhappy.

Lorna tried. She managed to smile stiffly. "Oh." She looked down at the table. "Deal the cards again, will you, Luke?"

He did so. When he left, she ripped her pillow to pieces in torment. She really wanted to help Luke Trudeau. She understood his loss. She even understood that this case was special to Andrew. His sister-in-law had been the innocent victim of a calculating murderer. But it hurt too. From the very beginning, Andrew's interest in her had been manipulative. She was instrumental in pinning Simson. Yes, he wanted to save her life, it was his duty. Had he not meant to go so far as to seduce her?

Lorna wanted to think sanely, to behave as an adult. But as the time passed, she started to write out the words: I hate Andrew McKennon. Or Drew Trudeau. I hate them both.

What a childish thing for an adult woman who had once considered herself mature and sophisticated to

25

do. It was the time, she rationalized, the never-ending time and the horrible loneliness, the feeling of being imprisoned by the walls that hemmed her in more and more daily.

Andrew came back. There was a knock on her door and she opened it to see him standing there. Had he been out on a date? He was wearing a suit that was wonderfully tailored. He was still shaggy, but no amount of shag could ever hide the arresting quality of his features. She despised him for looking so good.

"Go away," she told him, trying to close the door in his face.

He caught it with his hand and leaned against it, his eyes narrowing. "I thought you might like to know that your friend Donna is marrying my brother."

"What?"

"You heard me. Your friend is marrying my brother. It's a long story, but, well, they're getting married."

Lorna was stunned. And then thrilled for Donna. Yes! She would be perfect for Luke Trudeau.

Andrew was still standing there.

"Thank you," she said coldly. "When and where, please?"

A shield fell over his eyes. "Don't think that you're going, Lorna. You may be willing to set yourself up for target practice, but I'm not about to let you get killed."

She smiled. "I just want to know when and where. Donna is my closest friend, you know."

"And Luke is my brother, but I'm not risking an appearance."

"I just asked—" Her voice was rising. He answered her curtly, called her a "stubborn airhead," and left her.

She eluded her guard and went to the wedding, but

she never did get to see Donna. Lorna's nerves were so taut that she ran from the very person she was trying to see only to run right into a furious Andrew.

His face was white when he confronted her. He'd practically dragged her back to the apartment. She was hurt and angry and so emotionally charged that she fought his hold like a tiger as soon as the door to her elegant cell had closed.

"You might have been killed!" he raged, ignoring her blows.

"I don't care any more, I don't care . . ." she cried out, and then her energy drained and she was leaning against him sobbing.

He picked her up and held her, making her feel cherished and loved. "You do care . . . and I care, Lorna, I . . ."

And it happened again. The ferocity of anger became something very wild and beautiful. But it was painful too, deeply painful, because she couldn't understand herself, she couldn't understand him, she couldn't understand the bitterness. They were so furious, so passionate, so totally uncontrolled.

She wanted herself back, a Lorna she understood: a mature woman who never bickered or railed childishly, someone who would never consider going to bed with a man she so heatedly detested. A man who didn't need her and couldn't cherish her. A man who again stood up, raking his fingers through his hair, and apologized in a subdued and husky tone. Apologized!

Dreams . . . the last scenes were playing themselves out.

She couldn't see him but she could feel the touch of his fingers on her shoulder. He had apologized. Oh, dear God—apologized! Somehow it just made it all the worse. He called it a mistake, and she was still quivering, still fully aware that he could touch her like no

27

other man. With him she became a woman of warm and giving passion, abandoned, delighted, excited, and thrilled until she touched the sure-fire heat of the sun.

And he was apologizing.

"Lorna . . ."

"Andrew, leave me alone. Please, just leave me alone."

"Lorna, you don't understand. This isn't right, and I know that it isn't right, but you—"

"If you've any decency at all you'll understand that I never want to see you again."

"Now wait a min—"

"You stupid *cop!* Get out!"

She could still see his face so clearly. His eyes narrowed to glittering emerald slits, his jaw hardening to stone. Cold stone.

"Have it your way, Mrs. Doria. Cops just don't make the grade, do they?"

Mercifully the mist rose to obscure his features.

And with a start, the woman sleeping restlessly on the bed in Paxton awoke, trembling with misery.

She picked up the flower vase on her nightstand and sent it hurtling against the fireplace. It crashed with a furious sound. "I'd like to knock his head against a wall!" she shouted.

Absurdly, it made her feel better. Lorna Doria, she reminded herself, was a mature woman. She had common sense, a cool philosophy, and poise. She never allowed things to ruffle her.

Not things. Just Andrew Trudeau.

She walked to the fireplace and gazed woefully at her vase. It had been one of her favorite Au Pierre pieces.

Tears glazed her eyes. Why, she wondered, a silent moan wrenching her heart, did this man have such powers to change her, to hurt her?

CHAPTER ONE

Art Deco.

As he stood on the sidewalk looking through the glass at the woman and her handsomely appointed store, they were the first two words of description that came to Andrew Trudeau's mind.

Like her *objets d'art* from that period, Lorna was smooth and sleek. Tall and poised, with a unique grace of stance and movement, she was all elegance. Her hair was a gleaming blond, worn in a short, sleek wave that complemented the clean and graceful lines of her features. Her eyes were blue, the sky blue of a cloudless day. They could be cool, sharp, and astute; they could challenge and defy with a sizzle of fire and ice. Andrew could also remember—vaguely, he reminded himself, and not without an ironic bitterness—that the blue in her eyes could soften to a powdery shade and, when her luxurious lashes half fell to shield them, she could look at a man with such sweet and sultry abandon that it made him ache with longing and a thirst only she could slake.

He shifted from foot to foot, thoroughly disgusted with himself. She was a job, nothing more, he reminded himself.

Liar! a voice inside him charged. From the moment he had first seen her lying on that sidewalk, she had been something more. He should have been sympathetic but impersonal. He had spent enough time on the streets to know that you couldn't become involved. . . .

He had become involved. Not realizing it himself at first, he had become more enchanted with each visit to the apartment where Lorna Doria was housed. He hadn't been able to stay away.

He was a cop, had been her protector. He was a professional . . . Yeah, professional.

Andrew felt the bitterness again. He had let himself forget that once—no, twice. Twice he had forgotten all sense of duty, forgotten all sense of right and wrong, of obligation. He had glanced into her beautiful blue eyes when they had been wide and frightened, stripped of all restraint and liquid with her need to trust, to reach out. She had needed something, to feel protected, or perhaps cherished, or perhaps she had needed only a sense of security. And he had fallen. Damn, how he had fallen. He had trembled when he touched her, as nervous as a kid out on his first date.

He shifted again uncomfortably. Just thinking about her made him flush with a sudden heat. His hands were clammy and something coiled tight and hot within him. He shook his head slightly, as if by doing so he could shake away the disturbing recurrence of desire.

He stuck his hands into the pockets of his trench coat, clenching his fists. "I never met such a shrew in my life," he muttered aloud, determined to shrug away the knowledge that he wanted her still, just as he had since that first time he had seen her and every day after that. The feeling had been with him day and night, when he worked and when he slept, distracting him. . . .

And now he was back, watching her and trying to

convince himself that he could swallow all his emotions and do the job properly. Could—and would.

He remembered their absolute fury and how it had culminated ridiculously in the two of them in one another's arms. He still didn't know quite what happened; he was just so damned . . . beguiled by her. She could ignite his passions and make him shake with the strength of his desire. He had wanted her, needed her so badly that nothing else on earth mattered.

Andrew stiffened. He'd apologized, hadn't he? It hadn't all been his fault—she had been a sweet blaze of fire herself. But even though he'd tried to tell her how sorry he was, she'd been furious at him again, ordering him out and reminding him that he was a "stupid cop." Her and her damned superiority. He'd like to wring her superior little neck!

Andrew's jaw twisted and locked as he stared in the window.

He was good enough for her to fool around with when there was no one else, but offer to set her free and she was gone with the speed of a lark. Not that he'd tried to see her after Simson had been jailed; he'd crawled out of his brother's window to avoid seeing her. At that point, he had had no intention of inflicting his presence on a woman who considered him nothing more than an earthy and stupid cop.

But that was then and this was now. She might hate him; she might rather greet Frankenstein's monster than him, but, by damn, she was going to have to accept things. He was going to play it light and cool—and mercilessly determined. Whatever she had to say, he'd go after her implacably, he thought grimly. His case—and her life—depended on it.

Andrew hesitated again.

No, she definitely wasn't going to be pleased to see him, he thought dryly. Ah, well, cops were a little bit

31

like mailmen; through rain, through snow, through sleet—through feminine tempers that ignited like dry tinder. And damn it, he thought, his teeth clenching hard in his jaw, he'd been assigned to save her life. Whether she was pleased or not, he was going to do just that.

His own temper flared as he squared his shoulders and grasped the old-fashioned doorknob. Then he forced himself to count to ten. He was a professional. He was going to walk in and handle the situation with a very professional, calm objectivity.

Hell, he could even try to be nice.

He pushed the door open. A little bell jangled overhead and she looked up from her papers, an inquisitive smile forming on her lips.

When she saw him the smile faded. Her eyes took on the icy frost of a Massachusetts winter.

Andrew walked up the three carpeted steps from the entryway to the showroom floor and leaned lightly against the decorative wrought-iron railing. He didn't need to look around to know that the shop was filled with antique knickknacks, period furnishings, and fine art, all tastefully and artistically displayed. He had stared at the shop long enough to practically memorize its contents.

Nor did he need to look at the woman to know that everything about her was as quietly elegant as the shop. But he did need to look at her. He also needed to hold fast to the attitude of casual impatience that had sprung from the bitterness—and the pain he refused to acknowledge—of their last parting.

"Hello, Lorna." He offered her a dry half smile.

She was silent for a moment, returning his stare. She leaned back in her chair with a slow and negligent grace, idly running her fingers over the gold pen she had been using.

"Andrew Trudeau," she murmured politely, her lips once more forming a smile, but one that was frigid and grim. A tawny brow rose high against her forehead and she blinked with a feigned and sardonic confusion. "Or is it Andy McKennon I have the honor of greeting?"

Lorna was stunned by his appearance, shocked and dismayed. But she was determined not to let him see the flurry of emotions that gripped her. Andrew . . . fascinating her, as always, with something so simple as his appearance and the sound of his voice.

No! How in God's name did he have the nerve to come there! The damned jailer who had seduced her twice, torn her soul to pieces, and then walked out as if she had been no more than an occupational hazard! Dear God, he couldn't really be there, haunting her life in the flesh when she was trying so hard to pull all the pieces back together. She wouldn't let him near her again—couldn't let him near her again! She had to make him realize that she never wanted to see him again, never wanted to be used by him again.

"Get out of here, Andrew," she said, straining to keep a cool and distant tone in her voice. "You turned my life into absolute misery and I don't want you anywhere near me. Ever."

Andrew scowled and took a few steps across the Oriental carpet toward the desk. "Cut it out, will you, Lorna? I knew that you wouldn't be particularly pleased to see me—"

She was on her feet instantly. In booted heels, she was almost his height, and he stood well over six feet. But she didn't look extremely tall. She looked sleek. She was slender, but built with all the right feminine curves.

"Pleased?" she inquired sharply. That damn, imperious brow of hers remained arched, but he could see

33

that she was losing her poise. He'd always admired her composure; it was ironic that he seemed to be the one man capable of shaking it completely.

Andrew lifted his hand in the air. "Come on, Lorna . . ." He tried an awkward, more sincere smile and perched on the edge of her desk. She was no longer smiling, not even a polite smile or a grim smile. She was just staring at him. They were barely two feet from one another, so close that he itched to touch her. Not with logic; a blind man would have sensed the tension in her. But she was even more exciting when she was angry. When her pulse raged silently but visibly against her smooth, creamy throat. When her eyes snapped with fire and her breasts rose and fell with the rapidity of her breathing . . .

It was impossible to forget that he had held her, that she was as smooth and curvaciously exciting naked as she was in this white wool designer dress.

She had given him a depth of tenderness, sensuality, and sexuality such as nothing he had ever experienced. He had never forgotten. How could she?

"Lorna," he said softly, giving in to the urge to reach for her, to touch the silken and refined line of her cheek. His knuckles grazed her flesh, his grin deepening as he met her eyes and tried to remind her of all that had passed between them.

She smiled very briefly in return.

Then her hand—her long, elegant, soft hand—shot out with the speed of a bullwhip and cracked with just such force across his jaw. The impact sent him off the edge of the desk.

His reflexes were good. Good enough, at least, to keep him from sprawling to the floor. But he just caught himself, buckling his knees and ankles to cushion the spring and hunching carefully for a precarious moment before standing.

He stared at her again, ruefully rubbing his injured jaw, feeling all his muscles constrict. She was glaring back at him. She wasn't afraid. She hadn't moved a hair away from him, and her eyes were still shooting sparks. If she had been a dragon, Andrew thought, she would have been breathing fire.

He crammed his hands quickly into his pockets as he felt his fists clench. He ground his teeth together, tensing his jaw. Lady, I'd like to give you one—just one—good swat somewhere on your anatomy that would wipe that look clean out of your eyes.

Andrew smiled.

She had a right to stare at him with smug superiority. She knew damned well he wasn't going to do a thing to her. She'd slam a charge of police brutality against him so fast that his head would spin.

But one day . . .

"Well, I can see that you *really* aren't *pleased* to see me, Lorna," he offered dryly. Then his forced smile left his handsome features so quickly that it might have been a mask dropped at a second's notice.

He spoke coldly, flatly. "I hope you've got all your little streaks of vengeance out of the way because, pleased or not, you're going to be seeing a lot of me."

Her expression underwent a subtle change. The anger did not leave her face, but another emotion joined the wrath in her eyes. She was evidently startled—and dismayed.

"Why?" she demanded, a note of panic in her voice.

Andrew didn't answer her immediately. He started to idly roam through the showroom. The window display and the front of the shop were given over to a quiet and understated elegance. Small signs, done in exquisite calligraphy, explained the pieces: "Loveseat, Art Nouveau, 1893. Original Brocade." "Gaslamp, pink glass, Paris, 1903."

There was older pieces as well, Duncan Phyfe sofas, French Provincial dining chairs, silver candlesticks, picture frames, and fascinating, tiny sculptures.

"Andrew!" She snapped out his name. He turned. She was still standing behind her desk. There was nothing negligent about her pose. She still held her gold pen, but the tension in her fingers showed him that if it had been a pencil, it would have broken in two by now.

He smiled a little. His jaw still ached from her blow and he couldn't help feeling a certain—only slightly malicious—pleasure in the discomfort he was causing her. Hell, slightly malicious? He was still wishing he could take his itching palm right across her sleek and elegant posterior.

"Andrew." He heard the hardness in her voice, the threat that made it husky and breathy. "Andrew, you can tell me what you came to say or you can hurry yourself—whoever you are today—out of my store." She sat down, pretending a renewed interest in her work. "I'm busy," she added as she stared at her papers again.

"Well," he said lightly, leaving the front of the store and passing her desk as he wandered to the back, "you're going to have to get accustomed to being busy with me around."

"What?"

There. He lowered his head to hide a grin as he idly picked up a statuette of a young girl. Lorna was trying very hard not to turn around, but there had been a definite note of alarm in her tone. He knew, just as he knew the sun rose in the east, that she would not be able to stand his being behind her.

"You heard me," he said casually.

She was out of her chair again. He heard her footsteps on the rich carpeting as she hurried to him, explosively snatching the statuette from his hand. "It's a Lladro!" she snapped, "with an extremely low edition number. I'll thank you not to handle the merchandise."

He lifted a taunting brow. She flushed, eyes snapping angrily as she stepped away from him, her fingers tightly curled around the statuette.

"Even when it's obviously marked for sale?" he asked innocently.

Her lips tightened and he saw that unmistakable narrowing of her eyes. A slight motion, but one that promised violence. Andrew backed away from her quickly.

"Lorna! That's a Lladro you're holding," he reminded her with outrage and indignity. "One with an extremely low edition number! Besides which," he added, dropping the taunt in his tone and adding his own warning, "I'm a cop, not a punching bag. You might look like a lady, love, but you've got a right jab that could probably match Ali's in his prime. Try it again and I just might be tempted to put a number of equal rights theories to the test."

She watched him for a moment without bothering to answer, then she spun around and carefully set the statuette back on its pedestal. Then she walked to her desk, keeping her back to him. Her shoulders were straight, but her head was slightly bowed.

A feeling of remorse swept through Andrew, along with dismay. He was being awfully hard on her. After all, nothing that had happened had been her fault. Lorna had been in the wrong place at the wrong time. Then they had become too involved, and the guilt, the anger, and the bitterness had set in. He had been an officer of the law, sworn to protect her. Not to seduce her . . . or be seduced, whichever it had been.

It was a pity that they hadn't been able to start off

on the right foot this time. Not his fault, he tried to tell himself. She was the one who had belted him.

But he had known. He had known damn well that she wasn't going to want to see him. She had made that clear enough the last time he had seen her.

He emitted a tired sigh. Her life was more important than anything that had passed between them. A mask of grim determination set his jaw. He was the man for this job, and he was going to do it whether she —or he—liked it or not.

"Lorna," he told her back firmly, "I know this isn't going to make you happy, but the D.A.'s office is worried about you. They think it would be advisable for you—"

"What?" she whispered incredulously, not turning around.

"The D.A.'s office thinks you should come back to New York."

She spun around to face him, her features betraying her dismay. Then she set her shoulders firmly and strode to the displays at the rear of the store, straightening things that didn't need to be straightened.

"No," she said firmly, "I am not going back to New York. I am not going to hide. I am not going to be a prisoner again. It doesn't make any sense. Simson is in jail; he's been charged with murder. The D.A. has all the evidence, everything he could possibly need to nail Simson. I was given the option of protection when he was arrested in case he tried anything from jail and I turned it down, remember?"

"Lorna, listen—"

"No!"

A few long strides brought him to her. He gripped her shoulders, but she shook off his hold and stared at him, bristling with fury.

"Andrew, I mean it. I'm not going back—"

"Lorna—" he gripped her shoulders once again as he faced her, and this time his grip was such that she couldn't shake free—"you're starting to sound hysterical."

"Hysterical?" Her voice rose. Yes, she was getting hysterical. "Andrew, you people took months of my life! I was a prisoner—"

"You were never a prisoner."

"By my definition I sure as hell was! Locked into that little apartment—"

"You had over a thousand feet!"

"I wasn't free!"

Andrew closed his eyes for a minute, sighed, then met her eyes again, releasing the tightness of his grip, but holding her still. He couldn't let her turn away from him.

"It was necessary, Lorna. You know that."

For a minute he saw it, that touch of vulnerability in her eyes. And he knew it had been hard, terribly hard. She *had* been shut away, was basically a prisoner. So alone that she had been ready to turn to him . . .

"Lorna," he said more sharply than he had intended, "your life was at stake."

She made no undignified attempt to escape him. Her head fell back and she met his eyes with new fury.

"I was never a criminal," she said. Although he knew how it dismayed her to plead with him, there was a note of beseechment in her voice. "I wasn't even really a victim," she added.

"But you were a witness," Andrew interjected softly. "You still are."

He felt her shoulders stiffen beneath his hands. Her voice lost all trace of emotion and became flat. "But Simson has been arrested. What's the problem now?"

Andrew hesitated. He didn't want her feelings

39

against the system to be bitter—even though he was bitter himself.

"Lorna, Simson isn't in jail. He was released on bond."

Just as he had felt her shoulders stiffen, he felt the cold that suddenly permeated her. She was more than frightened. Good, he thought, she needed to feel some fear for her own sake.

"They let him out?" She gasped.

Andrew nodded.

"How could they? It's a mockery! What good are you, what good are any of you—"

"Damn it, Lorna, stop it!" He didn't mean to, but he shook her hard—too hard. He saw the anger resurface in her eyes, and he wasn't about to let her start talking again.

"I try to enforce the laws, Lorna, I don't make them! And I'm afraid the law is very complicated on this one. For one thing, I have no physical evidence against the man; I only have your word against his."

"Donna was kidnapped—"

"But not by Simson, and they didn't cross any state lines. I've got a case, Lorna, but one that isn't half as solid as it should be. The attorneys tell me I was lucky to bring most of the charges to a hearing. The law says that a man is innocent until proven guilty. The judge set bail at some ridiculously high figure, but Simson was able to raise it. He's out, and the underworld rumors say that he's made some pretty wild threats against you and Donna."

"Donna!" Lorna gasped with dismay, and Andrew knew she was more worried about the friend she had inadvertently dragged into the situation than she was about herself.

He was worried about Donna himself, but Donna

40

had married his brother, and Luke was about the best protection a woman could have.

"Don't worry about Donna," Andrew said quickly. "Luke has gotten a leave of absence and they plan on leaving New York."

"When?"

"Soon."

"But you want to take me back there?" she inquired, puzzled.

"Lorna, right now I can't make you do anything except tolerate my presence. We don't want to have to lock you up again because of threats, but your life is probably in danger again."

Something of the wild panic left her eyes. Her lashes lowered. "Andrew, let go of me, please," she said in a subdued voice.

He did so, watching her as she returned to her desk. "So what do you want me to do?" she asked, idly drawing lines over the blotter with her pen.

He exhaled a long breath as he walked back to the desk, perching at its edge once again.

"I'd like you to come back to New York," he told her.

"And move back into my prison?" she inquired.

"It was a rather luxurious prison," he returned dryly.

"A prison nevertheless. With no one around but a pack of watchdogs at my door."

"Hey, you're the one who said you didn't want company."

"Only yours," she admitted softly.

"That's funny. I could swear I was distinctly told I was not welcome on a few occasions when I entered the sanctuary."

He saw the flare of her temper in her eyes and the

rise of color to her cheeks. He winced slightly. He was baiting her, but didn't seem to be able to help himself.

He also saw her scrape her nails over the blotter. She didn't seem to be able to help herself where he was concerned, either. In a minute her hand was going to snake out again, this time with the perfectly polished nails digging.

He was trained to move more swiftly than she. He leaned forward slightly, encircling her wrists and pinioning them to the blotter before she could strike. Slim wrists with a fine bone structure. Her wrists seemed incredibly delicate, a definite contrast to the sharp venom in her crystal blue eyes as they seared into his.

"You son of a—get away from me. You used me, Andrew, you used the entire situation. You knew that I was frightened and alone too often. How could you? I should have reported you. And now you have the gall to come back to me—"

"Damn you!" Andrew raged suddenly. "I'm trying to save your life! Don't talk to me about reporting things! You report whatever you like, just make sure you report the truth. Like the fact that you invited me in. And that you—"

"Let go of me!"

He did so, taking care to sit a good arm's distance away from her. But he wasn't quite finished with his reminders.

"And don't forget to report," he reminded her coolly, "that you came racing into my arms dressed in one of those silk nightgowns that's designed to be more . . . enhancing than concealing."

"I heard a noise—"

"A truck in the street."

"You were supposed to be protecting me!"

"I did protect you."

"Oh, my God! That's what you call protection?

That's a nice job you have, Trudeau. Very accommodating."

She could be so remote and sound so gratingly cool at the same time. He felt an irritating urge to strangle her, slap her, do anything to rip her from that pedestal and force her to admit that—

That she had wanted him as badly as he had wanted her.

He smiled with an offhand shrug. "Dynamite job," he said agreeably.

She returned his smile. "Mr. Trudeau—or McKennon, whatever you're calling yourself this week—I don't want any more of your protection."

"But you're in danger!" Andrew snapped irritably. What was he going to have to do to get that fact through her thick skull?

"I believe you. I am in danger. *But I'm not the criminal.* I'm not going to be hauled back to New York to hide for however many months are left before this man can come to trial. I'll hire my own protection and inform the Massachusetts authorities, thank you."

She turned back to her work, entirely dismissing him.

Andrew counted to ten very slowly. She looked up at him inquiringly, as if she waited patiently to discover just exactly why he was still sitting on her desk.

"Lorna." He was trying very hard for patience. Lord, was he trying! Andrew crossed his arms over his chest. "The New York authorities have already been in contact with the Massachusetts authorities. It's gone farther than that. The Feds are in on it because Simson was crossing over state lines with his business. Now, I didn't come here today to haul you back to New York. I said that I'd *like* to take you back to New York and hold you in total secrecy—where protection can be secure. But it's your choice. For the moment, I was sent to act as a bodyguard until we could see just which way the wind was blowing."

"Why didn't they send someone else?" Lorna stood again, carrying an assortment of papers from her desk to an old wooden filing cabinet that added to, rather than detracted from, the artistic decoration of the showroom.

Andrew followed her. "They had to send me. It's my case. I've been on it more than a year. I know the street people, I know you—"

"Oh, yeah, you know me, all right," she said bitterly. A drawer groaned in protest as she pulled it out with vehemence.

"Lorna, quit acting like a child—"

"I've been treated like a child!" she snapped, eyeing him with a cold glare for a quick second before slamming the drawer shut. Andrew stumbled and almost crashed into the cabinet—whether by chance or purpose, she had managed to close his tie into the drawer.

She walked past him, apparently oblivious to his difficulty.

For at least the tenth time in the half hour, he ground his teeth tightly together and prayed for a cold wind to ease his temper.

He didn't follow her again. He released his tie from the cabinet, planted his feet firmly on the floor, and spoke harshly and condescendingly from behind her. "Lorna, whether you like it or not, I'm yours. Day and night. A haunt you'll never be able to shake. Now, you can continue to make this an absolute misery for us both, or you can come to terms with the situation."

She turned very slowly. She seemed a little pale.

"A haunt . . . day and night? What are you talking about?"

"I'll be with you *always,* Mrs. Doria. That's what a bodyguard does. Day and night, wherever you go."

"Wait a minute! I have rights. I was a witness, remember, not the criminal."

"I'm sorry," he replied coolly.

"It's my life—"

"Not really, not at the moment," he interrupted with a dry shrug. "The State of New York needs you, and it looks like the United States government has taken an interest too. So I'm sorry. Others have a vested interest in your life right now, others who don't want it thrown away because you can't handle a situation like an adult."

"I can refuse to testify!" She exclaimed.

"I'd only ask for a subpoena."

She threw her arms up in sudden and desperate aggravation. "Andrew! Don't you understand? I think I'd rather be shot than be forced to spend any more time with you!"

"And don't you understand? It isn't your choice."

"Andrew—I'm going to call my lawyer."

"Call him. Call anyone you like."

He should have seen it then. The way she was standing, she was a perfect target, a framed silhouette in the shop window. The glass was patterned with smoky designs in all the corners, but it was crystal clear in the center.

And she was in the center, dead center. Her sleek blond hair shone like a beacon and her shapely height was unmistakable.

But he didn't see it. He was too involved emotionally, too embroiled in the argument. Andrew was tempted to grab her, wrestle her to the floor, and force her to admit that she wanted him. That there was something more between them and she did want him around, that she wanted a whole lifetime with him around. . . .

Bad train of thought, he told himself. And not very

believable. There might be a thin line between love and hate, but he was pretty willing to bet that he was definitely on her hate side.

You're a cop, he reminded himself over and over again. This was business. The business of saving her life.

"Lorna." He began walking toward her once again, his palm extended as an offer of peace. She started to move away.

And thank God she had.

Because at that moment, the sharp crack and the horrible shattering of glass broke in upon their argument.

They both turned to the window, just in time to see it fall in a million pieces.

"Down!" Andrew roared. And though she moved instantly, it wasn't fast enough for him.

He did grab her with rough and vigorous determination; he grappled her to the floor, shielding her body with his own. A strange whisper over their heads was the next sound he heard, followed by a loud thud behind them.

Lorna's security system began to wail, then there was nothing but the screech of tires to be heard from the street, and the roar of a racing engine.

Andrew was shaking slightly. He twisted his head and saw the missile that had been thrown. A large brick. Not a bullet, but a projectile that could have killed her, had it caught Lorna in the head or neck. He had to get a grip on himself. This was his job, this was what he did for a living. . . . But fear had never affected him so. He had almost lost her. A second more . . .

She was such a fool! She kept fighting and resisting him. He had never meant to hurt her. Had he hurt

46

her? Maybe she had decided that a cop was okay for a lonely fling but nothing more.

He was still shaking, and that made him mad as all hell. Did she feel it? Perhaps not. He could feel the strident pounding of her heart, the quaking in her limbs and the rise of her breasts against his chest.

He could feel too much.

He rose above her and questioned her in staccato fury. "Still willing to die, Lorna?"

Her teeth were chattering and her voice warbled when she tried to talk. "It might have just been a thief. Or a vandal. Or kids . . ." She allowed the sentence to trail away. She knew as well as Andrew that no petty thief was throwing a brick at her shop.

She flushed. Her fingers were clenched tightly into the material of his jacket. She swallowed with an effort, willing her heart to abate its frantic rate.

"Not a kid, vandal, or thief," Andrew said.

"We could never prove it."

"You need me, Lorna."

"I . . . maybe," she admitted, her eyes wide with shock and fear. But could she handle more time with Andrew Trudeau? She closed her eyes, breathing deeply, but she still saw, despite her closed lids, the face of the man above her.

She could never forget that face. She saw it continually in her dreams. Strong, rugged, masculine planes, beautiful, hypnotic eyes. She knew him with a beard and overgrown hair; she knew him clean-shaven and well groomed. She knew him as a Skid-Row bum, she knew him in a tuxedo. His personality was as multifaceted as his undercover disguises.

A strange sensation swept through her, tingling, warming. She knew him as a man. Completely. And even now, in the midst of danger, she was responding

47

to the man. The hardness of his muscles, his body heat, his breath that whispered against her cheeks.

She had known so much hurt, so much uncertainty. What he wanted, it seemed, he took, casually, easily. He had wanted her.

The hurt . . .

It seemed they had been born enemies. Animosity rose between them like a storm that formed at every meeting.

"Lorna!"

Her eyes flew open in instinctive response. His eyes were upon her, a dark and stormy green, insinuating and much too astute. She searched them out. The hardness of his gaze, the heated impatience and anger, made her wince.

She had been acting like a child. Her temper had soared and flown, no matter how determined she had been to remain calm. Only he had this effect on her.

She couldn't do it. She couldn't have him by her. Not again. Not day in and day out.

She had to if she wanted to live.

And he had given her no choice in the matter.

Lorna closed her eyes again. He was hard; she would have to be harder, colder and stronger.

"All right," she said bleakly, trying desperately to keep her voice from naked despair. "I'm in danger. New York wants me alive." She exhaled a long sigh, forcing herself to open her eyes and stare at him frigidly. "And you're going to be my bodyguard. Day and night." Lorna allowed her voice to betray a wealth of sarcasm. "Well, bodyguard, where do we go from here?"

She didn't really have to ask. The sounds of sirens were already filling the street.

Andrew smiled grimly, returning her taunt. "My

dear prisoner! I hop to my feet and gallantly help you to yours."

He did so with a grin that was full of wicked pleasure. "Ah, but if you were really my prisoner," he murmured.

He didn't need to say more. A devilish brow rose high and she knew he was imagining a dank cell, a few rats, large shackles, a muzzle . . . and what else?

No! She lowered her eyes quickly.

Because she wanted to think that he was imagining her as they had once been, when she had fallen in love with him. . . .

Don't imagine, don't think, she told herself. She didn't want to remember that her prison was absolutely beautiful as long as he was there.

There were hurried footsteps on the sidewalk and two police officers rushed in to the shop.

Lorna turned to Andrew. He would handle the police. He would handle everything. She had learned all about his efficiency.

She smiled. "Lead on, warden."

He slipped an arm through hers. Green eyes touched her briefly and he returned her tight smile. "I intend to, Mrs. Doria. I definitely intend to."

"But I'm not leaving Massachusetts, Andrew. I'll accept a bodyguard, but not a prison."

"That's fair—for now."

"Not for now—"

"For now," he repeated firmly, squeezing her arm. "And will you hush up for a few minutes, please? There's a nice officer coming in to question us. Let's not give him the impression that we're a pair of bickering teenagers."

"We're not. We're a pair of bickering adults."

"Lorna—"

"All right, all right! I'll shut up!" She pursed her

lips together, waiting for a grim-faced officer to pick his way over the broken glass and approach them. But then she found herself repeating Andrew's words. "For now."

CHAPTER TWO

"This is your house?"

Andrew stared at the building in question as Lorna led the way up the winding path to her front door. Lorna glanced at him quickly; his expression was totally bland.

"Yes," she said briefly, opening the front door with a single key. Andrew followed her into the entryway, but he didn't allow her to close the door. He inspected it instead, frowning.

"Lorna, anyone could pick this lock."

"No one ever has."

"First thing tomorrow morning, Mrs. Doria, you need to call a security company and a locksmith."

She wanted to argue with him, just because his tone was the one that made her long to argue. But he was right; if she was determined to try to live a normal life when a powerful man seemed to have dedicated his life to killing her, she had to take all precautions.

Lorna didn't argue with Andrew. She dropped her shoulder bag on the deacon's bench in the foyer, then hung her coat in the hall closet and stared expectantly at him. During the long and painfully silent drive from downtown Worcester to Paxton, she had gotten a very good grip on herself. She was not going to be spiteful. She would not lose control again, she would not shout, and—heaven forbid—she would not strike out at him again like an angry child. She would be . . . polite. Polite meant hanging his coat in the closet for him, just as she would do for any guest.

Andrew handed her his coat. Lorna hung it up efficiently, closed the closet door, and continued into the house. "Would you like some tea? Coffee? A drink?"

"Whatever you're having," he responded.

He didn't seem at all uncomfortable in her house. He had followed her into the parlor and was idly scanning the room. And probably thinking that she was a neat freak! Lorna thought with a little bit of annoyance. Maybe she was, a bit—in some ways, a perfectionist—but it all came from her love of the old and the artistic. More than a hundred years ago, some talented craftsman had laboriously carved her sofa from rosewood. That craftsman had tendered each curve and line by hand to create a thing of beauty. And so, to Lorna, it was more than a sofa, it was a testament to the artist.

And her house . . . well, that was a monument to architecture and design. The little walnut end tables were also hand carved. Only the brocade on her loveseat and matching king and queen chairs was new. Of course, her television was contemporary, as was the stereo system, but even the looped sectional rugs were reminiscent of a past era.

Lorna hesitated a moment, watching Andrew. She still could see no emotion in his eyes. He didn't appear to be judging her, only assessing all that he saw.

She hurried into the kitchen and filled her percolator with water. Only then did she realize that her hands were shaking.

The police had duly recorded the brick that had flown through her shop window. They hadn't bothered to ask her many questions; Andrew had flipped out his badge—just as they did in the movies—and taken charge of the situation. It had all been handled very smoothly and efficiently, even to the temporary boarding of the window. She thought that the uniformed officers had looked at her a little pityingly when they left. They had assured her that the flying brick might have been the result of malicious mischief, but she knew they didn't believe it. And if someone with financial power was trying to kill you . . . then you were dead.

Lorna forced herself to measure the coffee and start it perking, then she sank down into a chair at the kitchen table, running her fingers through her hair and pressing her temples between her palms.

She felt like screaming, hysterically screaming with the bleak and total terror of it all. She had made the mistake of walking down the wrong street at the wrong time, and her life had been irrevocably changed by that one action.

Lorna started, not quite screaming, but gasping out a weak yelp, when she felt a pair of hands descending on her shoulders. She spun around to find Andrew staring down at her. His eyes now betrayed emotion, and the emotion that she saw in their striking green depths was pity.

Lorna shook off his touch and stood, going about the business of pulling out mugs for their coffee.

"You startled me," she told him coolly. "Black?" she asked. She didn't need to ask. She knew that he drank his coffee black, but she felt a little more distant by pretending she had forgotten.

"Yes, thank you."

Lorna stared at the percolator as she poured the coffee, trying to think about the man objectively. He looked different today, but that was part of his character and part of his talent. The first time she had seen him, he had been totally . . . overgrown. Bushy,

53

with the beard and shoulder-length hair. The last time she had seen him, the morning before she had left New York, he had been clean-shaven and his hair had been cut to a contemporary length; not really short, but normal. He had resembled his brother Luke so much that it had been startling. Except that Luke always smiled at her; Luke was always kind and gentlemanly.

And Andrew, well . . .

Today he was still clean-shaven, but his black hair had been growing out again. It was a little longer than hers, styled differently, of course, but it was actually longer, curling an inch or two over his collar. Was he preparing to hit the streets again as Andrew "McKennon," New York City down-and-outer?

Lorna handed him a mug of coffee, picked up her own, and headed back out to the parlor. She kicked off her shoes and sat in the center of the sofa, hoping that he would assume he should sit somewhere else. He did. He took the Queen Anne chair across from her, his eyes roaming the room again before falling on her.

"Andrew," Lorna said, meeting his gaze squarely over the rim of her mug, "I know that you're bluffing."

"Really?" he inquired politely. "About what?"

"About yourself. I don't have to be saddled with you. I'm a citizen with rights. If I were to call the N.Y.P.D., they would have to assign someone else as my bodyguard."

Andrew blinked, but just barely. His features, rugged but clean-cut, didn't change a hair. You could hit the man with a baseball bat, Lorna decided, and he would give nothing away.

He shrugged. "Are you planning to do that?"

"I don't know yet," Lorna answered honestly.

"It's my case," Andrew said flatly, his eyes holding hers.

"Simson is your case—not me."

"Simson is the man interested in your early demise."

Lorna lowered her lashes quickly and sipped her coffee. There were a number of things she couldn't deny. Andrew had worked very hard on the case. He had spent most of his time for a year living like a gutter rat to gain information from the street people. He'd stayed away from his family and friends all that time, and his sister-in-law had been killed.

Then Donna had gone to New York, met and married Luke Trudeau, and had almost been killed when she had been kidnapped by thugs determined to find Lorna. Kidnapped and brought to Simson. Yet if Donna hadn't been kidnapped, they would never have been able to arrest Simson.

It was Andrew's case. He was in it all the way.

And so was she, Lorna thought. She was in "it" way over her head, trying to save her life—and her heart.

"Lorna," Andrew said quietly, "I'm aware that you have a definite aversion to me. You do have a choice. If we were to return to New York, we could set you up in an apartment again. You could be alone, with officers on guard at all times. In that case, you wouldn't have to see me. It would be the smartest thing to do. Sometimes, Lorna, I don't think you fully realize that it's your life at stake."

"Andrew, you're wrong. I realize everything fully. But I think that I would lose what's left of my sanity if I were to be locked away again."

"Simson's trial comes up on February tenth."

"That's two months away," Lorna murmured.

"Which is not that terribly long a time."

Lorna didn't reply. She was pleased to see Andrew stand and walk restlessly to the window. She smiled a little bitterly. He was worried. He knew that she could make a phone call and, maybe not definitely, but possibly, get him off the case.

But did she really want to do that? He was good. Damned good, and she knew it well. If she were to demand that he be replaced, might she not be slitting her own throat?

He turned back from the window, apparently relieved by something. "They're here," he told her.

"Who's here?" she demanded with a frown, standing and hurrying to the window herself.

There were two police cars outside. Marked police cars from Worcester.

Lorna glared sharply at Andrew. "What are they doing here?"

"Protecting you, Mrs. Doria," he said politely, so politely that she was certain that there was an edge of sarcasm to his statement. "They'll be here just for tonight. By tomorrow night you're going to have a security system installed."

"What good is a security system against flying bricks or bullets?" Lorna inquired.

"Where security leaves off," Andrew replied cynically, "intelligence and common sense are supposed to come in."

"Meaning that I possess neither?" Lorna retorted. Her temper was rising. No! She warned herself. Be cool and civil. Think of him as hired help, think of him as a big German shepherd! He was a safety factor, nothing more. Look down your nose at him and do not let him goad your temper!

A grimace twisted his lips. "I'm not sure what you possess, Mrs. Doria. It was not, however, intelligent for you to escape a police guard to go to a wedding, or try to sneak into Luke's house to see Donna. If she had been seriously hurt or killed, it would have been your fault. You led those men to that house."

56

Lorna turned quickly from him. She had brought Donna into the danger. She had written that cryptic note and Donna had come running after her. And it was true that Lorna's clandestine sneaking into Luke Trudeau's home had led the thugs there. It was true that Donna had been kidnapped because of her. But hadn't she agonized enough because of it?

"Do you like kicking dogs that are already down, Lieutenant Trudeau?" she inquired, staring him in the eye.

"Not unless it can keep them alive," he answered with a voice as cool and bland as her own.

Lorna suddenly laughed. The situation wasn't funny in the least, and yet, in a way, it was. She was in a position that gave her a certain amount of power over Andrew Trudeau. He wanted to be the man on the case, and she just might have something to say about that.

"Lieutenant!" she exclaimed in mock reproach. "I'd had my doubts before about this situation working out. And now, well, I can see it might very well be absolutely impossible. We just don't get along, do we?"

He stared at her without a response as seconds ticked by. Lorna began to regret that she had rushed to the window. She was too close to him. So close that she was forced to remember an awful lot about him. Things she shouldn't be thinking about, like the little mole at the base of his spine and the small scar on his chest—the result of a knife wound from a scuffle with a burglar when he'd been a rookie. Move, she warned herself, and do it quickly.

There seemed to be a little magic circle around Andrew Trudeau. As long as she stayed outside of that circle, she could remember he was a cop. A rough and independent man who was very determined never to be tied down. A man who had been annoyed because

57

he had wound up in bed with her. But once she stepped inside that circle all she could remember was that he was a man who had a very definite power over her, a power that was confusing and painful and, at times, exquisite. She could remember the touch of his hands and how very gentle he could be.

It was truly a nightmare that he was back in her life just when she had been getting it back to normal.

She didn't have to move away from him. Still watching her with guarded green eyes, he wandered to the sofa and sat, spreading his arms out over the back. He smiled.

"You like to see people crawl, don't you, Lorna?"

"Crawl? What are you talking about?"

He didn't answer her question, he offered her a warning—or a threat—she wasn't sure which. "Crawl, Mrs. Doria. It's something done on one's hands and knees. Well, I don't crawl—for anyone, or anything. Have you got that?"

"Oh, I think so, Lieutenant."

"I don't," he muttered ominously.

"Well, then, Andrew, you tell me exactly how this is going to work out. We've been arguing since you stepped into the store. If Simson doesn't get to me, it's very likely that one of us will strangle the other."

Andrew laughed. She was reminded of how very charismatic he could be. His mouth was full and nicely shaped, sensual. The little lines around his eyes gave credence to his thirty-three years; they weren't deep lines, just enough to give him a pleasant look of character and strength. His cheekbones were high and wide, his jaw was square, his nose a little long but straight—except for the slight irregularity where it had once been broken. His eyes, when he laughed or smiled, danced with a sparkling green light.

But they didn't dance or sparkle at all when he was

angry. They gleamed like cut glass and were every bit as sharp and dangerous. And his mouth could compress until it wasn't full at all; it could be a slash of anger against his face.

"Lorna," he told her now, apparently impressed with the humor of the situation, "I'm sorry, I find it very difficult to imagine you strangling me."

She arched a tawny brow. "Vastly amusing, Lieutenant."

"And I'm hardly likely to strangle you—I need you alive and healthy, remember?"

"Ah, yes! How could I forget?"

The smile left his eyes. His mood could change with a startling and disturbing ease. "Now, as to keeping you alive." He sat up, resting his elbows on his knees and forming a steeple with his fingers. "The drapes remain closed at all times. That leaves no target for a brick or a bullet. You do not enter or leave the house without me. And from now on the car goes in the garage, and the garage is locked. As of tomorrow, we'll have a dog—"

"A dog? Wait a minute," Lorna interrupted. "I do not like dogs. They shed all over the furniture, they drool, they get muddy pawprints on everything, and they bring in fleas and ticks and—"

"Lorna, I'm not talking about a cute little Pekingese or some kind of poodle. This will be a police dog."

"A dog is a dog—and I hate poodles."

"Sounds like you hate all dogs."

"I don't hate all dogs, I just don't want one!"

"Don't worry, we won't be giving you the dog, but you need him for now, Lorna. I'm talking about a specially trained shepherd, the kind who can scent out bombs and the like."

Lorna turned away and stared out the window. She could still see the two police cars, but she shivered anyway. Bombs? Oh, God. She thought about Simson and she hated him with renewed fury. What kind of a man was he? He had conspired to murder his own grandmother, had murdered April Trudeau and mugged other women just to throw suspicion off of himself, he would have cheerfully killed Donna, and he was probably doing his damnedest to kill her now. How did a man become so cold and twisted?

It was a mystery—and yet it was a fact. There were a lot of cold and cruel people in the world with their own calculating brand of insanity.

"Okay," Lorna murmured. "We get a dog. What else?"

"You don't pull any tricks."

"What are you talking about?"

"You. You don't try to sneak away from me. As in the day you duped your guards and went to Donna and Luke's wedding."

She was glad she wasn't facing him. "But, Andrew, those were just regular men! How could I possibly sneak by the illustrious lieutenant and talented bum, Andrew 'McKennon' Trudeau?"

She turned around at last. Andrew was smiling but his eyes had a cut-glass gleam in them.

"You know, it's a pity we can't lock you up with Simson for a week. You'd have him crawling the walls begging to confess."

"Do you think so?"

"I'd guarantee it."

"Then what about you, Lieutenant? Won't you be crawling the walls?"

"I told you, I don't crawl."

"Ah, yes! That's right."

"Let's quit with the sarcasm for a minute, shall we? I want a promise, Lorna."

"And what's that?"

60

"That you will never go anywhere without me."

"Sorry, I insist on a private shower."

He made a clucking sound of annoyance. "Lorna, you're more than welcome to a pristine shower. And I mean it, quit with the flippancy."

Lorna took a minute to think. She stared at him, and she felt a wave of heat and dizziness sweep over her. She knew then that she couldn't do it, she just wouldn't be sane if she had him underneath her feet for two months.

But she might not be alive if she didn't. Andrew—if nothing else—was totally determined to protect her. Because he was absolutely determined to nail Simson. But another man, a man not so determined, might not be so willing to risk his own life. And there was probably no other cop in the world quite so good at survival as Andrew Trudeau. And . . .

What else? She asked herself mockingly. Wasn't she still a little bit in love with him? Didn't she catch herself harboring dreams that he really did care for her, that he'd had reasons for his strange and insulting behavior? Didn't she really want to be with him?

The thoughts were painful. Very painful.

Right now, Lorna warned herself, right this very second, get all those thoughts out of your head. Make it absolutely impossible for the two of you to come close together in any way, shape, or form. Save yourself from total humiliation, for God's sake!

"Lorna?"

"All right, Andrew. For the time being I'm going to accept the fact that you are my bodyguard and I'll respect my life and your position by never making a move without reporting to you. But I want a promise from you too."

"And what is that?"

"When we're in this house, you're nothing more

than part of the woodwork. You stay out of my way and out of my life. You don't come near me or touch me."

A very dry and mocking smile curved his lips. One dark brow arched and—annoyingly—he laughed again. "I'm just a servant of the people, Mrs. Doria."

"I want a promise."

"That I won't touch you? Granted. But, tell me, what am I supposed to do if you touch me?"

"Oh, I wouldn't worry about that, Lieutenant."

"Are you sure?"

"Quite sure."

He kept smiling at her, his mouth cynical. Ignore the man, she chastised herself, ignore him completely. But she couldn't help thinking of a standard joke that had gone around when she was in high school: "He's got a kind face. Yeah, the kind you want to slap!"

Andrew had that kind of face, all right. Very handsome, very alluring—and so damned mocking it made her steam inside. Maybe they had both been to blame, but he had no right to be looking at her that way now. Still, she thought a bit sheepishly, she had already slapped him once and received a warning in return. The warning hadn't mattered; she didn't like herself when she behaved in such a fashion and she'd be damned before she'd let him change what she was inside again.

He stood up, putting his hands in his pockets. "I'll take the couch at night—if that's all right."

Lorna hesitated. "That sofa is an antique."

"You want me to sleep on the floor?"

"I—"

He shrugged. "I've slept in worse places, I suppose. At least your heat is good."

Lorna's mouth twitched. "No, Andrew, I wasn't going to make you sleep on the floor. There's a den to your left there, one with a pull-out bed. It's got a bath, a closet, and a television."

"My God," Andrew murmured, lashes falling over his eyes momentarily. "She's offering me the Ritz!"

"Oh, I do try to be decent to 'servants of the people,'" Lorna murmured in response. She smiled sweetly. "And to keep them out of my way."

"My own little cage, eh?"

"Something like that. Now if you'll excuse me . . ." Lorna wasn't at all sure what she wanted to do. She just wanted to be alone, and she started for the kitchen.

"Lorna!"

She turned around and was startled by his appearance. He was still standing very straight, with his hands shoved into his pockets, but she couldn't read the expression in his eyes at all. His lips were tight, compressed, and his features appeared strained and tense.

"What?" she asked, pausing by the kitchen doorway.

"Don't—please don't take any risks because of our past relationship."

"Past relationship?" Lorna echoed. "We never had what I would call a relationship, Andrew."

"You know damned well what I'm talking about. You want blunt? I'll give you blunt. Don't let the fact that we slept together make you act stupid."

Oh, Lord! The steam inside of her was threatening to explode. No, no, no! she told herself fiercely. Be calm.

She smiled. "Andrew, I think you're mistaken about a number of things. The fact that we went to bed together does not bother me. I'm not a child, or an innocent. I believe, Lieutenant, that you were far more bothered than I."

63

The tension went out of him. He smiled, and she didn't like the sparkle that touched his eyes.

"Want to resume our lack of relationship?"

"No!" Lorna snapped. She turned again, pushing at the swinging latticed doors that led to the kitchen.

"Hey!"

"What now?" she demanded in exasperation. The door that she had just pushed slammed back to hit her bottom and sent her stumbling back into the parlor. She was ready to scream when Andrew made no pretense of hiding his laughter.

"What?" Lorna exploded.

"I just wanted to ask a humble question," he told her with a grin. "Before I get sent to my cage for the night, would you consider allowing me to scrounge in your kitchen for some dinner?"

"Dinner!" Lorna repeated.

"Dinner, yes. I'll be happy to replace the groceries, but at the moment I'm starving."

"Oh, no!" Lorna moaned.

"It isn't that severe," Andrew replied, puzzled at her stricken expression. "Look, if it's that upsetting to you, I'll just keep starving until—"

"Oh, shut up, will you? Good heavens, I could care less whether you eat or not." Lorna moaned. "I completely forgot!"

"Forgot what?"

"I'm having company for dinner. What time is it?"

Andrew glanced at his watch. "Five of seven."

"Damn! They're coming at eight!"

"Who?"

She glared at him coolly. "Friends, Lieutenant. I am allowed to have friends in for dinner, aren't I? I'm sure this seems highly unlikely to you, but before this all began, I led a normal life just like other normal peo-

64

ple, with friends, acquaintances, business associates, and the like."

He smiled dryly at her sarcasm. "Yes, you're allowed to have friends in for dinner."

Lorna spun around, pushing on the kitchen door again. It didn't swing shut right away because Andrew followed her.

"Far be it for me to intrude," he said with exaggerated courtesy when she spun around again to stare at him questioningly, "but perhaps I could grab a sandwich or something?"

"Didn't you just tell me that you were a servant of the people?" Lorna asked.

He cocked his head, watching her suspiciously. "Why?"

"You can start serving, that's why. I need some help."

"Command, and I will obey," he responded, sweeping one arm to the side as he bowed.

"I wish," Lorna muttered. She opened the refrigerator and started pulling things out. Onions, peppers, garlic . . . How had she forgotten? Easy, she told herself, someone had thrown a brick through her shop window and Andrew had made an unwanted reentry into her life. That was definitely a good enough excuse for forgetting something as undramatic as dinner with friends.

"What do you want me to do?" Andrew asked her. She realized that he was standing right behind her. He wasn't touching her, but she felt his warmth. And there was that scent about him, not so much aftershave—whatever he wore was very subdued—but something that was natural, clean, and arrestingly masculine.

Get away from me! she wanted to shout. "Start slic-

65

ing the onions," she said. "There's a chopping board right below the sink."

Dutifully he bent beneath the sink. "How do you want them?" he asked her. "What are they for?"

"Onion soup," she replied.

"Mmm—sounds good. What else are we having?"

"We?"

"Oh, come on! If I'm going to 'serve,' I get to eat!"

"Sausage and peppers," Lorna replied shortly. She dragged her largest skillet from a cabinet and set it on the stove. She had to brush past Andrew to get beneath the sink for another cutting board. "Hey, don't touch!" he reminded her.

"Gag it, will you Andrew?"

"Your rules, lady, not mine."

Lorna began to chop the garlic with a controlled vengeance.

"How many onions?" Andrew asked.

"Five."

"How many people are eating?" he asked.

She was tempted to tell him it was none of his business, but then she relented, reminding herself that she was not going to behave spitefully—for as long as she could hold out. "Four. Sorry, five counting you."

Lorna threw a touch of oil into the skillet and then the garlic. A second later she threw in the sausage, then started slicing green peppers.

"Am I interrupting a date?" Andrew asked her politely.

She was tempted to tell him yes.

"Andrew, don't worry. I wouldn't let you interrupt anything. As it happens, you're related in a round-about way to the company I'm having tonight."

"I am?" he asked curiously, reaching past her to steal a slice of green pepper. He didn't touch her in any way, shape, or form—and smiled annoyingly when her eyes met his and they both knew that she had made a slightly ridiculous demand when the two of them were working together in the kitchen.

Ridiculous as it might be in a kitchen, her demand was one she meant to stick with, and he was going to do so too. "Who are these people that I'm related to in a roundabout way?"

"Two of your brother's brothers-in-law and your sister-in-law's sister-in-law."

"That was a mouthful," Andrew commented. "Donna's family?"

"Yes. Had you made the wedding, you would have met them."

"Some of us knew that making the wedding could easily cause trouble," Andrew said quietly.

Lorna remained silent, and the only sound in the kitchen was a faint crunching sound as Andrew chewed his pepper.

A minute later he reached for another. Lorna slapped his hand indignantly.

"You're not supposed to touch," he reminded her.

"Sorry. You're ruining dinner."

"One pepper less will ruin dinner?"

"You've got it."

"Then I do stand reprimanded! By the way, your onions are done."

Lorna dug out another skillet and set the onions on to sauté, adding a touch of garlic.

"Put the kettle on for water," she told Andrew, "and get the cheese out of the refrigerator. Then start slicing some of that French bread."

"Yes, ma'am!" He saluted, bringing a smile to Lorna's lips.

As Andrew did as he was told, she saw that he was smiling a little secretively.

"What is that stupid smirk for, might I ask?"

He straightened, having chosen the mozzarella without having had to ask her. "I was just wondering if I was going to be allowed to sit at the table."

Lorna put the last of the ingredients into the skillet and set the lid over it. "I'll think about it," she told Andrew. I don't even want you in the damn kitchen! she thought. But she had been a bit desperate.

She stood on tiptoe to reach the soup bowls. Again, he brushed past her. When she was barefoot, he was at least five inches taller than she, and it was far easier for him to get the bowls.

"Thank you," she said grudgingly. When the water started to boil she put instant bouillon in the soup bowls and filled them with boiling water, then added the sautéed onion and garlic. Andrew seemed to know what he was doing. He followed behind her like an assembly line, plopping a square of the bread and a few slices of cheese on each.

"I must say, Lieutenant, you're capable of being helpful," Lorna murmured.

"We strive to please," he commented.

"I'll bet you do," she muttered. "What time is it?"

"Only seven-twenty."

"Good. Put some ice into the bucket, will you? I'm going to set the table." And get into another room—away from you for a minute! she added silently to herself.

She walked hurriedly through the parlor to the formal dining room, drawing her good china from the sideboard. As she set out five dinner plates, salad plates, bread and butter plates, and cups and saucers, her mind persisted in repeating one train of thought: This isn't going to work, it just isn't going to work, it isn't, it isn't, it isn't . . .

Lorna folded napkins, then set out the wineglasses.

She was just setting the last spoon in place when the phone began to ring and then abruptly stopped.

For a minute she paused curiously, then a flash of anger swept over her. Damn him! He'd answered her phone on the kitchen extension. Of all the nerve!

Lorna charged back to the kitchen. "What the hell do you think you're doing?" she demanded, hands on her hips. Andrew was leaning against the counter, chewing on a piece of French bread and looking quite at home as he covered the mouthpiece with his hand, ready to reply.

Lorna didn't give him a chance. "Woodwork, Andrew. I told you that you were supposed to blend in with the woodwork. You've got no right to answer my—"

"I knew it was going to be for me," he interrupted her.

"What?"

He pushed away from the counter, stretching the phone wire to put some distance between them.

"No, I don't think she'll take to the idea even after today. But sure, put her on, let her try."

"What's going on now?" Lorna demanded, frowning.

He handed her the phone with a polite smile. "Donna wants to talk to you."

Lorna took the phone. Andrew took his bread out of the kitchen. Lorna noted that he had also poured himself a glass of wine. He scooped it up just before passing through the swinging doors.

"Make yourself at home!" she muttered irritably. And then she remembered that she was holding the phone and that Donna was on the line.

"Donna! How are you?" Lorna feigned a cheerful voice, fitting the receiver between her cheek and her neck so that she could pour herself a glass of the burgundy.

"Fine, Lorna! Worried silly about Simson being on the streets, but physically fine. Listen, Lorna, Luke has been very uneasy about this whole deal, and he wants to get out of town until the trial starts."

Lorna sipped her wine, feeling a bit of a chill. Luke Trudeau had been blessed—or cursed—with some kind of strange sixth sense. If Luke was uneasy, it was time to be worried.

"I think it's a great idea for you two," Lorna replied. "You're still newlyweds, to a point!"

"Yes, I guess we are. And I suppose it's a real blessing that Luke is a priest because he would have lost his job by now if he wasn't. I didn't mean to make a pun on that," Donna murmured over the wire, and Lorna smiled, thinking of her friend. Where she was five ten, Donna was a petite five four. Donna's hair was a dark sable and she was very amply curved. Lorna was more slim than curved, and when they went out together, she couldn't help but think that they looked like a feminine set of Laurel and Hardy.

Lorna had also always thought of Donna as being sweetly innocent. She was a lovely, caring person, and for all the danger Lorna had brought to her friend, she could only be grateful that she had, at least, been the cause of Donna and Luke getting together.

"Lorna, are you listening to me?"

"Yes, yes, go on!"

"Anyway, it's up in the mountains. Very lovely, they tell me, private and protected. There's a barbed-wire, electric fence around the place, the ranger's office is at the gate, and it really sounds just perfect. What do you say?"

Lorna took another sip of her wine. "I'm sorry,

Donna—I must have missed something. What are you talking about?"

She heard a long sigh of exasperation. "Lorna, I want you and Andrew to come with us to South Carolina. To the mountains. I'm convinced that it would be the safest place to stay until the trial."

Lorna choked on her sip of wine. "Me . . . and Andrew?"

"Well, of course. Andrew has to stay with you until the trial. Andrew or another policeman. But since Andrew is on the case already, and he is my brother-in-law, you know . . ." Donna's tone was slightly reproachful and Lorna felt a bit guilty, but only a bit.

"You should come," Donna concluded.

"I—" Lorna began, then she stopped, draining all the wine from her glass. "I don't think so, Donna. It seems we've figured out a way for me to try and lead a halfway normal life here."

"Oh. Well, think about it, will you, Lorna?" Donna's disappointment was evident. "It won't be the same as it was before; you wouldn't be alone."

"I know," Lorna murmured. She knew that she was hurting Donna's feelings but she didn't dare risk her own. Being locked away with Donna and Luke was one thing, but adding Andrew to the brew for a foursome in the mountains—no way!

"I will think about it, Donna, I promise."

"Please do," Donna said. "Lorna, I'm really worried about you. I wish—oh, well, I won't repeat myself. I'm just so glad that Andrew is with you. How are things going?"

"Just great," Lorna said into the phone. Could Donna hear the rich sarcasm in her voice? "Things are going just lovely here." As lovely as a night with a saber-toothed tiger, she added silently.

71

And then she poured herself another glass of wine and cheerfully changed the subject, telling Donna that her brothers and Theresa were coming for dinner and that, certainly, she would pass on Donna's love.

CHAPTER THREE

Andrew lifted the cover from the pot that held the heating spaghetti sauce. It smelled delicious. No store-bought here, but the homemade stuff, recently taken from the freezer. It reminded him that he was really starving, that he hadn't eaten anything other than a few slices of green pepper and two pieces of bread since early that morning.

He looked around the kitchen a little guiltily, as if he expected to find Lorna behind him, ready to jump down his throat if she caught him snitching more food before her company came. But she wasn't in the kitchen. She was upstairs dressing.

"A formal meal?" he had asked her when she had hung up the phone and told him—without any reference at all to Donna's suggestion that they join her and Luke—that things were simmering in the kitchen and she was going upstairs to change.

"Don't be ridiculous" had been her reply. "I'm just having a few friends over."

But once she had left him—smoothly sweeping up the stairway, of course—he had decided his own appearance was not the best. He'd retrieved his bags from the rented Mustang that was parked behind her Ferrari—a red Ferrari, no less—hastily showered, and changed into dark pants and a white pullover sweater. There had still been no sign of his grudging hostess, so he'd put on some coffee for the patrolmen who were keeping watch on the drive.

And now . . . well, the sauce was just too tempting. He took another thick slice of bread and dipped it into the bubbling sauce.

It was good. The woman could definitely cook.

Andrew gazed out the kitchen window. The patrol cars were in place, parked just past the driveway. Officers Brent and Buchannan were leaning against the hood of one car, talking, the collars of their leather jackets pulled up against the cold evening. Their partners were out back. Andrew felt a momentary pang of guilt; there he was inside, munching on French bread, and there they were outside, probably freezing.

Then the guilt faded. He still felt sympathy for the men, but no longer the guilt. He had spent many a night in far worse positions. Miserable nights were part of the job, and if you took the job, well, you took the bad along with the good. Like this, sipping burgundy and eating messy bread with homemade sauce.

Andrew grinned, using his free hand to boost himself up to the counter. He allowed his legs to dangle as he finished the bread, washed it down with a sip of burgundy, and lit a cigarette.

Things weren't going so badly, he thought. True, she'd given him a good smack to the jaw and threatened to pull some strings and have him replaced, but he was still there. Things weren't going that badly.

His grin disappeared and he inhaled on his cigarette. He was there because Simson was out of jail and a brick had come flying through Lorna's shop window. The Worcester police were welcome to think that it had only been a case of malicious mischief, but Andrew knew it wasn't. Apparently someone in the Worcester hierarchy believed the same, or else they

74

were willing to oblige their New York counterparts, because the two patrol cars *were* sitting outside.

For tonight, he could breathe a little easier.

But it wasn't tonight that was bothering him. He could accompany Lorna everywhere she went and tomorrow he would see that she had the best security system installed. He could bring in the best-trained dog in the world and still . . .

Still, it was almost impossible to protect a life when someone as determined as Simson wanted that life snuffed out.

A total disappearance was the best bet, but Lorna didn't want to disappear, and Andrew didn't know whether he wanted to be completely irritated or give in to a touch of empathy. Hiding out *was* hard. Very hard.

Thank God that Lorna, at least, was in a decent financial position. Andrew had seen men and women financially and emotionally ruined by being witnesses to crime. But still . . .

Well, he thought, his grin returning slightly, Lorna wasn't doing so badly. She certainly didn't appear to be dispirited or depressed. And she was sure as hell ready to keep fighting. Fighting him, at any rate.

Andrew flicked an ash into the sink, noticed how it sat on the spotless stainless steel, and ran the water to rinse it down. Didn't she have any ashtrays? he wondered. He was afraid to use any of the elaborate little dishes that sat on the end tables in the parlor; they just might be priceless art treasures.

The thought irritated him again, and he wondered about his own motives. More than he had ever wanted to nail anyone in his life, he wanted to nail Simson. The man hired assassins as easily as other men hired gardeners. He did so impersonally and very coldly. Human life meant nothing to the man at all. Simson

75

had never seen, met, or heard of April Trudeau, but because of Simson, she had died. Because the man wanted to kill his own grandmother, for God's sake, and did manage to kill her, he involved Lorna.

Lorna. Well, she was the crux of the matter now. They had thought at the precinct house that he'd been too involved when his sister-in-law had been killed; if they only knew how involved he was now. . . .

And just how involved was he? he asked himself ironically. She had informed him that they had never had a relationship. He'd wanted to challenge her on that, but he hadn't, of course. If he had, he would have had to fathom his own behavior, and he'd be damned if he could figure any of it out at all. Point: He had wanted her from the moment he had seen her. Point: There was an air about her, something that put her a little above the normal breed of humanity. Point: She was stubborn, temperamental—and capable of being so imperiously cool that he longed to drag her down into the dirt and grass of the earth. But point: He wanted to hit the earth alongside her.

Point: Most important of all, he had really believed once that he was falling in love with her, and it had been a frightening feeling. It had added to the power she could already wield over him, and he wasn't accustomed to feeling that way at all. He was thirty-three years old, and he'd been a cop for ten of those years. He was good, and he knew it, useful, and he knew it. But nothing had ever stood in his way, wife or kids. Marriage was not a good institution for cops. Andrew had seen the best relationships go sour when one partner was a cop. And who could you blame: the one out pounding the streets with the gun or the one who sat home, wondering if that was the night she—or he—might be left alone?

Andrew sighed softly. He'd never thought he had

anything against marriage, but then he'd never thought about marriage until he'd met Lorna. And from that point on, he'd been one big set of contradictions whenever he'd seen her. He hadn't really known what he felt, or what she felt for that matter, and he should never have taken her to bed under those circumstances.

"Cheer up, old boy," he said aloud, using his best Basil Rathbone–Sherlock Holmes accent. "The picture isn't at all as bloody bad as it looks."

No, it wasn't, because he was there, talking to himself while his cigarette burned down on her kitchen counter. But damn her! Why wouldn't she listen to Donna? The guarded house in the mountains would be perfect. They could take real care getting there—airline tickets under assumed names, rental cars that could be changed after a few miles—it could work. In the city, any city, she was a target. There were buildings, alleys, streets, and people everywhere. There was no way to tell who was just going about their business and who had lethal business on their minds.

Maybe she'll change her mind, he thought, but not with any great hope. And then he felt a chill assail him. He didn't want her risking her life because of *him.* Maybe if he offered to pitch a tent in the yard. . . .

But they hadn't gotten on so badly fixing dinner. Of course, that had been because she needed help, but still . . . Andrew's wanderings came to a stop when he heard a sharp, almost frantic pounding on the front door. Then he heard a feminine voice, muted by the closed door and the distance, but it was almost as frantic as the pounding.

"Lorna? Lorna! Let me in!"

Andrew jumped from the counter, dropping his cigarette into the sink, and hurried to the door. When he

77

pulled it open a small woman almost fell on top of him in her haste to enter.

Then she was drawing back, very startled by the sight of him. She was young—in her late twenties, he judged—very pretty with huge dark eyes and glossy hair. She was also agitated.

She stared at him for several seconds, and then he smiled. "Hi."

"Hi," she responded. The agitation seemed to drift from her as she stared at him with puzzled assessment. Andrew noted over her shoulder that there were two men following her up to the trellised porch.

His smile deepened. "You're Theresa Miro, right?"

"Right," she replied, still puzzled. "And you're . . . a friend of Lorna's?"

Andrew laughed. "Something like that. Actually, in a roundabout way, I'm also a relative of yours."

"You are?" Theresa's puzzled frown deepened.

Andrew stuck out a hand. "I'm Andrew Trudeau. Donna's brother-in-law."

"Oh!" Theresa exclaimed, eagerly taking his hand and pumping it with a friendly warmth. "Then that's why—I'm sorry, I was staring frightfully, wasn't I? But you see, I was sure I'd seen you before, and certain that I hadn't. You're very much like Luke—not quite so dark, and your eyes are green, aren't they? I think Luke is just a little taller, isn't he? A bit heavier—"

"Theresa!"

The two men had reached the door. If Andrew hadn't known who was arriving, it wouldn't have mattered. Both men bore a strong resemblance to Donna, with their big, bright-blue eyes, thick, sable hair, and striking smiles.

The first, apparently the older of the two, was the one who had interrupted Theresa. He set one hand on her shoulder as he offered the other to Andrew. "Stop dissecting the man! Andrew, I'm Joe Miro. Sorry we didn't get to meet you at the wedding, but we've heard about you and it's a pleasure. You've met Theresa"— he paused, giving his wife an affectionate squeeze on the shoulder while rolling his eyes above the back of her head—"and this is Tony, my younger brother."

"Joe, Tony," Andrew acknowledged, "my pleasure."

"But what are you doing here?" Theresa demanded. And then she let out a long gasp. "Oh, something has happened! The police cars outside—oh, Joe! I told you something was wrong."

"Theresa," Joe murmured to his wife, "let's get out of the doorway, shall we?"

They stepped in and Tony closed the door behind him. They were all looking at Andrew, so he decided to answer them honestly.

"I'm here because . . . well, I'm not sure how much you know of what happened in New York."

"Everything," Tony Miro told him. "Lorna explained her part in the affair to us, and Luke told the rest to Dad, and Dad is pretty good at repeating things word for word."

I would be willing to bet, Andrew thought dryly, that Lorna didn't tell you everything. But that wasn't really important, not in the long run when the long run meant lives. "Simson is out."

"Of jail?" Joe asked incredulously.

"Yes."

"How?" The eldest Miro seemed very angry. "The man kidnapped and threatened my sister, put Lorna through pure hell, is guilty of murder—"

"Joe!" It was Theresa who chastised her husband this time. "Don't yell at Andrew. It isn't his fault."

Joe Miro quickly lowered his voice. "I'm sorry, it's just so incredible. It's just not right."

"The man has to go to trial," Andrew said. "And until then, well, the law reads that a man is innocent until proven guilty."

"Oh, my God," Tony murmured. "Donna!"

Andrew smiled reassuringly. "Tony, please don't worry about your sister. She and Luke are aware of everything. They're planning on doing a disappearing act, and until then, there are men assigned to guard them. Besides, I've got a lot of friends on the force, so I can guarantee you that no one can get near their house."

"That's good to hear," Joe said softly.

"What about Lorna?" Theresa asked.

Andrew grimaced. "Lorna is stuck with me. I'm trying to get her to pull a disappearing act too, but—"

"I already spent too much time as a disappearing act!"

The foursome turned toward the stairway at the sound of Lorna's voice. Andrew was certain that she hadn't planned an entrance, and yet she did make one. Informal? Well, all right, maybe she was informal, he thought, but her black pants were velvet, and he was sure that the slinky red top she was wearing was silk. Somehow she didn't look informal, but she was the type of woman who could probably look elegant in old denims and a worn, oversized flannel shirt. Mmm. She was the type of woman who could take a man's breath away just by walking down the stairs in *informal* velvet and silk.

She seemed to glide into the room—or sweep, Andrew wasn't sure which would be a better description —and yet there was nothing phony or artificial about the quick hugs and kisses that followed when she greeted the three Miros. Andrew felt a twinge of some-

80

thing like envy; he was an outsider there. It was obvious that the friendship between the group was deep and sincere. He told himself that he didn't feel jealous —he refused to feel jealous—when both Joe and Tony kissed her. But it did bother him, and he was very glad when he remembered that once, before things had gone too far, Lorna had told him all about the Miros. She had practically grown up in their house, so she must surely think of Joe and Tony as brothers. And Joe Miro was married. Tony Miro wasn't.

Well, hell, if she was going to fall for Tony Miro, she would have done so years ago, right? he asked himself. Right. The assurance wasn't really there. He was jealous.

He forced himself to smile politely until the greetings were over. And then he noticed that Lorna was staring at him. "Andrew, you didn't *serve* anyone drinks!"

His smile deepened as his teeth grated. "Sorry, Lorna, we just didn't get that far yet."

"What would you like?" Lorna asked her guests.

"Scotch all around, I guess," Joe said, "but I know where to get the ice and the Scotch."

"Oh, no, sit down, Joe. Andrew will get the drinks. He's made himself right at home and knows his way around." She spoke pleasantly, sweetly. Joe looked as if he was about to protest, but Andrew stepped in before he could say anything.

"Scotch all around?" he inquired cheerfully.

"Thanks, Andrew, a small one for me please," Theresa called. Andrew was already halfway into the kitchen. He raised a hand in acknowledgment, then passed through the swinging doors.

He dug into the ice as if it were a long-lost enemy. Big deal, he told himself. Who the hell minded making

81

a few drinks? It wasn't the drinks, of course, it was the tone of her voice. . . .

He poured too much Scotch in Theresa's glass and decided to dump a little down the sink. He saw his wet cigarette there. "Damn her!" he muttered, pulling the butt out of the sink and tossing it into the trash— which was neatly hidden below the pipes.

He practiced a smile again, forced it into place, and balanced the three glasses as he returned to the parlor. Lorna was sitting on the sofa, her arm draped elegantly over the curved back, and she smiled at him sweetly. "Why, Andrew, I believe you've forgotten mine."

"Why, Lorna, I'm so sorry! I'll rectify that immediately." He returned to the kitchen, wondering what the hell her game was.

Andrew returned and handed Lorna the drink. He was glad to see that Joe and Tony Miro were giving her a lecture on safety.

"Thanks, Andrew," she murmured, accepting her glass. "Oh, would you mind terribly? I like a little soda in mine."

Yes, I mind, he thought. I'd like to take the damn soda, pour it over your head, and douse that too-sweet smile from your face.

But then he grinned. She wanted a "servant" of the people? Fight fire with fire, he reminded himself.

He took the glass from her, noticing her hands and the nailpolish that matched her slinky top. May all the saints preserve us! he thought. Do her damn nails always coordinate with her clothing?

"Be right back."

Soda. Soda was no big deal. Well, if this was going to be the night, he might as well get into the act.

He brought out her glass with ice, Scotch, and soda. What problem could she possibly have next?

She sipped it. "Andrew—"

"Will you excuse me for a minute?" he interrupted politely, addressing the group. "I made some coffee for the guys outside. I know what it's like to sit in the cold."

"Oh, of course you do!" Theresa exclaimed. "Wait a minute, I'll come with you."

"You don't need to."

Lorna's expression changed to one of concern and a touch of shame. "I should have thought of those men myself! I'll bring the coffee out. And maybe they're hungry."

"You won't go out at all, Lorna!" Andrew said far more sharply than he had intended. He took a breath and started over, realizing he had no right to yell at her for wanting to offer a simple courtesy. "Lorna, please, I just don't like you going outside unless you have to, okay? Let's not take chances when we don't have to."

For a minute she looked as if she wanted to argue. Then her lashes lowered and she ran a finger around the top of her glass. "Okay. But ask them if they'd like something to eat, please."

"I will," he promised.

He returned to the kitchen. By banging around for a minute, he found cups and a tray. There were four guys out there, Brent and Buchannan and their two partners. Somewhere around midnight the shifts would change, and two new patrol cars—also from Worcester, since Paxton's force was too small to supply such a guard—would replace those now parked near the driveway.

He set the cups on the tray, poured the coffee, found a cream pitcher in the refrigerator, and added sugar packets from a copper cannister marked "sugar."

He gazed down at the tray. He was going to look

83

like a waiter when he walked outside with this, he thought disgustedly.

Just as he was about to begin his trek out to the patrol cars, the kitchen door swung open. It was Theresa, smiling brightly but uneasily.

"I just wanted to see if you needed any help finding things," she told him.

"Nope, sugar was marked sugar, and luck was with me—the cream was in the refrigerator."

"Yes"—Theresa laughed—"Lorna's is a well-ordered existence."

"Always?" Andrew's tone was teasing, but he really wanted to know.

"Always!" Theresa assured him. Then, as if she didn't really trust a man to serve coffee properly, she glanced at the tray.

"Spoons, Andrew," she reminded him.

"Oh, yeah." He dug into Lorna's silverware drawer and produced four spoons. "They probably all drink black coffee anyway and they're going to laugh their heads off at me when I appear with all this paraphernalia."

Theresa chuckled. "Would that bother you?"

"What?"

"If they laughed at you."

"No. I'd be glad if it brightened up the night a bit."

Theresa smiled as she lifted the top off the sauce pot and stirred it. "Brighten them up with dinner. They'll love it."

"I'm sure they will."

Theresa dropped the lid back into place and turned to him, not smiling any more. "Andrew, this is really bad, isn't it?"

He thought about lying to reassure her, but reassuring anyone wasn't going to change things.

"Yes. I think so."

84

"Isn't there anything that can . . . really be done?"

"Short of trying to shoot Simson, no. It would help if Lorna would agree to go back to hiding, though."

"Can't you make her?"

"No, not legally."

"Maybe I can help," Theresa murmured. "And Joe and Tony are talking to her now." She grimaced. "Lorna can be very stubborn."

"I know." Andrew started to pick up the tray, then he hesitated, trying not to be obvious.

"Is she always stubborn?" he queried, trying to sound casual. "Or is it just with me?"

Theresa laughed. "Always, but politely so." She shook her head slightly. "Donna can talk to her sometimes. The two of them were always the strangest pair. I mean, Donna is an absolute mess! Oh—don't get me wrong, I love her just like a sister, but Donna is totally unorganized and Lorna is fanatically neat. They roomed together in college, and I, for one, would never have thought it could work. But it did. Opposites and all that, I guess . . ."

When she hesitated, Andrew became increasingly curious. "What, Theresa?"

"Oh, I was just thinking about Jerry, Lorna's husband. He was a very nice guy, and his death was a real blow to all of us. But . . ." She paused again, as if embarrassed that she was talking so to a relative stranger. Then she shrugged. "You *are* my sister-in-law's brother-in-law, aren't you? Jerry was so much like Lorna that I wondered sometimes if they would stay married. They were both so polite and organized, almost staid, if that makes any sense. It often occurred to me that in another ten years, they would have bored each other to tears. I'm not making much sense, am I? Like I said, Jerry was a great person. I shouldn't have

85

said anything—Joe would be ready to gag me." She grinned.

Andrew thought she was adorable—a lot like his sister-in-law.

"Don't worry, I won't give away a word." He picked up the tray and started for the swinging doors.

Theresa stopped him. "Andrew?"

"Yeah?"

"I—it really is great to meet you. I just love your brother. He's great for Donna and she's so very happy."

"Luke is pretty special."

"So are you," Theresa told him, her eyes sparkling.

He should have just said thank you. He didn't. He smiled ruefully. "I don't think Lorna thinks so."

"Then she's as blind as a bat, but she'll come around. I'll bet you!"

He grinned. "Are you a good cook too?"

"Not bad."

"You're on. We'll bet a dinner."

Theresa laughed. "You're on."

As he at last walked out of the kitchen with Lorna's elegant tray, he heard Theresa muttering to herself. "Where would I like to go to dinner? I think I'll make him take me to some extravagant place in New York . . ."

He started walking toward the front door as Lorna was coming toward the kitchen. She paused and he saw that she, too, was checking out his tray. Joe and Tony were sitting in the parlor. Lorna had apparently left them because they were still talking about the brick episode.

"Got everything?" she asked Andrew.

"Yes, thanks."

"I'm going to fix them some dinner," she said.

86

"They'll appreciate it, I'm sure," Andrew replied, dismayed by their stiff exchange.

It was a crisp, cold evening, one that promised a snowfall. Andrew shivered a little as he walked out to the patrol cars.

Buchannan, a young guy in his early twenties, did laugh when he saw the tray. "Hey, Brent! This isn't such a bad detail. No Styrofoam here!"

Andrew laughed and set the tray on the hood.

"Sugar! Lots of it!" Brent exclaimed happily.

"Ah, you drink the stuff like maple syrup!" Buchannan teased him. Then he looked at Andrew. "Thanks, Lieutenant, this is great."

"No problem," Andrew said. "Dinner is coming shortly."

"Dinner!" Buchannan sighed. "I've been smelling the aromas from that house since I've been here. Thought the devil himself was on my tail, but if we're actually going to get fed—"

"It sure beats chasing the pickpockets in town," Brent finished.

Andrew smiled and then sobered. "Seen anything?"

"Not a thing. And believe me, Lieutenant, if anything was coming, we'd know. This is a dead-end street, one way in, one way out."

"The only car that's come down the street belonged to Mrs. Doria's company. They understand why we stopped them, don't they?"

"Sure," Andrew replied. Joe and Tony seemed like reasonable men; if the cops had asked them questions, they had answered them.

Reasonable. Why the heck couldn't Lorna be reasonable?

Andrew glanced toward the forest on the opposite side of the street. "That seems like a danger spot to me."

87

Buchannan shrugged. "I've lived in Worcester all my life, Lieutenant. That forest is thick with shrubs and brambles. Not many people would be willing to crawl through it."

Andrew nodded. "Just don't get too comfortable, okay?"

"We won't, sir," Brent promised.

Andrew turned back to the house. Coming from Brent, the "sir" made him feel incredibly old.

At the door he ran into Tony and Joe, who were coming out with dinner plates piled high for the patrolmen. Andrew grinned, holding the door open for them. "Anything left for us?" he laughed.

"Plenty," Joe assured him. "It's an Italian trait to always cook as if an army might be stopping by."

"Want some help?"

"Yeah, go inside and pop the cork on the wine, will you?"

Andrew let them pass. Through the parlor he could see that Lorna had lit candles in the dining room. The crystal wineglasses were sparkling and most of the food was on the table. Theresa came through the kitchen carrying a large salad while Lorna followed with an overflowing bowl of pasta.

Andrew moved quickly to her side, taking the bowl from her hands.

"What are you doing?" she demanded.

"Just trying to serve!" he exclaimed. He placed the bowl on the table and pulled out a chair for her. Deftly, and with his own peculiar brand of grace, he repeated the gesture for Theresa.

"Thanks!" Theresa said, just as Joe and Tony reentered the house.

They took their places at the table, leaving the fifth chair next to Lorna for Andrew. He started to pour the wine.

"My Lord, you're a helpful man!" Theresa said appreciatively.

"Hey, when a cop gets invited to dinner, he does his very best to serve," Andrew said.

"But you're not a cop, you're family," Joe replied with a grin, passing the sausage and peppers to Theresa. Then his grin slipped, and he was looking at Lorna again. "Now, about this brick incident—"

"Joe!" Lorna exclaimed impatiently. "Please, let's talk about winter, or your kids, anything else."

"But I don't think you realize—"

"I realize," Lorna stated firmly. "I also realize that I have a floundering business and that I'm sick of being locked away. Besides"—her eyes met Andrew's, as hard and sharp as the crystal wineglasses—"I have Lieutenant Andrew Trudeau on guard. How could I possibly be safer?"

Mockery and challenge so sweetly spoken that no one else in the room could have possibly caught her undercurrents of tension.

But then, maybe they did.

"Oh, I don't know." Theresa laughed, raising her glass to Andrew. "That all depends on what kind of safety you're talking about!"

"Theresa," Tony admonished, "this is serious."

"Very serious," Joe agreed.

Lorna sighed. "Please, I beg you! Let me have some normalcy in my life. If you will all promise to drop the subject, I will promise that I'll run and hide like a good citizen if anything else happens. Agreed?"

There was silence for a minute, then Joe started talking about a play he and Theresa had seen in Boston the week before. After that Theresa told Lorna all about the dance class her daughters were taking, and Tony engaged Andrew in a discussion about his work in New York City.

As the other discussion began to die out, Tony said, "Luke told me that you couldn't attend his wedding because you were working undercover. I don't think I understand that completely. Donna told me later that as Andrew 'McKennon,' you spend time with the bums and crooks. If they're crooks, why don't you just arrest them?"

Before Andrew could answer, he realized that all eyes were on him. Lorna's were very intent. He shrugged. It was difficult to explain that there were crooks and then there were crooks.

"Sometimes," he said at last, "we need to keep a rapport with the little guys so we know what the big guys are up to."

"So they go free?" Joe asked.

"In a way." He frowned. "I know a lot of petty thieves who are real nice guys. There *is* honor among thieves, you know," he said, only half joking. They were still staring at him, so he tried again. "There are guys who will steal your watch and every cent you have in ten seconds, but they'd never hurt you. They're as antiviolent as the next guy. There are also street gangs that would never involve anyone in their warfare but themselves. All of them are an independent lot, but they can be invaluable when we need assistance. So, yeah, a lot of the time they go free."

"You get to know them well, huh?" Joe asked.

Andrew picked up his fork and stabbed a piece of sausage. "Yes," he said, before biting into it.

The conversation shifted again, but when Andrew looked up from his plate, he caught Lorna watching him intently. For one brief second she appeared puzzled—and concerned.

But when he looked at her questioningly, she shivered with an involuntary motion, one that was almost imperceptible. A cloud of bleak depression settled over Andrew. She was afraid of him.

"I don't mean to be nosy," Theresa said to him, "but who's older, you or Luke?"

"Luke," Andrew told her, "by three years. Do I look that decrepid?"

"No!" Theresa answered with a laugh. "You just look . . . harder somehow."

Andrew broke off a piece of bread. He knew that when he looked at her again, Lorna would be staring at him.

She was. And she wore that puzzled and frightened look again. Then she quickly lowered her eyes from his.

Yes, she was thinking, he did look "hard." And that was a word of description that Theresa had used when comparing him to Luke, who sure as hell wasn't the type of man you would describe as a cream puff!

There was something about Andrew that was controlled but volatile. He looked wonderful in the pants and white sweater. The sweater played off his coloring and made his hair look darker, his eyes very green, and his color attractively tan. When he smiled and the lines creased around his eyes, he was very appealing, arrestingly handsome. But he wasn't smiling now. She could see the tautness of his features; they were almost gaunt, as sharp as his eyes. His looks alone revealed that he was a man accustomed to action, always on the alert. He was rough in a way; always wary, but never afraid. Lorna got the impression that Andrew, if faced with ten angry men, would weigh his odds, shrug, and enter in the fray. He might lose, but he would never give up.

Hard. Was it a hardness that had also closed around his heart? Was he a man who was incapable of giving a woman more than he had already given her?

91

She saw him gaze about the table. Noting that everyone was finished, he rose and gathered the empty plates.

"Andrew," Lorna began, frowning. Earlier she had wanted to taunt him about his willingness to "serve the people." Now she felt a little guilty. He had risen admirably—and cheerfully—to her bait.

"Are you finished, Mrs. Doria?" he interrupted her very politely.

"Yes, but—"

"Andrew, sit down!" Theresa broke in. "Entertain Tony and Joe while Lorna and I pick up. We know the system."

"The system!" Andrew protested in grinning outrage. "My dear Mrs. Miro, I assure you that I can handle things in an order that will meet even Mrs. Doria's high standards!"

"Oh, I didn't mean—" Theresa laughed, realizing that Andrew was teasing her.

Lorna lowered her eyes, pursing her lips to hide a smile. Was she really such a fanatic?

Balancing all the plates carefully on his arm, Andrew gave a slight bow that would have made the most experienced waiter proud. He disappeared between the swinging doors and reappeared before Lorna could stand to collect the food bowls.

"Mrs. Doria!" he exclaimed, eyes sparkling in what she definitely considered their most dangerous mode. "Please, sit down! You're going to mess up the system." He quickly balanced the pasta and salad bowls and the platter that held the sausage and peppers.

"Andrew—" There was a low warning note in her tone as she started to protest, but Joe Miro suddenly laughed.

"Andrew, I take it that one of your undercover jobs was in a restaurant."

"Yes. An Italian one at that. A great little place on the West Side."

Joe stood. "Listen, don't get too good at this or Theresa will start to think that I should be more helpful than I am. Oh, the heck with it. Think I could fit in with your system?"

"Sure," Andrew replied with a smile.

Tony threw his napkin on the table. "Might as well join the crowd," he told Lorna.

Theresa broke into delighted laughter.

"Wait a minute!" Lorna protested as the three men headed for her kitchen. "I've got fruit, and I was going to make espresso."

Joe and Tony looked at one another and shrugged.

"I can handle that espresso machine of yours," Tony said.

"And I can get the fruit. I can also find the after-dinner liqueurs," Joe said.

Andrew, grinning at them both, disappeared into the kitchen.

It fits right in, Lorna thought. I started this thing, and he's ending it with some real showmanship.

As Joe and Tony disappeared into the kitchen Lorna started to follow them.

"Lorna, stop!" Theresa persisted. "My mother-in-law spent her life waiting on those two. And as my father-in-law would say, This is America! Let them handle some of the domestic labor!"

Lorna gave Theresa an uneasy smile and settled back in her chair. Theresa's gaze followed the men's departure to the kitchen.

"He's wonderful," Theresa murmured.

"You mean Joe?" Lorna asked dryly.

Theresa laughed unabashedly. "You mean my husband? Yes, he's wonderful too, but I was talking about

Andrew. He's so much like Luke, and yet not like him at all."

"I agree with the 'not,' " Lorna said a bit stiffly.

"How do you mean?"

"I—uh—I don't know," Lorna murmured, unwilling to share her feelings about Andrew with anyone. "Maybe because Luke is a priest. He's always courteous, always thoughtful. He never shows the least bit of a temper—"

Theresa's chuckle cut her off. "I promise you, Luke does have a temper. Ask Donna. Any man tends to be temperamental toward a woman who—well, take Joe. He's one of the nicest, quietest guys you'd ever want to meet, but he can sure yell at me when we get into something. You see, I can make him mad because he cares so much. He worries about me, and my opinion counts. If none of it mattered, he'd have no reason to fight with me." She paused, then asked a little incredulously, "Do you actually fight with Andrew?"

Lorna stiffened again, then lied through her teeth. "Of course not. What would we ever fight about?"

Theresa shivered, but it was a delightful little shiver. "Mmm, I just love that aura of danger about him. It makes him sexy as hell!"

Oh, yeah, sexy, Lorna thought. She would never deny Andrew Trudeau "sexy," but things went beyond sexy, and beyond sexy was intimidating. Beyond sexy was a man accustomed to violence, primed to face it, toned to fight it; always tense, always ready. So ready he turned his back on a woman seconds after they had made love.

Ah, well. You could take the man out of the cop, but you could never take the cop out of the man.

A short time later she and Theresa were ushered into the parlor. Joe produced the plate Lorna had prepared earlier with apples, grapes, and pears. Tony was smugly pleased with his espresso.

Along with their little demitasse cups, she and Theresa were given the Tia Maria they both liked, served in the right glasses.

"Andrew was in charge of cleaning up," Joe explained. "And don't worry—he rinsed all the plates before putting them in the dishwasher."

She couldn't stand it any more. Lorna set down her demitasse cup and smiled at them. "I'm not worried, but I will check things out!"

As she sailed through the kitchen doors, Andrew was slipping the last plate into the dishwasher. She looked around her kitchen. It was spotless.

Andrew straightened to lean against the counter, half smiling as he lifted his arms to indicate the kitchen.

"Any problems, boss?"

"No," she said grudgingly. "It looks perfect. Andrew, I know that I started this . . ." She couldn't find the right word, so she, too, indicated the kitchen.

"I have to get the stuff from outside, but I'll do it in a few minutes," he told her. "I've been on a lot of K.P. duty, it's no big deal. If I ate, I don't mind picking up." He reached into a pocket for his cigarettes and grimaced. "What I would like is an ashtray."

Lorna frowned. "There are ashtrays all over the place."

"You mean all those pretty little dishes? Do you really use them?"

"I don't smoke, but yes, they are ashtrays."

He laughed, and she felt her mouth compress. "What's so funny?"

"Nothing. Not a thing. Isn't your espresso getting a little cold?"

"Probably, but so is yours."

"Then let's join the others, shall we?"

His hand briefly touched her back as he propelled her toward the swinging doors. Lorna felt a little quiver within her abdomen. Sexy. Yes, the man was definitely sexy. But what was worse was that all he had to do was look at her to remind her just how sexy he could be. And when he touched her, however briefly . . .

They were futile thoughts. She was not going to let things get out of hand again. Out of hand . . . she could tell anyone exactly what his hands looked like, and exactly how they felt . . .

She slipped away from his touch. His fingers had seemed like a brush of flame through the silk of her blouse.

She needed to keep her distance from him, she reminded herself. And it was getting very difficult to do so. It had been so easy to work with him in the kitchen; it was easy to have him there, seeing how he got along so well with friends she had had all her life.

Lorna closed her eyes briefly, inhaled, exhaled, and curved her lips into a bright smile with which to greet those friends.

Her smile faltered for only a moment as her heart took on a frantic beat. Soon those friends were going to leave and she would be alone with Andrew.

A man who was sexy, yes. And a man who was also very, very dangerous to her heart.

CHAPTER FOUR

Lorna had probably never talked so much in her life. She wasn't really sure what she was doing; no matter how long she talked, the Miros were eventually going to get up and leave.

And, of course, they did.

At twelve-fifteen Joe glanced at his watch, gave his wife a rueful smile, and reminded her that his parents were watching their children. Theresa immediately got up to clear away the demitasse cups. Lorna begged her not to bother.

What was the problem? Lorna asked herself. They would leave, and she would tell Andrew good night. She would go upstairs, he would disappear into the den. Why did she dread the moment so much?

Lorna kissed each member of the group as they all prepared to leave. Theresa looked at her worriedly, Tony begged her to be careful. Andrew volunteered to walk the group out.

The door closed, and Lorna was alone.

When the Miros had left, there was very little left to do. While Andrew was out with them, Lorna hurried around the parlor picking up the cups and pony glasses. The dishwasher was already swishing away, so she quickly ran some hot, sudsy water and started washing the few things in the sink.

The pans Andrew had washed earlier were still in

the drainboard. She was somewhat surprised to see that he had actually found the copper cleaner to shine the bottoms of her pots.

"I don't suppose you ever let anything sit until morning, do you?"

Andrew's voice, close behind her, startled her so badly that she swung around, slamming one of the pony glasses against the stainless steel sink.

"My fault," Andrew said briefly, as a couple of long strides brought him to her side.

Lorna stared blankly down at the broken glass, bringing her forefinger automatically to her lips when she noticed the spot of blood on the tip. Andrew started to pick the pieces of glass out of the sink. Then suddenly he was looking at her, and for no apparent reason, she was blushing. His eyes just seemed so . . . intense.

A nervous laugh escaped her. "Klaus Kinski," she said.

"What?"

"You remind me of Klaus Kinski in his roll as Dracula."

He laughed. "Great, I remind you of a vampire. How badly did you cut yourself?"

She backed away a step. "Not badly."

"I'm sorry, I didn't mean to startle you." He finished retrieving the pieces of glass and opened the cabinet to drop them in the trash. "I made you break the glass. It isn't a priceless antique, is it?"

"No, don't worry. It's replaceable."

His gaze met hers and lingered. She wondered fleetingly what was going on in his mind; his eyes gave nothing away.

He turned back to the sink. "Why don't you go on up to bed? I can finish up here."

"Why should you? It's my house."

"Ah, but I'm the servant of the people, remember?"

"Andrew—"

"Look, Lorna, it's been a long day. Please go up-stairs. Give us both a break for tonight."

Give us both a break? The evening hadn't been that unpleasant!

Lorna spun around quickly, said a brief good night, and started up the stairs. She went into her bedroom and closed the door, wishing it had a lock. Well, it did have a lock, but it locked with a key, and the key had probably been missing for a hundred years.

Why bother? she mocked herself. She knew damned well that Andrew Trudeau would never come sneaking up to her bedroom—or pounding, for that matter.

She switched on the light and kicked off her shoes as the room sprang to life. She looked at the huge four-poster bed with its light-blue comforter, the polished floorboards, the Oriental sectional rugs, her dresser with its smoky Colonial mirror. This is my home, she reminded herself, and I will be comfortable here!

Impatiently she moved to the huge armoire in one corner of the room. She slipped off her blouse and slipped it onto a hanger, hung up her pants, and dug around until she found a flannel nightgown. She pulled the nightgown from the closet, then paused. She felt so . . . sticky. Her palms were clammy, the back of her neck felt soaked. It was really ridiculous. The night was very chilly. Of course, her house was warm, but not uncomfortably so. And she was still . . .

Accept the truth, kiddo, she told herself firmly. He makes you nervous. And that's why you're so *sticky*.

She'd had a long shower less than five hours ago. Lorna sighed—not caring that the sound was very loud for a sigh. She was alone with her mixture of emotions for the moment.

She wasn't going to be able to sleep for a long time yet, anyway. A hot tub full of bubbles and a long soak with a good book might be right in order.

She carried her gown into the bathroom and hung it on the door, then started running a bath, smiling ruefully as she uncapped the swan depression-glass decanter and added the bubble mixture to the tub. Even the bathtub was indicative of her personality—or of her personality quirks. It was a massive thing with huge, clawed feet and old, elegant faucets.

"Well, I like big bathtubs, and I like antiques!" she murmured aloud, realizing that her tone was defensive. Feeling impatient with herself, she stripped off her lingerie, searched the glass and brass shelves above the commode to find what she called her "bathtub" book, and crawled into the tub. Holding the book carefully out of the water, she grabbed the swan and poured more bubblebath beneath the spigot, then balanced the decanter on the edge of the tub. She settled back with her head resting over the rim and opened her book.

But the book was a murder mystery, and Lorna noticed that her hands were shaking. She set the book down, turned off the water, and leaned back again, closing her eyes.

Was she being a fool? Shouldn't she be willing to go anyplace—with anyone—where she might be safe? It wasn't a matter of courage that made her determined to live her life as normally as was possible, it was just an abject horror of being locked away again.

It would be nice to fall asleep, nice to forget all about Andrew's reappearance in her life and the brick that had flown through her shop window. It would be even nicer if she could stop thinking about this thing on so many levels. She didn't want to die and she didn't want to get too close to Andrew. But then

100

again, she didn't want Andrew to go away because, as far as her life went, she did trust him.

"Idiot!" she whispered aloud when a new wave of shivers enveloped her despite the heat of the bath. "You should run, you should do anything in your power to live and worry about the rest later!"

Maybe it wouldn't be quite so bad if she did what Donna suggested. Donna was her best friend and Luke was a terrific guy. Even with Andrew around, it wouldn't be so bad. They wouldn't be alone, there would be barriers between them. It wouldn't be like it had been in New York.

She opened her eyes, then closed them again. Her business was going to be in shambles if she closed it up again. Yet it would be better to be alive with a faltering business than dead with a prospering one. An associate had called her the day before to tell her about an estate auction in Boston next week. The estate had belonged to the Cannarys, a family that had settled in Boston when it had still been part of the Massachusetts Bay Colony. To Lorna such a sale was what Christmas was to a child. Well, maybe, just maybe, she could get to the sale and then go hide out. That was it! Perfect, she thought.

If Andrew would just agree. Well, it could be a deal. She would promise to hide out if and only if she could go to the sale. After all, Simson wasn't psychic; he would expect her to be in Worcester or Paxton, not Boston.

With that settled in her mind, Lorna sat up and reached for the soap. As she bent a knee to raise her foot out of the bubbles, she knocked over the glass decanter. It hit the tile on the bathroom floor with a shattering crash.

Lorna looked over the side of the tub a little blankly, then muttered, "Damn!" First the glass in the

101

kitchen and now her little swan. She was becoming dangerous to her own belongings.

She was still staring at the glass when a new sound startled her. She swung around to face the door, a loud, terrified scream escaping her as it banged in.

Then her scream died. If the situation weren't so uncomfortable, she would have laughed.

Andrew was standing in the doorway looking very tense and anxious. His mouth was compressed to what she had come to think of as its "scowling cop line," and his eyes were darting quickly around the room. One white-knuckled hand was tightly curled around the doorknob, the other was clenched against the door frame.

And then his eyes were on her. She returned his stare—her challenge dying on her lips before she could voice it.

"What happened?" he demanded.

Lorna lowered her lashes, praying that not too many of her bubbles would burst.

"I broke my swan."

"You *what?*" His voice was puzzled and aggravated.

"My swan. I broke a decanter, that's all."

"Oh, my God." He exhaled with relief.

But he was still standing in her bathroom doorway and she just didn't know how long her bubbles would last. Lorna realized that it was very difficult to look remote and sophisticated while sitting naked in a bubble bath.

"Andrew—"

"You're all right?"

"I'm fine. I told you, I just broke the stupid swan."

"Well, you almost made me a candidate for an early coronary!" he said, his words crisp with irritation.

"Well, I'm sorry!" she answered in kind. "It wasn't

my intention to frighten you. Or to break the swan. Now—"

"Clumsy lately, aren't you?"

He wasn't gripping the door handle anymore, nor was he tense. And if he was still angry from the scare, she couldn't tell by looking at him. He had shifted so that he was leaning nonchalantly against the door frame, watching her with amusement.

"Andrew, could we discuss my coordination—or lack of it—at another time? You're supposed to be woodwork, you know. And woodwork doesn't usually interrupt my bath."

"But this woodwork is protecting you. If you don't want me showing up in intimate places, you should try not to make so much noise while you're occupying them."

The bubbles were breaking all around her at an alarming rate. Maybe it had something to do with the sudden rush of air, or maybe it had something to do with her own body heat, which was rapidly rising.

"Andrew."

He waved a hand jauntily in the air. "But then again, Lorna, I wouldn't let any of it bother you too much. I mean, we aren't talking about unfamiliar territory here, are we?"

She felt his eyes, sparkling and unabashed, raking over her. They seemed to have a tangible touch as they brushed over her breasts, her stomach, to the end of the tub and the region where her feet were buried beneath the suds, then back to her breasts and to her eyes. His lips were twitching.

"Andrew, get out of my bathroom!"

He lifted his hands innocently. "I'm going. Have a nice night."

And he was gone, closing the bathroom door behind him.

Lorna stared after him. "You royal pain in the—"
She realized that her hand was squeezed so tightly
around the soap bar that she had formed indentations
in it. At least she hadn't thrown it.

Still muttering, she rose, grabbed a towel, and nervously slid into her nightgown. She cleaned up the
broken glass and the puddle of bubble bath it lay in,
still muttering and swearing softly. Leaving the bath
immaculate, she forced herself into bed. She was still
far from sleepy, so she turned on the portable television on the far side of her dresser. A Worcester station
was showing reruns of an old sitcom. Not exactly
stimulating, but far from the subject of murder.

Her mind wandered quickly from the television.
Maybe she was handling things all wrong. Maybe she
should have crawled out of the tub with the bubbles
clinging to her and flung herself into his arms. "You
want to resume a relationship, Trudeau? Then hold
me. . . ."

She was going crazy again—and she wasn't even
locked away. She didn't want to have an affair with
the man, she wanted more. She wanted to understand
him.

No.

Yes.

That's where all the problems lay, she realized. Before he had been sexy, Andrew had been kind. And
before they had become lovers, she'd had that strange
feeling that she'd waited all her life to meet him.

Lorna tossed in her bed, plumping the pillows. If
only she had handled things differently that first time
when he had jumped out of bed so angrily. If she had
asked him why instead of turning her own back in
anger. . . .

No one was going to be thinking logically at such a
time, she reminded herself sadly. The first normal hu-

man reactions would be the exact ones she had experienced. She had been stunned, hurt, and angry. And then, of course, she had wondered what was wrong with her that could draw such a reaction from him.

She stiffened, remembering their second encounter and his apologies. She'd never been so bewildered or hurt.

On one level, she could make some sense of it. Andrew was a cop, and their relationship—or lack thereof, as she had reminded him—was certainly not in the bounds of duty.

But still . . .

No, she would never be able to make morning coffee and calmly ask him to sit down so that they could discuss their strange and brief sex life together. Besides, he probably wouldn't be able to explain his actions, and even if he could, she wouldn't like the explanation.

Andrew just didn't want to be involved. Superficially yes, but on a deeper level, no. And, as much as she liked him—yes, she could admit that she liked him very much—she wasn't sure about him. He meant more than danger to her heart. There was an aura of danger about the man himself. He knew humanity on endless levels, he had lived among the down-and-out and the street gangs and he could change his personality like a chameleon. Lorna wasn't sure she knew who the real Andrew was.

Besides, if she were ever really involved with a such a man, she would be constantly worried, wondering where his next assignment would take him and what new danger he was being exposed to.

Lorna got up and flipped off the television. Then she crawled back into bed, wrapped her arms around her pillow, and closed her eyes.

None of it mattered. Andrew didn't want to be

pinned down or involved. She was best off reminding herself that she wasn't too sure she would want him anyway.

Downstairs, Andrew was standing in the kitchen, staring at his watch and then at the kitchen extension. He looked at his watch again. One A.M. A little late for a phone call, especially when he didn't really know what he wanted to say. He just felt as if . . .

He shrugged to himself. His nerves were on edge, what with that sound of shattering glass and the terrible dread he had felt. And then—Lorna.

Her bright-blue eyes on him had been startled, then sparkling with anger. Cool anger, of course. She knew how to behave with elegant poise even when a man burst into her bathroom.

He'd been glad she'd been wearing a lot of bubbles. Well, maybe not quite enough bubbles. They'd foamed like white snow around her breasts, and yet he had seen a hint of rose color at their crests. Or maybe he just knew that the rose was there because he just knew how she looked when he cupped her breasts in his hands.

Hmm. Maybe there *was* very little to be seen, maybe it was all a figment of his memory, a vision he saw with painful clarity. He knew the length of her legs and the curve of her hips. He knew . . . that bubbles surrounding a beautiful woman were extremely erotic. So erotic that they made a man's mouth go dry; his hands would have trembled if he had let them.

His own early-warning system had been in effect long before she'd ordered him out. Andrew had been listening, he just hadn't managed to turn himself around. He'd been unable to stop himself from teasing her simply because the situation *had* been innocent on his part.

106

Andrew ground his teeth sharply together and stared at the phone again. Despite the fact that a brick had flown through Lorna's shop window, he felt strangely serene about the night. And feeling serene made him as nervous as hell. He didn't like to let his guard down, and because he felt the way he did, the compulsion to talk to his brother was a strong one.

He picked up the phone and started dialing.

The phone rang several times before a soft, feminine voice finally answered.

"Hello?" Her voice was breathy.

"Donna?"

"Andrew?"

"Yes, I hope I didn't wake you up—"

"No, no. Is something wrong? Has something happened?"

"No," Andrew said reassuringly. "Really, Donna, I promise you, everything is fine."

"Oh, thank God!" she murmured. Then she asked in a puzzled tone, "Andrew, do you know what time it is?"

There was the slightest touch of exasperation to her voice, and he chuckled. "Yes, I know what time it is. And I'm sorry, I guess I didn't wake you up, but obviously I did interrupt things."

"Andrew!"

"I'm sorry, but you two are married. You can crawl right back to bed. I'd like to talk to Luke, though, just for a second."

"Well, now you might as well take your time!" she told him dryly. "At least you didn't crawl through the window. Luke, it's Andrew."

While he waited for his brother to get on the line, Andrew grinned, remembering the first time he had met Donna. At that time he had always crawled through his brother's window to get into the house

107

because he hadn't wanted anyone to associate him and Luke. On one such occasion he had crawled through and come face to face with Donna.

"Damn, Drew, do you know what time it is?"

Andrew could understand Luke's irritation. He'd been dragged out of his bed—and his wife's arms, apparently—at one A.M., all because of a feeling, Andrew thought unhappily.

"Yeah, I just went through it with Donna, and I'm sorry, Luke."

"Well?"

"Well—" Andrew hesitated. "Luke, this is going to sound very strange, I know, but I felt like I *had* to call. I feel too easy about everything, as if—as if nothing is going to happen for a while."

"Drew, I'm *not* a prophet, you know." Luke's voice came over the wire quietly. Andrew knew that his brother was no longer angry and, absurd as it might be, he understood the feeling.

Luke wasn't a prophet, no. Nor did Andrew ever call his brother a psychic. They didn't call "it" anything, but the police had used Luke Trudeau's extraordinary mind many times, and now Andrew just felt that he had to know his brother's intuitions.

"Luke," he prompted.

A sigh came over the wire. "Okay, Andrew, I'll tell you what I feel as best I can. Remember, though, that my feelings don't come with signed guarantees. Tonight I get a feeling of calm. And I was enjoying that calm until you called."

"Sorry," Andrew repeated, grinning.

"You should be," Luke said, but Andrew could sense that his brother was grinning too. "I feel that Lorna is okay as long as she stays inside that house. For the next two days at least."

"*In* the house?"

Luke sighed with exasperation. "In the house, yes. Don't ask me why—these are just feelings. Keep Lorna inside and things should be all right."

"What about next week?"

"What do you think I am, Andrew, the *Farmer's Almanac?*"

"Luke, give me a break."

"I'm sorry. I just really don't know what to tell you. I feel that Simson will lay fairly low, but that doesn't mean that danger doesn't exist. Simson will be going for a hit-or-miss play. And he isn't invincible, you know. I think that if we take care, we'll all come out of it okay."

"That's good to hear."

Luke was strangely silent on the other end of the wire.

"Luke?" Andrew pressed him. "You're thinking something."

"Well, the thought just occurred to me that . . . oh, just that Simson isn't the only danger in the world."

"What does that mean?"

Andrew knew his brother well. He could almost see him shrugging. "I guess it doesn't mean anything except that you should be careful. I'd *like* to see you two at the mountain retreat."

"Yeah, I would too."

"I can't tell you anything else, Drew. Work on Lorna. See if you can't get her to agree to a vacation in the mountains. I'll call her again or I'll have Donna call her. It's the only thing that I really do feel good about."

"Okay, Luke. I'll do that." He paused. "I really am sorry for the hour—and the interruption."

"I guess I'll forgive you, especially since your friends are all over my street."

109

"Cops?"

"Yes. The ones assigned to us, and I'd say at least another five undercover guys."

Andrew grinned. The force did make for some solid, supporting friendships. "Good."

"Your old partner is out there, by the way."

"Tricia?" Andrew smiled again. When he'd been a rookie, his partner had been a gruff, but sharp old man named Lewis. When Lewis had retired, Andrew had been paired up with Tricia. He'd have been a liar to deny that he had had a whole lot of reservations about working with a woman, but Tricia had proven herself to be every bit as sharp as Lewis, and her sex had often proved invaluable to them as a team of detectives. But after Simson had been arrested, Andrew had been left on the case while Tricia had been pulled off. She was proving to be as good a friend, too, as any man on the force.

"Give her my thanks."

Luke laughed. "I don't know if I should approach her. She's pretending to be a prostitute—right in front of a priest's house!"

Andrew laughed. Luke promised to pass on Andrew's message anyway, then Donna was back on the phone, demanding to know how Andrew had liked her brothers and her sister-in-law. At last Andrew rang off.

He walked into the den, pulled off his clothes, leaving his shorts on, and tried to sleep.

It was no good. He was still too worried about feeling calm.

Muttering to himself that he was the biggest fool in the world, he took his pillow and blanket—and his gun—to the foot of the stairs. It was stupid, because he did have faith in the guys outside and in his broth-

110

er's words. But just in case—well, no one would be getting past him.

It wasn't terribly comfortable, but he had slept in much worse places. If he could just quit worrying!

He allowed his mind to wander to Lorna again, and the way she looked decked out in a million tiny bubbles. Mmm. He would have really loved drying off those bubbles for her.

Not a good path for the mind to take, he warned himself, but it was better than worrying about the days to come and he allowed himself the fantasy.

So he spent a lot of time tossing and turning on the hardwood floor, telling himself that it couldn't be, that he was being more of a fool than he would ever know.

Lorna awoke feeling a little groggy. She'd gone to sleep awfully late, but her inner clock hadn't allowed her to make up for lost time by sleeping late.

She had a strange sensation that something pleasant had happened during the night, and for several moments she lay there, puzzled. Then she jumped out of bed and raced to the window. A little cry of delight escaped her.

The sky had been promising snow, and that snow, the first of the season, had fallen during the night. Her sloping lawn was blanketed with beautiful, fresh white flakes. The pines behind her yard were also covered, their branches dipping beneath the weight of the snow, and the entire picture was a winter wonderland.

Lorna hurried to her dresser for thick socks, jeans, and a bulky wool sweater. She rinsed her face and gave her teeth and hair a quick brushing, finished dressing by pulling on boots, gloves, and a jacket, and raced down the stairs.

Andrew was nowhere to be seen. He was probably still sleeping, she decided, which was just as well. He

111

might have had something caustic or irritating to say and she didn't want this first touch of winter to be marred in any way.

The back door was through the cellar, which had been converted to a game and family room. The steps to it led down from the kitchen. Lorna thought about putting some coffee on, then saw that Andrew had apparently started it already, which meant that she should hurry out before he made a reappearance.

She pulled open the cellar door, raced down the steps, and hurried to the back. The main door and the screen door were latched; in her gloves she fumbled with each, then hopped up the few steps that led to the lawn.

The air that touched her cheeks was wonderfully crisp and invigorating, and the snow was beautiful. By the end of January, or probably before, she would be tired of snow and winter weather, but right now . . . now it was just wonderful.

She stepped out into the yard and knelt down to cup the snow in her hands. She stuck out her tongue to taste a bit, then threw the handful back into the air. She started to walk again, hearing the snow crunch beneath her boots.

She noted that the little pond that sometimes hosted a variety of birds was also covered with snow. The water must have frozen and then been covered by the snow. She'd have to get something put up around it before someone slipped and fell, not expecting the patch of ice.

Lorna stared out at the pines again, smiling once more. They looked so pretty against the clear blue sky that contained a few light clouds as white as the snow.

"Lorna!"

She spun around as a voice that was harsh and annoyed cut through her happy observations of the day.

Andrew. Who else? Clomping after her through the snow, he was wearing a scowl that would have become Genghis Khan. Her heart fluttered a little as she remembered that she had promised not to walk out of her house without his okay. But she was sure she was in no danger; after all, her road was a dead end and the patrolmen were still on duty.

"Lorna, I swear you are an obstinate mule with no sense of self-preservation whatsoever. Will you please get back into the hou—umph!"

Andrew had walked right onto the bird pond and was now sailing toward her like a child on a slip-and-slide. His expression was so startled, his flight so comical, that she couldn't help but burst into laughter.

He came to a stop at her feet and looked up at her. His features twisted into a mask of stunned chagrin, then anger flashed briefly through his eyes, and finally he was laughing too.

Then Lorna was the one to gasp in sudden shock when his hands closed around her ankles, jerked, and sent her flying backward to land on her rear in the snow.

"You—" She began to sputter.

But the sparkle in his eyes was not worthy of her words, it was worthy of a whole lot more. She clenched her gloved hands around the snow beneath them and pelted him with the moist flakes. They showered over his face, turning his eyebrows to a frosty white and melting on his cheeks.

"War, is it?" he cried. The next thing she knew, he was grabbing his own fistfuls of the newly fallen snow.

"No, wait!" Lorna decided belatedly. She pushed herself to her feet, trying to balance on the slippery snow. *His* handfuls of snow were *big* ones.

She turned and started to run, but didn't get very far at all. His body catapulted against hers and they

113

were down on the ground again, rolling in the snow until they were covered in the white flakes. The impetus of his movement at last came to a halt, and when it did, Lorna found herself lying on her back staring up into his eyes.

He was straddled over her hips, pinning her in place. His eyes were still full of laughter, his brows were still snow white, and his fists were still full of snow.

"No!" Lorna screamed, but she was laughing too. Andrew didn't *throw* the snow at her, he just picked up his hands and let it fall. She was suddenly sputtering to get it out of her mouth, and then she was staring into his eyes again.

A silence fell between them, a silence like the snowbound day. Nothing rustled in the wind, no bird cried to break that crystal moment between them.

Lorna felt as if she were holding her breath, and yet she was breathing. She felt his thighs about her, and they were very warm against the cold.

But his eyes . . .

She could never read all the emotions that churned and swept through the guarded depths of his eyes. Andrew's smile faded as he reached a gloved finger to her cheek and gently pushed the flakes of snow aside. He touched her brows, clearing them of the clinging snow, and she longed to reach out and touch his cheek, to slip her arms around him and pull him to her.

She didn't. And at last he withdrew his hand. He stood, reaching down to help her up.

She could have just stood; she intended to, but suddenly the opportunity seemed too good. She wrenched hard on the hand that had been offered her, shifting her weight. Delightfully, to her great triumph, Andrew fell face first back into the snow.

He twisted around quickly, but for once Lorna was quicker. Her snow was ready in her gloved hands, and she allowed it to simply fall on his face.

"Think you're a comedian, huh?" he challenged. Before she could move, she found that she was the one beneath him again, wearing most of the snow.

This time she did reach out. She was laughing so hard at the snow caked to his brows that she had to dust it off. But when he caught her hands, her laughter faltered. That expression was back in his eyes, sharp and yet guarded. And, as she had felt last night, his eyes touched her more surely than his hands.

Lorna thought he was going to lower his head until his lips touched hers, until they both denied the lie of any argument.

But then the tense, unfathomable expression in his eyes and features disappeared. He released her hands and moved away from her. His tone was clipped and mocking. "No, no, no, Mrs. Doria! You're not supposed to touch!"

Lorna quickly drew her emotions into herself with a lot more self-preservation than he would ever understand.

"Lieutenant Trudeau, I believe you started this fiasco. You pulled me down by the ankles."

"The best of us have our lapses," he said, and she sensed the bitterness behind the words. Why not? she thought. She was one of his "lapses," wasn't she?

"Come on, Lorna, get up," he commanded. "We both must be crazy. You shouldn't be out here to begin with."

He offered her his hand again. She could see no reason to take it, but neither did he give her time to think. His eyes were scanning the pines, as if he expected danger was lurking behind them. When she didn't take his hand, he took hers, half dragging her to her feet.

"Andrew—" she began.

He gave her a little shove from behind, following closely. "Yell as soon as we get in the house, will you please?"

She started walking toward the house, irritated that he was practically on top of her.

Yet he would be. He was her bodyguard.

CHAPTER FIVE

Lorna didn't yell at anyone, because from the time she returned to the house to the moment she fell into bed, it proved to be one of the most hectic days of her life.

The doorbell was chiming and the phone was ringing when they got inside. Andrew told her to answer the phone; he would get the door. The men at the door were from Freholt Security Company. While Lorna was still on the phone, Andrew invited the men in and started showing them where he found the greatest weaknesses in the house.

The woman on the phone was from the New York D.A.'s office; she wanted to see Lorna that afternoon to take another deposition. She intended to be on a shuttle flight within the hour, and could reach Lorna's by one or two in the afternoon at the latest.

"But I don't understand," Lorna protested, watching uneasily as Andrew led the security men around the house. "I've already given dozens of statements. I gave you a statement before the arraignment and I identified Simson in a line-up before I left New York!"

"I'm sorry, Mrs. Doria, I'd like to go over it with you just one more time."

Lorna sighed. "Whatever you want. I'll be here."

"You'll be there? The time is convenient?"

"Yes." When Lorna hung up, Andrew was leaning against the kitchen door frame, watching her.

"The D.A.'s office?"

"Yes. A Miss Latham is coming out here."

Andrew raised a brow. "That's a courtesy, you know."

"A courtesy?" She asked bitterly.

"The D.A. was the man who ordered special protection this time. That's why his office is coming to you."

"Great," she murmured, but she wasn't really paying attention to Andrew anymore. One man was walking around her house with a pile of wires while another was drilling away at her front door.

They were both—not intentionally, she knew—leaving wet tracks on her floors. So much for enjoying the first snow of the season, she thought ruefully.

Andrew must have been reading her mind. "The floors will clean, Lorna."

"I know," she said. She turned her back on him and poured herself a cup of coffee. Thinking twice, she poured one for him without asking. He accepted it with a murmur of thanks, turned around, and left the kitchen.

Lorna ran upstairs to change her snow-drenched clothing, leaving it in a pile to run down to the dryer. Then, despite herself, she was thinking about Andrew again. He was still drenched. Maybe he didn't mind being wet, but she should at least offer to throw his things in the dryer too.

When she came back downstairs, there were four men from the security company in her house. Things were definitely out of her control.

She found Andrew helping a thin, white-haired man stretch a wire across the parlor window. She raised a brow, indicating the new arrivals. The man gave her a jaunty hello.

"I told them it was a rush job," Andrew explained. She had to stand over him as he was lying on the floor

118

to follow instructions and bring the wire up through the wall.

"Oh," Lorna said briefly.

They were still drilling at the front door and the sound was giving her a horrible headache.

Andrew finished with the wire and stood up, dusting his hands on his pants. "Is that it, Mr. Martin?" he asked the white-haired man.

"For now, Lieutenant Trudeau. Thanks for the help."

"Not at all, I'm here to help. Lorna, why don't you put on some more coffee for these guys?"

She nodded, then indicated the bundle of clothing in her arms. "I thought you might want to change and give me your wet stuff to put in the dryer."

He looked at her peculiarly for a minute. "Thanks."

He disappeared into the den.

Mr. Martin smiled at her while he was fitting a thin wire across the glass. "These old places are real hard to do right," he told her, "but I promise you, ma'am, no one will ever get in here without you knowing when we're through! And the alarm system will go straight to the local police."

Lorna made herself smile because the man was so nice. "I'm sure you're right," she agreed.

Andrew reappeared, wearing a beige pullover and clean denims. He handed her his wet clothing with another thanks.

Lorna mumbled something and retreated to the kitchen. She hurried down to the cellar and started stuffing things into the dryer, then retraced her steps to the kitchen and put on another pot of coffee. Andrew wandered into the kitchen just as the percolator began to bubble.

"I've got another problem, you know," she told him with her back to him.

"What's that?"

"The shop window."

"They boarded it up last night."

Lorna turned around quickly. "But I can't leave it like that, Andrew, it looks horrible!"

"Does that matter—for now?"

"Of course it matters!"

He walked past her and watched the coffee as it perked. "I think it would be a good idea if you stayed away from the shop."

She began to protest, then remembered that she wanted to bargain, and she smiled sweetly. "But, Andrew, I thought you were here so that my life could be normal."

"I am."

"Well, it isn't normal to close down a place of business. Still—" she frowned, as if in concentration—"I do need to replenish some stock."

"Meaning? What are you getting at, Lorna? I know you aren't in any financial trouble. Donna told me once that your parents left you quite comfortable, and your husband had a sizable life insurance policy."

"I'm comfortable," Lorna agreed, "but not so affluent that I don't have to worry about the future."

Andrew decided that the coffee had perked enough. He found his empty cup on the counter and filled it again. Lorna wandered to the kitchen table and sat, watching his back as he got his coffee. She shivered a little, noting the breadth of his shoulders. Andrew gave the appearance of being slender, but he wasn't really. He was just tall and tightly muscled.

She started when he spoke again. "What are you getting at, Lorna? You don't smile that way unless you want something."

"Oh, really!" she snapped.

"Really," he said, turning around and leaning

120

against the counter as he watched her. The fact that he knew something was coming and seemed to be patiently waiting to hear what it was irritated her.

"All right," she said bluntly, deciding honesty would be her best policy. "You still think I'd be better off in hiding, right?"

"Right."

"And if you look at the situation logically, the greatest danger does lie around my 'known' habitats, my home and my store."

"I'd say so."

She suddenly found a great fascination in her thumb and stared at it while she talked. "I have to go to Boston, Andrew."

"What?"

"I have to go to Boston. Just for a day."

"Where does this come in?" he demanded. "You were just talking about the relative safety of going into hiding—"

"And," Lorna interrupted, firmly reminding herself that she was the private citizen and that the two of them were more involved than they should be, "I was pointing out the fact that anyone who was looking for me would be looking for me here."

Andrew closed his eyes and massaged his temple with his thumb and forefingers. "I see."

"Do you?"

"I see your logic. I don't know if I agree with it. We'd be back to square one in Boston."

"Andrew, I need to go to an estate auction. If I could get to that auction, I could purchase enough stock so that I wouldn't have to worry about it for a long time. If I did that I'd be all set to reopen if I did decide to close down again for a while."

"Close down?" His eyes opened. He set down his coffee cup and reached into his pocket for his cigarettes. Lorna automatically stood to offer him an ashtray. Her hands were trembling and she was annoyed with herself. She shouldn't have to be making a deal with him, but that was exactly what she was doing.

As soon as she had placed an ashtray by his coffee cup, she sat again. The kitchen seemed very small, and it wasn't small at all.

He's not my keeper! she tried to tell herself. But in a way he was. He had completely taken over, and she couldn't really argue, because he was trying to keep her alive.

He inhaled on his cigarette, watching her through half-closed eyes, eyes that gleamed with a catlike wariness.

"I take it that if I let you go to Boston, you'll agree to spend the rest of the time in hiding."

"Yes," Lorna replied stiffly.

He sighed. "I really don't like you going out at all."

"But I can't spend the rest of my life crawling beneath rocks! Believe me, I don't want to die, but I've thought this through. How the hell would anyone know I was in Boston? And even if someone did figure it out, I'd be gone by then."

He inhaled and exhaled again.

"You smoke too much—and you drink way too much coffee," Lorna commented.

"Maybe," Andrew murmured.

As silence prevailed, Lorna felt the tension increasing with every second that passed. He just kept watching her—and thinking, she assumed. She wanted to shake him for an answer.

"Andrew," she said sharply. "I am still a free citizen. I don't need your permission to do anything."

Well, it was true. But it had been the wrong comment to make. His eyes narrowed further and there was a visible tightening about his jaw, but he still said nothing.

Just when she thought she would absolutely explode, the white-haired man from the security company walked through the swinging doors, apologizing for the interruption.

"Lieutenant Trudeau, there's an officer out here to see you."

"Oh, thanks." Andrew crushed out his cigarette and started to follow the security man out of the kitchen.

"Andrew!" Lorna snapped, jumping from her chair. He paused, annoyed, at the doors.

"You're expecting someone, I take it?"

"Yes. Your dog."

"My dog?"

"The shepherd," he reminded her. He continued out the door. It almost swung into her face, but she caught it and followed him, her annoyance growing stronger. She wouldn't need a damned dog if she went to Boston and then to South Carolina.

"Andrew—" Lorna stopped in the center of the foyer. The security men had already finished with the front door. There were two new shiny brass bolts and she could barely see the wires that had been fitted to cross-grain in the woodwork where it met the small lookout panels of glass.

Two of the security men had moved into the dining room. From the footsteps overhead, she assumed that the other men were at an upstairs window.

But now there were two more intruders in her home. A small man in uniform was talking to Andrew. He held a leash that led to the collar around the largest German shepherd she had ever seen.

The shepherd was just sitting there, panting slightly.

"Lorna"—Andrew turned to her—"come here and meet Sergeant Wilkes and George."

"George?" she said weakly.

"That's his name, Mrs. Doria," Sergeant Wilkes explained. The man was chewing gum and he spoke with a slow drawl. He was the shortest cop she'd ever seen —he was no more than five foot seven—but he had a nice, easy grin to go with his voice. She liked the sergeant on first impression, but George was another matter.

George was drooling on her floor. Then the animal gave a big shake and riddled her floor with melting flakes of snow.

Lorna stepped forward tentatively. She shook Sergeant Wilke's hand, then stepped back again to look down at George. He didn't look ferocious, he just looked messy.

"Shake with the lady, George," Sergeant Wilkes said.

The shepherd obligingly lifted a paw. Lorna looked at that paw. It was huge, and damp and grimy with snow and dirt.

"You want me to—"

"For heaven's sake, Lorna," Andrew said impatiently. "Shake with George. He needs to know that you're his friend and that you're the one he's protecting."

Oh, my God, Lorna thought. I not only get stuck with super-cop Trudeau, but a miniature horse as well.

She swallowed and took the dog's paw. "Hi, George," she murmured. George returned the greeting by thumping his tail against the floor and whining slightly. Before Lorna could drop his paw, he licked her hand.

"I'll stick around today, Lieutenant," Wilkes was telling Andrew. "Get you and Mrs. Doria acquainted

124

with George, and George acquainted with the house. You ever work canine, Lieutenant?"

"Yeah, about a year ago. We had to team up with a bomb squad."

Wilkes nodded, as if the brief answer made sense. "Then you'll know what you're doing. I'll take George around the house and grounds now."

He started to turn. "Wait!" Lorna called out.

Sergeant Wilkes looked to her expectantly. "I—I don't know what to do with him. I mean—"

"Just feed him and let him be near you. George will do the rest, ma'am. Oh, if you have friends over, introduce them to George just like I did now." Sergeant Wilkes touched his cap and led George back outside.

"This is insane!" Lorna muttered.

"What is?"

"George!"

"Lorna," Andrew said, shoving his hands into his pockets in a way she had come to learn meant that he was going to be impatient and obstinate, "there is nothing in the world as good an alarm system as a good dog."

"But he'll bark at everyone!"

"That's right."

"My mailman, my friends—"

"And he'll give you the opportunity to determine whether or not it *is* just your mailman or your friends."

"But—"

"But what happens to George if we go to Boston?"

"Yes, exactly," Lorna said, every bit as stubborn as he was.

"He goes with us."

"You are crazy. They don't allow dogs in hotel rooms!"

"Yes, they will. They'll allow George."

125

"Andrew—"

"Lorna, believe me, I know what I'm talking about. A seeing-eye dog can get into a hotel room, and so can George. *If* we go."

"What do you mean, 'if'? I'm a private citizen and I'll do what I damn well please. You've turned my home into a circus, my business into a joke, and my life into a disaster! I'm sick of this, all of this. I should just refuse to testify."

His lashes fell briefly over his eyes. When he looked at her again, his eyes registered a chill that seemed to touch her and rip cruelly along her spine.

"You'd let a murderer go free, Mrs. Doria?"

"Why shouldn't I? It seems that the law does."

"That isn't true."

"The hell it isn't!"

"We're all doing our damned best, Mrs. Doria."

"Well, it doesn't seem to be enough, does it?" Lorna challenged him. "Simson is running around free, and I'm the one in the cage again."

"The law is trying to *help* you, Lorna!" Andrew grated quietly. Then something in him snapped, just as it had in her. He moved swiftly, grasping her shoulders and holding them tightly as he gazed down into her eyes. "I'm not the one who threw the brick through your window, Lorna. And if I've made a circus of your well-ordered house, I'm sorry as hell. As for your life, well, you've needed or deserved everything that you've gotten—from me at any rate. It's been a jolt out of that pristine little shell of yours." His voice lowered dramatically when he apparently realized that the security men were not beyond their hearing. "I keep apologizing to you, don't I, Lorna? Well, I won't anymore. A hob-nob with humanity was just what you needed. You were on the same human plane with the rest of us—for a few minutes at least."

She felt her facial muscles tightening and could hear the sandy grind of her teeth as she clenched them together. She could also feel the color draining from her face, and she longed for the power to send him crashing against a wall. Lorna tried to tell herself that he didn't mean what he was saying, that he was angry and spouting off, just as she had been when she had threatened not to testify.

But he did mean it—that was exactly the problem between them. Or part of the problem between them.

She jerked from his touch, tears of anger and confusion stinging her eyes.

"I don't put myself on any pedestals, Lieutenant. If you've done so, then that's your problem." She turned around, heading for the kitchen. She wanted to get there quickly, before she could burst into tears of frustration and start asking herself the same futile question again—why me?

"Lorna!" He called her back sharply.

"What?" She didn't turn around.

"Did you mean that? Are you going to refuse to testify?"

She paused a long time, but still didn't turn to face him. "No, Lieutenant. I plan on being an honest, law-abiding citizen. A credit to that plane of humanity. I'll be testifying."

She hurried into the kitchen and started to pour herself more coffee. Her hands were not trembling, they were more like shaking branches in a snowstorm.

She decided on a brandy instead.

By one o'clock Lorna had recovered a semblance of her composure. She'd cheerfully made sandwiches for the security men and the new set of patrolmen parked beyond her driveway.

She was in the kitchen, and though Andrew was

127

still combing the house with the security men, she was not alone. George was at her feet.

He was stretched out on the floor, panting as seemed to be his normal state. Every once in a while his tail thumped against the floor. Lorna just kept watching him. She wondered why he kept panting when it was so cold outside. She also wondered if and when she was going to be able to pat his head and "get close to him," as Sergeant Wilkes had advised.

"Oh, George!" Lorna murmured. "It's nothing personal—really. It's just that you're a dog. Dogs shed. And they pant. And they drool."

George wagged his tail.

Then Lorna almost went flying from her chair, because George was on his feet, barking very loudly. She wondered how she could have ever thought he looked docile; his teeth were bared and he looked like a real killer.

He bounded past her into the front hall, jumping on the door and barking, if possible, even louder.

"George!" Lorna screamed, but by the time she could follow him Andrew was already there, gazing through the small glass panes on the door.

"Down, George," he said. "It's a friend."

George immediately dropped to his feet. The barking stopped and he sat on his haunches a step or two behind Andrew.

Andrew opened the door to admit a small woman in a fur-lined trench coat and a brown fedora.

"Hi, Milly," he greeted her pleasantly.

Milly? Lorna raised a brow.

"Andrew, how are you?" Milly entered, tugging at the belt of her coat. She stood on tiptoe to plant a kiss on his cheek and then gazed past Andrew to Lorna.

"Mrs. Doria"—Milly walked toward Lorna with her hand extended—"I'm Milly Latham. I'm sorry I never had a chance to meet you in New York, and I do apologize for this intrusion on your privacy."

What's private anymore? Lorna wondered sourly, but she smiled and accepted the woman's hand. "There's nothing to apologize for."

"I'd just like to get one more statement from you, if you don't mind. As the trial approaches, we'll be talking more, of course, but for now we just want to make sure that your memory remains fresh. Do you mind if I use a tape recorder?"

"No, not at all." Lorna lifted a hand, indicating the kitchen. "I believe it's the quietest room at the moment, Miss Latham."

"We're going to be working together frequently, Mrs. Doria, and I don't have any great title, so please call me Milly."

Lorna returned the gesture and asked Milly to call her by her given name. She led the way into the kitchen, poured coffee while Milly set up her tape recorder, and then joined her at the table. Milly Latham was, Lorna judged, in her late twenties or early thirties. She was attractive in a no-nonsense way, and Lorna couldn't help wondering just how well she knew Andrew. It made sense, of course, that they were acquainted, Lorna told herself. The police and the district attorney's office had to work closely together.

"Now, let's start with your name, your reason for being in New York, what you were doing on that particular street, and then exactly what happened as you saw it."

Lorna took a deep breath. She had done this so many times! She stated her name, explained that she had been a tourist, and then described the crime exactly as she had seen it. Occasionally Milly asked a question.

What seemed like hours later, Milly at last turned

off the machine and smiled. "Thank you so much, Lorna. You're an excellent witness. You didn't falter once. You're entirely credible, which will be very important when we come before a jury."

Lorna arched a brow. "I still don't see where there can be any difficulty prosecuting Mr. Simson."

"Prosecuting is always difficult, I'm afraid. Mr. Simson is an important man, and a very affluent one. There's only your word that he was driving that car on the night of the murder, and the police haven't found the man who was the actual killer."

"But what about Donna Trudeau? She was kidnapped."

"But not by Simson. Simson is claiming that those two men were acting on their own behalf. He claims that he didn't know what was going on when he was called."

"But he threatened her!"

"Her word against his."

"It's ridiculous," Lorna murmured.

"Oh, it's not that bad, Lorna. Have some faith. With your help, we intend to see that he's found guilty of at least two counts of murder." Milly Latham paused. "The State of New York has no death penalty, you know. And I have no intention of waving flags on the morality of that issue. But, if we were shooting for the death penalty, we'd be prosecuting Simson for murder one, premeditated murder."

Lorna frowned. "I don't understand. Are we letting him get away with anything?"

"No. In New York, the legal wheels roll more smoothly when we prosecute someone for what they call second-degree murder. We want Simson shut away—especially since he's a very dangerous man. Fifteen years to life is the minimum sentence, twenty-five years to life is the maximum. We'll be shooting for the maximum sentence. If we work it right, Simson will definitely be locked away for a quarter of a century."

"If we do it right?"

"That's why all this is so very important. I know this is horrible for you, and I know my being here today is an intrusion into your life, but we need you. I can only promise that we intend to make it all worth your while by giving it our absolute best."

Lorna smiled. "I appreciate that." She had to admit that she liked Milly. The woman was determined and positive.

"Well, I guess that's about it," Milly said, standing to collect her papers and belongings. "Thanks for the coffee and the cooperation. I'll be seeing you soon."

Lorna stood too. "Thank you," she echoed.

Milly smiled. "Take care, Lorna. I mean that in the deepest sense."

Shivers touched Lorna's spine. "I know."

"Luckily you've got Andrew."

"Luckily."

"He's the best there is."

Best at what? Lorna wondered waspishly. Then she felt a little bit ashamed of herself; she was allowing confused emotions to turn her into a vindictive shrew.

Milly smiled again and disappeared through the kitchen door. Lorna heard her talking briefly to Andrew in a low voice, and then she heard the front door open and close.

Lorna sighed, then remembered the clothes were still in the dryer. She tripped over George on her way to the stairs.

"Mutt!" she exclaimed. He wagged his tail. She hadn't even realized that the dog had returned to the kitchen.

When she started down the cellar stairs, she heard

him following her. And when she reached the cellar, she found two of the security men there, working on the two basement windows and the back door.

She smiled at them uneasily, pulled the clothes from the dryer, and tripped over the dog again.

"George! You're not my damned shadow!"

But apparently George had decided that he was. He followed her back up the stairs.

Lorna folded Andrew's things and left them on the kitchen table. She started to the second floor with her own and realized again that George was following her.

"George, I don't allow German shepherds in my bedroom, and you are a dog. You're going to shed all over everything."

George whined and thumped his tail. Lorna gave up and allowed the dog to follow her into her bedroom. He didn't try to jump on the bed as she had expected, instead he curled up at its foot. Lorna put her things away, then flopped onto her bed and stared up at the ceiling, wondering how life could change so drastically from one day to the next.

She must have dozed briefly, because the next thing she knew, George was growling furiously. His ears were sharply raised and his eyes were pinned to her door.

"What is it, George?"

He ran to the door. Lorna hadn't closed it completely and he nudged it open, then raced down the stairs, barking at the front door again. Only then did Lorna hear the chimes. She hurried to the staircase and saw Andrew heading for the door. As if he knew she was above him, he turned to her.

"It's all right, Lorna. I sent out for pizza." He stroked the dog's head. "Down, George, it's all right."

Lorna went into the bathroom and rinsed off her face, then went downstairs. There was something curious about the house, and it took her a moment before she realized that it was the lack of commotion. There was no one around. George wasn't even there any more because he had followed Andrew into the kitchen.

Lorna did the same.

"Where is everyone?" She asked.

Andrew was opening the pizza box. "They put enough tape on this thing to have mailed it around the world," he grumbled, then he looked up at her. "Oh, the security men are finished and Sergeant Wilkes took a drive to see a little of the area."

Lorna nodded. "I'll get some plates," she murmured.

"Don't you ever eat off paper?" He quizzed her.

"Sure. At picnics," Lorna replied. She took out two of the everyday plates she kept in the kitchen, set them on the table, and started to get the silverware.

"Lorna, please don't tell me that you eat pizza with a knife and fork."

"I—"

"Try it with your hands. It's good that way."

She shrugged. "You *do* use a napkin, don't you?"

"Sure, if one's available."

She saw the flicker of amusement in his eyes and concealed her own smile. She turned around again, facing the refrigerator and the wine rack. "White or red with pizza, Lieutenant?"

"Beer. But if I have to make a choice on wine, I'll go for red."

"I've got beer."

She pulled two cans from the refrigerator. Andrew lifted a brow in surprise and pulled out a chair for her. She started to sit, then started up again. "I forgot the glasses."

133

"Try it out of the can. There's something about that added taste of metal!"

Shrugging, she sat again. And when he took the seat across from her and his knees brushed hers, she discovered that beer tasted just great from the can—she downed half of it in a gulp.

This isn't fair, she thought. She didn't like sitting there so intimately, as if they were friends. They were going to plunge into another argument, and if they didn't, it would be worse, because getting close to Andrew was even more painful and confusing and . . . futile.

Andrew served them each a piece of pizza, folded his, and took a big bite. He chewed, took a swallow of his beer, then suddenly looked at her. He was silent another minute before he spoke.

"I've made all the arrangements for George."

"I beg your pardon?"

"I made reservations at that new hotel in the center of Boston. They understand that George is a guard dog."

"Oh!" Lorna suddenly felt very warm and a rush of tremors seized her. It was like being grateful, and she didn't want to be *that* grateful, because she felt just like George looked when he got a pat on the head. But it was more than grateful, the rush of heat that touched her was because he cared about her wishes. Because he had ordered pizza and because it had been awful between them, but when they had come into the kitchen they were able to sit together at the little table and tease each other once again.

"Thank you, Andrew," she murmured, casting her gaze to her pizza. She didn't say it with subjective gratitude, just courtesy.

She was startled when his free hand touched hers, not gripping it but turning it so that his fingers played on her palm. Her eyes focused on his hand touching hers, then rose to meet his.

"Lorna, after Boston we go to the mountains, right?"

She nodded mutely, suddenly unable to talk.

Andrew was still gazing at her. He lifted his piece of pizza. "It's getting cold."

Lorna started to take a bite of her piece, thinking that it couldn't be too cold since the cheese was dripping all over her fingers, when she was startled by something warm and moist resting on her lap. She looked down to find George gazing woefully at her.

"I think our canine friend likes pizza," she murmured dryly. Poor George. He looked at her so pleadingly! His tail thumped hard on the floor, and Lorna decided to give him a taste.

"Don't you dare give that dog pizza," Andrew said indignantly.

"But he wants some."

"And his diet includes Alpo only. Want to wreck a good dog?"

"No, I suppose not."

"George! Where are your manners?" Andrew demanded of the dog. "Get away from the table. You know better than to beg."

With his tail between his hind legs, George walked across the kitchen dejectedly.

"Andrew, has it occurred to you that I haven't got any Alpo?"

"It occurs to me that, for a woman who doesn't like dogs, you're showing gorgeous George here a great deal of consideration."

"The animal has to eat!"

Andrew laughed. His eyes were sparkling. "Wilkes will be back soon with a large supply of Alpo."

With his eyes still carrying an intriguing glint, Andrew took another bite of pizza.

"What's that look for?" Lorna demanded.

"What look?"

"That one."

Andrew's lids closed halfway over his eyes and he lowered his head, ostensibly readjusting a piece of pepperoni on his pizza. "I was just thinking, I guess."

"About what?"

He shrugged. "Well, if you're getting soft toward George, there's no telling what you might actually be feeling for a person."

"That's right," Lorna said smoothly, "there's just no telling."

Andrew finished up his pizza, wiped his fingers with his napkin, and walked over to pat George on the head. "That's how it goes with the lady, huh, pal? Cops and dogs get to sleep on the floor. At least you've made it into the bedroom!"

Lorna took a sip of her beer, feeling a flush of heat, but not from embarrassment.

"Unless my memory is faulty," she told him, meeting his eyes steadily, "the cop was never asked to sleep on a floor. He's also been more than inside a bedroom."

Andrew lowered his head again, but as he hunched down on the balls of his feet by the shepherd, a secret smile played about his lips.

"Ah, but the circumstances were strained," he murmured. At last he looked at her, his crooked, wistful grin tugging at her heart. "I always wondered if it was a matter of choice."

"A matter of choice?" Lorna repeated, puzzled.

He straightened, hands in his pockets, and started walking toward her. But George suddenly started to whine, thumping his tail against the floor. Andrew paused.

"Must be Sergeant Wilkes."

"How do you know?"

"I don't. George does."

The front chime began to ring. George barked, wagged his tail furiously, and stampeded through the swinging doors.

Lorna glanced at Andrew to see that the sparkle was gone from his eyes. They were enigmatic and distant once again. He bowed slightly, sweeping an arm with exaggerated politeness as he did so.

"Madame, your door. It will be Sergeant Wilkes, I assure you."

Lorna smiled dryly. "I see. I get to answer my own door all of a sudden. How nice."

Lorna followed George through the doors, thinking that Sergeant Wilkes had a knack for arriving at the wrong time.

Then again, maybe it was best that the conversation hadn't gone any further at that point.

But as she walked through the parlor, she noticed the fireplace. It would be a nice night for a warm, crackling fire she thought, to pull pillows down, and sit before the fire.

She never pulled any pillows down, nor did they build a fire. Sergeant Wilkes came in with a large bag of Alpo, fed George, finished off the pizza with Andrew, and stayed so late that Lorna was in bed long before he and Andrew had finished analyzing the new football season.

CHAPTER SIX

Andrew sipped his coffee the next morning, staring out at the white expanse of Lorna's lawn from the kitchen window. Light snow flurries were falling, catching and dancing on the breeze.

There were no more patrol cars in the driveway. Lorna had a new security system with a direct link to the nearest police station, and she had a detective from New York living in her house. The Worcester police were free to get back to their thieves, domestic disturbances, traffic jams, and other crimes.

The snow made Andrew feel restless, more restless than he was already feeling. The house in Paxton was isolated. Lorna had neighbors, but their homes were far away, across an endless expanse of snow. Andrew was accustomed to the city with its constant motion, bustling people, the neon lights and loud sirens.

There wasn't really much to do there except talk to Lorna—if she ever decided to make an appearance. And every time he talked to Lorna, he was skating on thin ice. He wanted to do more than talk, and a warning would thud away in his mind that he would proceed to ignore.

Just looking at the lawn reminded him again of the differences between them. This was her life. The beautifully restored old house, the isolation, the elegance, the perfection.

And what's your life? he quizzed himself. A small apartment, absurd hours, and the eternal chase. Strange friendships with hookers and small-time dealers. The old dating game when he wasn't on a case. Nothing that was permanent, he realized, nothing that touched the heart.

Something brushed his leg and he heard a soft whine. He looked down to see George staring up at him expectantly. "I haven't fed you yet, have I, old boy? Well, come on then, I guess it's Alpo time again."

Andrew fed the dog, lit a cigarette, and stared back out at the snow. Everyone knew that mixing business with pleasure was a foolish thing to do. He'd known it for years. Then Lorna Doria had walked into his life and, from that point on, he hadn't understood a thing.

He'd been almost desperate for the assignment to come up here. Because it was his case? He wasn't so sure anymore. This morning he was convinced that he had come for one reason only—Lorna. Not because her life was at stake, but because what had happened between them had gnawed and gnawed at him. One way or another, he'd had to know whether it had been right or wrong. Not the obvious wrong, of course, the wrong of a detective taking a woman who was virtually a prisoner of the state. A woman who was far too alone and frightened.

"Was it me she wanted," he murmured aloud, "or would anyone have done just as well in the circumstances?"

When George whined, Andrew gazed at the dog. "Sorry, George, snow makes me talk to myself. I've got an idea. Why don't you and I go put up some kind of fence around that little pool of ice out there? Not that we'll be here long, but there might be kids in the area, you know."

In the cellar he found some two-by-fours and wire

mesh. He whistled, but George was already behind him. The shepherd trailed happily after him as he walked carefully through the snow, looking for the little pond.

"This is it, George," he said to the dog. George was running over to a pine tree to take care of nature's call.

Andrew hammered the first stud of wood into the ground. He paused then, feeling as if he was being watched. He stared out at the rear field of pines, then turned around. He grinned and waved. Lorna was standing at her upstairs window.

He turned his attention back to his studs and wire and drove another stud home. I'm going to have to tell her to stay away from those windows, he thought, making a mental note of it. He moved onto the third stud, and then the fourth, and then started fighting with the mesh wire that just didn't want to go his way.

His concentration was broken when he heard George at his side. The dog was growling, a low, rumbling sound that came from the animal's throat.

Andrew looked at the dog, then around the yard. Nothing had changed. The snow-blanketed landscape seemed oddly silent, except for the rumbling in the dog's throat.

"George?"

The dog was staring at the pines. Andrew turned to stare at the pines too, much more intently.

"Andrew!"

He swung back around to stare at the house. Lorna, her hands in the pockets of her fur-trimmed jacket, was coming up the cellar steps to the lawn. She was smiling, intent on reaching him quickly with her long strides.

Andrew stared at her briefly, then back at the pines. A feeling of absolute foreboding rose within him. He saw the pines, he saw Lorna, and he heard George growling.

"Lorna! Get down!"

He saw her stop to stare at him with startled alarm. But he didn't see much more because he was racing for her, tackling her into the snow. He heard a blast, a whistle of wind beside them, then a thud as a bullet embedded into the back of the house. The shot had been wide and wouldn't have hit her whether he had tackled her or not, but where there had been one shot . . .

George was barking furiously as he raced for the pines.

Andrew rolled quickly away from Lorna. "Get into the house and call the police," he told her, scrambling to his feet and helping her up.

She nodded, her face as white as the snow. He started after the dog.

"Andrew!" she screamed.

"Get in the house!"

"You're going after a gun, Andrew!"

"I've got a gun too. Damnit, I'm a cop."

"Cops bleed too, Andrew."

"Lorna, get in the house!"

By the time she obeyed him, he was halfway to the pines. He could hear George, still barking and thrashing through the pines.

A few seconds later Andrew was in the maze of trees himself. Except for George's barking, he felt that strange sense of stillness and quiet again. The dog was way ahead of him and the sound of his barking seemed distant, part of another time or world.

Andrew stood still for a minute to listen, then he started walking carefully. George should be ready to corner their quarry, he thought, but there might be more than one man.

141

He heard a rustling behind him and swung his gun around, breath held. He let out the breath. It was just a nervous squirrel.

He heard George barking again, louder and closer. Then another shot rang out against the stillness of the snow.

Andrew paused. Oh, my God, he shot the dog! he thought. His gun was primed as he hurried toward the sound, but then he heard George again, growling. And then he heard a human scream of pain and terror and when he at last emerged from the trees into a clearing, he found his man on the ground, one wrist held in the vise of George's teeth.

There was a shotgun lying nearby in the snow.

"Call him off!" the man wailed.

Andrew strode over to the shotgun and picked it up, then he stared down at the dog and the man.

"Good work, George."

The man's wrist was bloody. "For the love of God, call him off!"

"Don't fight him," Andrew said, "and you won't get torn up."

The man went still and twisted his face toward Andrew. It was a young face. The culprit probably wasn't even twenty.

"What's your name?"

"I ain't telling you."

"All right, don't." Andrew began to read the man his rights in his most monotonous, sing-song voice.

"What?" the man exploded. "You're a cop? I didn't do anything! I was just out walking when this hairy ape attacked me."

"Do you always go walking with a shotgun?"

"I just wanted to do some hunting. Would you call this damn mongrel off?"

"George, let him go. Okay, buddy, on your feet."

The young man staggered up to his feet, fretting over his wrist. Andrew took a closer look at him. Twenty had been a good estimation for age; the youth was of medium height, slim, and his cheeks bore traces of acne.

"I wasn't doing nothing," he began sullenly.

"Except hunting a blond woman, eh?"

"I don't know what you're talking about."

"Oh, I think you do. Get moving."

The man stared at Andrew. Andrew cocked his gun, "It's a Magnum. Special police issue. It could blow the side out of a barn, so I suggest you start moving."

George growled. It surprised Andrew that his culprit seemed more wary of the shepherd than the gun.

As they started back through the trees, Andrew could hear sirens. Lorna had called the police. When they neared the rear of the house, four men in uniform, armed and ready, were rushing around to meet them. Andrew could see Lorna's anxious face peeking through the panes on the cellar door.

"I didn't do anything!" the young man started yelling. "This idiot set his dog on me."

"There's a bullet embedded in the back of the house," Andrew said calmly. "I'm willing to bet it matches up with your shotgun."

One of the men in uniform stepped forward with a pair of handcuffs. "What's your name, son?" he demanded while clipping the cuffs into place.

"None of your business," the man spat back.

Andrew reached into the man's jacket and pulled out his wallet. He found a driver's license.

"Michael Henderson of Worcester. Well, Michael, I think you're going to have a lot of questions to answer. I'm just dying to hear your responses."

143

"Look, I was just out hunting. I didn't mean to hit anyone!"

"We'll see about that downtown," Andrew replied gravely.

Staring out through the window, Lorna was experiencing a strange mixture of relief and newfound panic. Andrew was fine. He and George both appeared undisturbed by their experience in the woods. Only the young prisoner looked ruffled, and a little bit bloody.

But then Andrew disappeared with the other men to the front of the house.

Lorna hurried up the cellar stairs and stared out one of the front windows. Andrew was getting into one of the patrol cars, sitting beside his prisoner. One of the patrol cars seemed to be staying behind. As the first car moved away, an officer started walking up to the house with George at his heels. Lorna left the window to rush to the front door. She threw it open before the officer could knock, and George immediately rushed in beside her.

"What's happening?" she demanded.

"Everything's all right, ma'am. We're staying behind to keep an eye on you until the lieutenant gets back." This officer was the perfect gentleman. He sounded as if he had originally hailed from Boston.

"Until the lieutenant gets back?" Lorna echoed.

"Yes, ma'am. I believe he thinks he can learn something important. Please don't worry. Officer Parkins and I will keep a sharp eye on things. Just make sure you've got the house locked up tight." He tipped his hat and started walking back to join his partner.

Lorna watched him. He signaled her to close the door. She did so, feeling again a confusing rush of emotions. She was so relieved that Andrew was all right—and so furious that he had gone off without a word to her.

Her eyes fell to the dog by her feet. She patted his head. "You're a good dog, George. Good boy."

Lorna wandered into the kitchen and poured herself a cup of coffee. She sat down at the table and tried to make a list of the pieces she would be interested in buying at the auction, but after writing one word on the sheet of paper she burst into tears, covering her face with shaking hands.

Her own backyard. Someone had tried to shoot her in her own backyard. Where would it end? When Simson was behind bars? Wouldn't he hate her even more then? Be more determined than ever to use his connections and resources to bring about her demise?

George whimpered at her side and stuck his cold nose onto her lap. Lorna, startled from her thoughts by the dog, patted his head.

"It's all right, George. I'm just being a little crazy." The dog whined again, swishing his tail uncertainly. Lorna grabbed a tissue and wiped her eyes. "George, I'm fine, I promise." Then she laughed out loud. "I must be going crazy—I'm trying to reassure a dog!"

But bless George! He was exactly what she needed. She no longer felt hysterical, just cold and dreary and a little bit hardened. If Simson was determined to get her, she would have to be just as determined not to allow that to happen. And, although she was terrified, she wasn't going to spend her life cowering in a corner. She would be careful because she wanted to live, but she would learn to play the game along with the best of them.

Look at Andrew, she thought. Yes, look at Andrew. He went into the streets daily. The living was deadly, and he survived. He'd had police training, of course, but more than that, he'd learned to be streetwise. Quick and clever.

She was going to start learning a few things herself.

She patted George on the head again. "George, I absolutely refuse to be a sitting duck for Simson or go mad and do his dirty work for him all by myself! I've got a few ideas of my own."

They were probably feeble ideas, Lorna realized, but they were better than sitting around the kitchen crying into her coffee. She actually smiled as she wondered what Andrew would think.

And then her smile faded as she passed by the fireplace. Last night she had wanted to build a fire and sit before it so badly. To watch the flames in warmth as the winter cold blanketed the house.

Her smile returned. Tonight she was determined to do just that. By the time Andrew returned, he would be greeted by a different woman. Lorna laughed out loud, not yet sure herself just how different that woman was going to be.

Lorna hurried up the steps and headed straight for the bathroom, staring with speculative determination into the mirror.

"Well, Lieutenant Trudeau," she murmured, "I hope you like the woman you're going to meet tonight, because she's feeling very differently—about a lot of things."

Lorna reached, opened the cabinet beneath the bathroom sink, and began rummaging. She paused suddenly, feeling a cold tremor sweep through her.

Andrew.

She'd never known such fear as when he raced into those pine trees, fear that he would be hurt, fear that he would be killed. And when she'd heard the second blast . . .

Tears stung her eyes again, but not for herself. "Oh,

Andrew," she murmured, "you're not a cat, and you don't have nine lives. But you're always rushing into the fray, aren't you? And you'll never change. But I do love you," she added, "and I guess we all have to learn to take life one step at a time."

Feeling her resolve strengthen, Lorna picked up a pair of scissors.

They were all grouped around a table in a small room with a single window. The walls were a dull green, the floor was bare—in fact, the room was bare except for that table and a scattering of chairs.

Andrew leaned against the wall near the door. Michael Henderson was seated on one side of the table with an attorney provided for him by the state. Captain Raill of the High Street station was doing the questioning.

"One more time, Mr. Henderson. Why were you shooting at Mrs. Doria?"

"And one more time, Captain, I'm telling you. I wasn't shooting at Mrs. What's-her-name. I was just out hunting."

"There is no hunting in residential neighborhoods," the captain responded. "Look, Henderson, as Lieutenant Trudeau suggested, the bullet embedded in the house matches up with your shotgun. Now, ask your attorney. I can book you on attempted murder and guarantee you a long stint in prison, or we can do a little bit of dealing here."

Andrew's eyes narrowed as he watched Henderson go pale. "No dealing," Henderson said. It was almost a whisper, hoarsely spoken.

Henderson, Andrew realized, was a terrified man.

"No deal!" he repeated.

"Now, Mr. Henderson—" the captain began again, but Henderson interrupted him.

147

"In prison, Captain, I'll be alive."

Andrew walked into the room, tapping the captain on the shoulder. The captain glanced at him, then stood, giving Andrew his chair. The state's attorney was trying to explain to Henderson that all the charges against him might be dropped if he would cooperate.

Henderson glanced at Andrew very warily. Andrew returned the look gravely. "Mr. Henderson, I'm not going to ask you to answer anything right now. I'm just going to talk. You see, I don't need you to tell me anything. I know that you were hired to kill Mrs. Doria, but you messed up, so now you're scared. Real scared. And you should be. Because now you just might be a target yourself. But let me warn you, Henderson, you've gotten into a league with the big boys. If you don't help us get them, it's very likely they'll get you."

Sweat broke out on Henderson's forehead in profusion. He stared at the table, knotting and unknotting his hands.

"I can't help you," he said at last. "I don't know anything. I was approached by men in a warehouse and I never even saw their faces."

"What about payment?"

"I was supposed to go back to the warehouse."

Andrew suppressed the desire to laugh. Henderson was nothing more than the lowest flunky. Just a kid. If he'd succeeded—Andrew took a deep breath and continued his thought—if Henderson had succeeded in killing Lorna, he would have gone back to the warehouse and received nothing for his pains but a bullet of his own.

"Where is this warehouse?" Andrew asked.

"I can't tell you."

"Henderson, no one will ever know, I promise you."

Michael Henderson looked ill. His face was the color of dough. At last he whispered out an address.

Andrew left the room along with Captain Raill. "We should close in on the place," Raill said.

"No, Captain, you do that and there'll be nothing there. Can you let me go in first?"

The captain watched him, then shrugged. "This isn't New York, Lieutenant."

"I know. But we owe Henderson something. And, unless I miss my guess, you're going to find out that the warehouse belongs to an absentee businessman anyway, someone legit."

"A case where the army would fall and the single soldier would get through?" Captain Raill asked.

"Something like that, sir."

Raill shrugged. "It's your baby then, Lieutenant. What can I do for you?"

"Got any shabby outfits hanging around?"

"Sure. See the desk sergeant. And make sure you fill out all the right forms, Lieutenant. I don't want the responsibility on this. You're a New York cop and this is Massachusetts."

"I'll keep the paperwork straight," Andrew promised.

"See that you do that. We'll keep Henderson locked up until we see what comes down."

Forty minutes later Andrew was walking along the street to the warehouse. He rubbed his cheek, glad that he hadn't shaved that morning. He carried a brown bag with a whiskey bottle that was three-quarters empty, his jacket was threadbare, and his hat was covered with dirt, real dirt—he'd sneezed his head off the moment he'd put it on, which had seemed to amuse the Massachusetts police.

That was all right. They were behind him now. He

needed to depend on their backup and he felt that he could.

Nearing the warehouse, he began to stagger his walk. When he reached the doors, he looked around, saw no one, and quickly slipped the lock. He left the door ajar.

The door was vertical with the loading dock, and it took no time at all to see that the warehouse was empty except for a few dusty boxes. Andrew moved over to a dark corner by a set of stairs and sat. Then he took a deep breath and started doing what he spent a large portion of his working hours doing—he waited.

The sitting wasn't so terrible today. He half closed his eyes and allowed himself to indulge in his daydreams. Not daydreams in the plural, just one. A daydream about Lorna.

He could see her sitting in a tub of bubbles, laughing in the snow, grinning as they shared pizza together, chopped garlic . . . made onion soup.

He imagined holding her again. No words, just holding her. Looking into her eyes, watching them as they looked into his. His arms would tighten around her and he would slowly lower his head, and he would finally be kissing her again, drinking her in, feeling her warmth, exciting and sweet . . .

It could happen. The dream was a touchable one. But if he held her in his arms, what did he do then?

Keep her alive, stupid.

Oh, God, yes, that had to be the first priority. But minutes stretched to hours, hours to days, and days could be endless—or too short, depending on . . . the two of them. He was still the cop guarding her, but he was also more. And if he intended to keep beating his head for having become involved, he was being all the more foolish because it wasn't necessary. Lorna was not a spiteful or vindictive woman, she didn't want to hurt him or pull him down. Neither of them could guarantee the future, but, by God, he could make his own actions better. He could at least open up and let her know what he was thinking and feeling instead of leaving her cold. She'd had every right to hit him the day he'd walked into her store.

But he didn't want to think, even now. He just wanted to imagine her. The way her long, elegant nails played lightly over his neck, the beauty of her eyes when they opened to his . . .

Andrew started suddenly, shrinking against the wall and opening his eyes. The warehouse door was creaking open.

A man dressed in a heavy coat walked in, his footsteps crunching over the concrete floor.

He looked around the warehouse, then lit a cigarette. Andrew studied the man's features. His face was heavy and jowled, but his complexion was sallow and pinched. He had lifeless eyes, like a man who had seen more than he wanted and wore mental shields against it all.

He smoked his cigarette, dropped it on the cement, and crushed it out with his shoe. He wandered around again within the same few feet, growing impatient.

Andrew kept his head low as he watched the man waiting tensely.

Finally the door opened again and a second man entered. This one, at least ten years younger, wore a tweed coat and was thin. The only similarity between the two was the look in their eyes that said they had seen too much and chosen to ignore what they saw.

"Well?" snapped the heavier man.

"Forget Henderson. He blew it."

"I told you not to hire an outsider. The man was an idiot" came the irritated reply.

"You said it had to be kept on the outside, that you didn't want anything traced back to you."

"And I told you not to hire that idiot."

"Hey, what do you think? That I had a line-up waiting at my office for the job?" the younger man asked sarcastically. "This damn thing isn't our problem to begin with. You got friends who need work done—it's their problem. I want out of it."

"Shut up!" the heavier man suddenly hissed.

Andrew felt his muscles tighten when he realized they had seen him.

The man with the jowls approached him. Andrew's chin was on his chest, his posture slumped. Jowls gave him a good kick in the leg. Andrew opened his eyes with the pretext of panic. He clutched his whiskey bottle tightly to him and stared at the two men.

"Hey, give a man a little peace."

"What are you doing in here?" Jowls demanded harshly.

"Just gettin' warm, man, just gettin' warm. Look, if it's your property, I'm on my way out." He shuffled slowly to his feet, grabbing the stairs for balance. The two men were still staring at him. "Hey, you couldn't spare a dollar, could ya? You look like the type of man who's doing okay out there in the world."

"A dollar? Get this!" Jowls laughed. "Whatever happened to 'Buddy, can you spare a dime'?"

"Inflation," Andrew grumbled drunkenly. "Can't buy no drink for a dime these days."

"Waste him," the thin man said.

Andrew put out an arm in protest. "Hey, man, no violence, please! All's I was trying to do was get out of the street. I've got this cough, you see." To prove it, he started hacking away and reached into his tattered coat, ostensibly for a handkerchief.

He brought out his police special instead and aimed it at the two men, dropping all disguise.

"Sorry, Slim, I'm not in the mood to get wasted today. You're under arrest."

The two men stared at him for a moment, then Jowls turned to make a run for it. When Andrew didn't shoot, the other man followed suit. Andrew smiled as he watched them go.

At the door, a foursome in blue were ready to take them into custody.

Andrew walked out into the sunlight and the snow. Slim and Jowls were being handcuffed. A few minutes later they were all driving back to the precinct. Andrew learned that Jowls and Slim were Norman Hewitt and Theo Medallo, respectively—loan sharks and bookies, among other things, suspected of underworld connections.

"It's going to be a long, long time before we get them to tell us anything, Lieutenant," Captain Raill told him.

"Then I think I'll go home," Andrew said.

"Home?" the Captain asked, puzzled.

"Sorry—back to base," Andrew muttered. What a fool. He was beginning to think of her home as his. He coughed slightly, a residue of that earlier cough that warned him—just as Lorna had—that he was smoking too much. "Whether they talk or not, it seems likely that they're the Massachusetts connection."

"I agree. I just hope I can get them arraigned on something to keep them off the streets for a while."

"Yeah, I hope so too."

"I'll get a car to take you back. You're heading for Boston tomorrow?"

"Yes."

"Good. This thing can be their problem for a

while." But Captain Raill smiled and promised to make contact with the chief of police in Boston.

It had long been day by the time the patrol car wound its way up to Lorna's house. As he got out of the car that evening, Andrew noticed that the house seemed dark. Not totally dark, just muted, as if the only lighting was from the fireplace in the parlor.

Lorna knew that Andrew had returned. She recognized the way George barked and wagged his tail at the same time.

She tensed as she heard his footsteps coming up the walk, and she looked around the parlor once again.

She had taken out two huge throw pillows covered in a burgundy silk. Her comforter was laid out over the back of the sofa so that she could spring to her feet to answer the door and make it look as if she had been dozing before the fire. A book—the murder mystery again—and a snifter of blackberry brandy sat at her end of the coffee table. There was a filled ice bucket in the center with a rock glass and a bottle of Jack Daniels at the other end. She'd made a call to Donna to check on the Jack Daniels. Between the ice bucket and the bourbon was a tray with cheese, pepperoni, olives, and crackers. She belatedly hoped that Andrew had eaten dinner somewhere along the line.

But the refreshments weren't really the big surprise for the night. She was.

George was still barking when Andrew knocked on the door. "Lorna, it's me. Andrew," he called out.

She stood up nervously, pulling at the hem of what she considered to be a too-short skirt. Then she walked to the door and pulled it open.

"Lorna—" he began, and then stopped short to stare. He gazed at the hair that was no longer blond, but tinted an ashen brown. It didn't look like the same

154

hair at all. It was cut into feathery bangs and layers that fluttered all about her features.

His eyes fell from her hair to her face. Different . . . her eyes looked much rounder, darker. Her lipstick was very red, and her cheeks were highly blushed.

Her short knit dress made her change complete. Her clothing was generally so elegant, but quiet and subdued. This garment was trendy! She could wear it, she could carry it off with her height and bearing, but she just looked so young.

"My God!" He gasped aloud. He couldn't believe it was she. She might have been a different woman, but still a very sexy one.

She didn't respond to his look. She was busy staring at him as if she, too, had seen a stranger.

"Andrew?" He suddenly remembered that he hadn't bothered to change the grubby street clothes. He was filthy.

"Yeah, it's me"—he grinned—"but is that really you?"

She laughed and backed into the hallway, spinning around. "Am I really that different?"

Andrew closed the door, locking both bolts. He stared at her as she made a model's circle for him once again. "You're different, all right. But . . . why? What are you doing?"

"Hey, it should be my turn for questions first," she reminded him. "What's going on?"

Andrew pulled off the tattered coat.

"Don't you dare put that thing in my closet!" Lorna warned him.

He smiled and dropped it to the floor.

"Are you going to answer me?" she asked.

"Could I have a shower first?"

"Andrew!"

155

"All right. The guy out back was a flunky named Michael Henderson. He led us to two other guys who I'm pretty sure are the main connection here in Massachusetts. They're at the station now, so it proved to be a pretty profitable day."

He stopped speaking to watch her. She was listening to him, but she had walked away. He noticed the setup on the coffee table as she dropped ice into a glass and poured a generous portion of Jack Daniels. He was wondering how she knew he had a penchant for Jack Black, but not even that thought could be cohesive in his mind as he watched her. The knit of the—whatever it was—was clinging to her curves like a second skin and when she dipped down, his heart began to flutter and his palms grew clammy at the wicked length of long legs exposed to him.

He cleared his throat. "I don't think Henderson was ever really any kind of a menace. But he was important because he gave us the other guys. It means nothing should be happening for a while—in Massachusetts, at any rate."

"Do you really believe that?"

She was still fiddling with his glass, still driving his libido insane.

"Yes, I do."

She stood, smiled, and brought him the drink. He accepted it, finding it a little hard to breathe.

"Why are you all . . . dressed up?"

"Because I went to the warehouse."

She frowned. "Andrew, you should have let the Massachusetts police handle this. They're servants of the people too, you know."

"I know, but I wanted these guys."

Her lashes lowered for a moment and he found himself fascinated with her mouth. The ruby lipstick

156

clearly outlined their full shape. He thought about his daydream, about holding her, kissing her.

"Okay, then. That's fair for the moment," she said at last. "Have a drink and a shower."

"What about that get-up you're in?" he asked her.

"I'll explain what I'm up to and you can give me the details when you get out."

He gazed into her eyes again and saw a wistful look there. He felt the cold drink in his hand and the warmth from the fire all at once.

And another warmth. One that was his just by standing near Lorna, inhaling her subtle perfume, seeing everything in the flickering, seductive light of the fire.

Dear God, she was something to come home to! He twisted his lips into his best semblance of a jaunty grin. "Sure thing, kid," he told her.

She smiled and he hoped he could walk to the den without tripping—or without looking back at her in awe, like a kid on a first date.

His mouth was dry. He took a sip of the drink and gazed at the pillows. "Is one of those for me?"

He noticed then that she was a little unsteady herself. She had her hands clenched together in front of her. To keep them from trembling? Was she as nervous as he was?

Her blue eyes met his squarely. "If you want it, it is," she replied.

"I'll be right out," he told her.

CHAPTER SEVEN

Lorna sipped her brandy and stared at the fire. She lifted her free hand and found that her fingers were shaking. She rolled her fingers into her palm and clenched her hand in her lap. She was so nervous that it was pathetic.

Why?

It was all going according to plan. It's just that the plan was to take a man to bed, and she didn't know if that was right, she didn't know if he would turn away again, and she didn't know if the whole thing made any sense in the long run.

But did she need to know all that? It was there, the thing between them, and she needed him.

And him? He had made enough innuendos, right from the start when she had been insanely angry just to see him again.

A log slipped and the fire flamed high, casting a beautiful glow around the room.

What about the future? she asked herself. But the future was a vague and distant thing, very uncertain. And did it matter? She knew that she liked Andrew very much as a man. If there was nothing for them in a vague tomorrow, she still would not look back in regret. This was her choice, just as it had always been. If she didn't entirely understand the nature of her particular "beast," well, it didn't really matter. People were unique, complex beings—Andrew especially so. She would have to accept that. For the most part anyway, she had some of her own criteria to be met.

"Oh!" Lorna jumped, startled, as his hands touched her bare neck lightly, then started a massage that was both firm and gentle.

"You startled me," she murmured.

"I didn't mean to." His hands kept moving. She felt more than their touch upon her nape and shoulders as a warmth swept through her, giving her a sense of both languid peace and stirring excitement.

His whisper touched her ear. She knew he had knelt down beside her. "You're very tense."

"I'm always tense on days when someone has taken a shot at me and my bodyguard disappears in a patrol car without a word." His breath, warm and smelling just faintly of bourbon, continued to touch against her bare flesh and whisper along her earlobe, fanning her shoulders like a brush made of angel's hair.

"I asked them to tell you where I was going," he said, just a little defensively.

"They did."

"Then?"

"Andrew, this may amaze you, but I was worried."

His fingers slipped lower, playing along her collarbones gently, growing firm again as they moved back to her shoulder.

"That's gratifying."

Lorna stared down at her brandy snifter. The fire was reflecting off the glass, giving it beautiful streaks of color. And just like that rainbow sheen on the crystal, his touch filled her with color, magenta rays that brushed upon her heart and her desires.

"Tell me more about this bit with the warehouse," she said, sitting up and turning around to face him.

He shrugged and stood. "Got another drink for me?"

She nodded as he came around the sofa and sat. "Where's your glass?" she asked him.

"I left it in the bathroom, but don't panic! I'll just run back and get it." He did, with an expression of amused tolerance that brought a wry smile to her lips. When he returned, she was still smiling.

"Am I really that bad a fanatic, Andrew?"

He took time answering the question, filling his glass with ice and pouring himself another portion of bourbon. He eased back beside her again, stretching an arm along the back of the sofa. "What's a 'bad' fanatic?" he asked.

"Andrew!"

"Are you a fanatic? Yes. But is it bad? That all depends on opinion."

"And what's your opinion, Lieutenant?"

"You're tolerable."

"Tolerable? Thanks a lot!"

"Okay, okay—you're more than tolerable. You're . . . pleasantly biddable. How's that?"

"I'm not sure that's much better."

He reached over and ruffled her hair, watching his fingers as they trailed through the feathery wisps. "I'm going to have to get used to this fluffy brown stuff." He frowned suddenly. "This stuff isn't permanent, is it?"

"The bangs? Yes, until they grow back out."

"The color."

"You don't like it?"

"I have nothing against brown hair on a brunette, but you were meant to be a blond."

Lorna smiled, but his frown remained. "Lorna, what is this"—he indicated her hair and dress with the wave of hand—"all about?"

160

"This, Lieutenant, is a little trick I learned from you. I thought that if I altered my appearance fairly drastically, I'd make a less conspicuous target."

Andrew kept looking at her as he reached slowly into the pocket of his beige chambray shirt for his cigarettes. Lorna anticipated his movement and plucked an antique matchbox from the end table. She struck a match. His eyes met hers as she lit the cigarette.

He inhaled and exhaled, still watching her.

"What did I do to rate all this?" he asked her curiously.

"I've decided to play the perfect hostess this evening, Lieutenant Trudeau. Fanatics are very good at that."

He smiled. "Yes, so I see." He leaned against the corner of the sofa, watching her languidly through heavy-lidded eyes. She knew he was still alert, assessing her every word and motion.

She plucked a piece of pepperoni from the tray and chewed it. His eyes were on her mouth. She sipped her brandy and his eyes were still following her.

"What do you think?" she asked him.

"About what?"

"My costume."

"I think it's fun to see you looking like a page right out of a teen magazine," he said with a wry grin. "Trendy."

"Will it work?"

"For what?"

"A disguise. If I were walking around."

He shrugged. "Some. But you've forgotten something."

"What's that?"

"You're about five ten. It's hard to hide yourself at that height."

161

She sighed. "I never thought much about it."

Andrew reached over and crushed out his cigarette. "It might help some. Face it, Lorna, you just shouldn't stay where you can be a target." He leaned back against the sofa again, sighing as his head rested against the pillow.

Lorna watched him, frowning. "I know that, Andrew, but you said we'd go to Boston."

"And we will. But right after we do whatever it is you want to do, we're leaving. Right?"

"Yes, I already said that."

He was smiling rather smugly, Lorna thought.

"Good," he told her softly. He paused before speaking again. "How far does being a perfect hostess go?"

Her heart took a soaring leap, then seemed to patter swiftly against her chest. "What do you mean?"

She saw his lips twist further. "I mean . . . that I'd just love a piece of pepperoni"—he opened his mouth and pointed toward it—"right here."

She hesitated, not sure whether to tell him to go to hell and get his own pepperoni or to laugh.

She shrugged, unable to stifle the laugh, then picked up a piece of pepperoni between two long fingers and leaned over to plop it in his mouth. As his mouth closed over the pepperoni, his arms encircled her and drew her to him.

Lorna braced herself against his shoulders. He chewed the pepperoni, watching her eyes. He swallowed and smiled wistfully. "Do perfect hostesses kiss their bodyguards?"

"They've been known to do more than that," Lorna said breathlessly.

All trace of humor was gone as he cupped her chin in his palm and slowly brought his mouth to hers. Their lips touched, and then she felt the gentle brush of his tongue over hers, parting them. He filled her

mouth with his own special warmth, the taste of bourbon and pepperoni and the bittersweet poignancy of
memory.

Lorna responded to him, sinking against him,
threading her fingers through the hair at his collar and
answering the sensual exploration of his tongue with
her own. She felt the brush of his freshly shaven chin,
smelled the faint scent of soap and shave lotion. His
hands moved over her back, one pressing against the
small at the base of her spine, the other moving over
her shoulders to mold her against him. She was pliant
for him, loving the touch of his body against hers. It
was a place she had been before, a place she had
longed to be again, and if the kiss stole her breath
away, it was not something that she cared to hide.

But at last his mouth moved from hers as he eased
back to watch her again. The firelight cast soft shadows upon both of them, flickering as they stared at one
another. Lorna made no effort to move, it was unnecessary. There were things to be said, and she would
say them, but she would not leave his warmth.

"I've wanted to do that all day," he told her huskily. Then he touched her lips with his forefinger.
They were damp from his kiss, still slightly parted,
and entirely beautiful. And her eyes, meeting his in
silent understanding . . . no makeup could ever
change their crystal brilliance when she stared at him
like this.

"I was more or less planning it," she murmured
honestly, and then she cocked her head slightly, as if
to better understand what he might say.

He touched his fingers to her lips again. "I want to
make love to you, Lorna."

She smiled and straightened a bit, not moving away
from him, but no longer touching him.

"Andrew, I want that too. But I have to ask you why you turned away from me . . . before."

He stood and, reaching for his drink, walked to the mantel to stare directly into the flames.

Then he turned back to her. "I think you know why."

"Because you were a cop—protecting me?"

He nodded.

"But it was more than that, wasn't it, Andrew?"

"Maybe. Yes." He walked back to the table and set his drink down, then came to her and knelt by her side, taking her hand, moving his fingers over her palm.

"Talk to me, Andrew," Lorna said, her breath catching in her throat. "Whatever you say," she whispered. "I'll want you tonight."

He stared into her eyes again. "Admit it, Lorna, you don't want a cop."

"And I don't think you want entanglements."

"I don't know. That's as honest a reply as I can give you, Lorna. I'm not used to . . . being worried about. To reporting to anyone. And—"

"And what?"

"I don't think that you want me as anything permanent."

She smiled and touched his hair, then his cheek. "Andrew, you scare me to death. That's true. I don't know what I feel, either. I just know that I'm past the anger, I'm past trying to hate you because I do like you."

"Lorna, you had a right to hate me. That's why—"

"It doesn't matter, Andrew. There's only one thing that I want from you now."

"And what's that?"

"I don't want you to turn away. I want you to hold

164

me, and I want you to stay with me through the night."

He brought her hand to his lips and kissed it gently, then stretched out each delicate finger and kissed them too. When he met her eyes, she saw only tenderness and caring.

"I would love to sleep with you through the night, to hold you next to me and be holding you still when morning comes."

He plucked the brandy glass from her hand and set it on the coffee table. Then he reached for her and pulled her into his arms. She slipped her arms around his neck, smiling as she rested her head against his shoulder. He carried her toward the stairs.

"We're wasting the seduction scene, you know."

He raised a dark brow. "The seduction scene?"

"The pillows, the fire, the drinks, everything."

"The pepperoni was extremely seductive. Were you planning on seducing me, Mrs. Doria?"

"Yes, I was."

"The fire will burn longer. Perhaps I could seduce you upstairs, then you could seduce me downstairs. And, of course, we'll be hungry by then, so the cheese will come in handy. Then, too, we'll be thirsty, and I've always wanted to taste blackberry brandy from an elegant navel."

Lorna kept smiling, but she lowered her head. Andrew took them up the stairs, and with every step, she felt more afire. If it was wonderful to lean against him, it was even more wonderful to anticipate the moments that were ahead. She was content, and still she was alive with energy to touch him and love him.

He pushed her bedroom door open with his foot. The four-poster loomed in the moonlight and he brought her there, setting her down gently. He sat by her side, leaning over to kiss her, to drink inexhaustibly from the brandied sweetness of her lips. She wrapped her arms around him as his tongue played over her mouth and he brushed light kisses over her forehead, cheeks, and chin.

He broke the kiss and set his hands to the belt around her hips, and when it gave, he tossed it to the floor. He stretched out and pulled off her shoes, and when they were gone, he massaged her feet, and the massage led back up the length of her legs, pushing up her dress and skimming her hips until he found the band of her pantyhose. He slipped them from her, touching the fire of his mouth to the bared flesh at her navel, then at each hip, and then down the length of her leg as he peeled away the hose. They, too, fell to the floor with a soft flutter, caught like gossamer in the moonlight.

Lorna lay very still, barely breathing, and yet feeling each breath as it caught and then quickened. When he touched her again, hands sliding to her waist to catch the dress and draw it higher, she at last moved to assist him. When the dress had disappeared over her head, she threw her arms around him and held him tightly to her.

"Andrew" was all she could murmur.

He held her, but then his hands were busy again, trembling as they released the catch on her bra.

"When I was working today, I was imagining you the way you looked the other night in the tub. The bubbles were all around you, but I knew . . . I wanted so badly to walk straight to the tub and sweep the bubbles away, to hold and caress your breasts . . ."

Her bra fell to the floor and he gently pressed her back to the bed. The moonlight bathed her with a rare, silver beauty. All that she wore was a wisp of lace about her hips, but he did not touch the bikinis yet. He

166

sat by her, smiling. He touched her cheek and then the breasts he had so admired, cupping their round weight, cherishing her nipples with the graze of his thumb until she cried out softly, reminding him that she needed to love as she was loved.

He pulled off his shoes, and she moved, raking her long nails lightly over his back as he shed his socks. He shed his shirt, and her nails touched against his bare flesh. He turned to her again, wrapping his arms around her, succumbing to a kiss that brought his naked chest against her breasts and filled his senses with both bliss and burning arousal. He broke apart from her, tugging at the buckle to his belt. Her hands replaced his, more sure, yet trembling too. Andrew stood and shimmied out of his jeans and shorts, and for a minute he remained still, watching her.

She returned the stare, smiling as she drank in the sight of him, the pale moon glow against breadth of his shoulders, his sinewed length, the tension of his body primed for hers. And then she cried out softly again, jumping from the bed to slip her arms around him and hold him in a thirsting kiss.

He held her from him, and his lips touched her shoulders, moved slowly to touch against a breast and caress it gently. His teeth rasped lightly against a nipple, and then his lips molded over it again, his tongue rolled again and again as he sucked against her flesh.

"Andrew . . . stop." She moaned, raking her fingers through his hair, over his shoulders as the sensations streaked through her like mercury, making her deliciously weak. She both burned and shivered and the need for him wound in her tightly and sweetly until it was both so painful and so sweet she would scream if it could not be eased. "I won't be able to stand!" She gasped.

"I don't want you standing," he told her huskily, his voice muffled against her.

"Andrew . . ."

When he knelt, she clutched his shoulders and his fingers found the elastic to the wisp of nothing that was her panties. He touched her hip with his tongue through the material, slowly, savoringly.

"Andrew . . ."

His fingers tugged at the elastic, and where the lace had been, he touched her afresh, exploring the texture of her flesh. The elastic slowly moved down her legs. She faltered slightly, grabbing his shoulders tighter as he tugged the material from beneath each of her feet. His hands returned to her hips, steadying her, and he forged a trail of kisses along her calf, to her kneecap, and along her thigh. She closed her eyes, knowing the splendor that was about to burst around her. Her nails dug lightly into his back and she gasped once again, feeling a surge of almost unbearable sweetness from the intimacy of his mouth's caress.

Lorna cried out, falling to her knees before him and taking him into her arms. She nipped at his shoulder, then smothered the nip with a heated kiss.

And then she was lifted in his arms and borne to the bed again. His face was beautifully taut before hers, drawn with desire. She opened herself to him as she felt his weight shift between her thighs. There was a wondrous moment of gratification as her body welcomed his, and she felt, once more, that she had waited a lifetime for him. He was vital and electric, and when he came to her, touching her, filling her, and then just holding her, she was vital and electric too.

He moved . . . and their rhythm caught fire. Sensations streamed like a tide against the shore, lashed and receded, rose again and again; his body penetrating hers like the brilliant warmth of the sun. It was

168

where she was meant to be, loving him, knowing his energy, making it her own, allowing it to soar. It was as if he made her all that she could be.

Moonlight graced his shoulders with its silken sheen. With the hungry caress of her fingers she felt the coiled strength of him, given to her beautifully with both tenderness and boundless passion. She enveloped him with her body and heart, ankles lacing around him, nails grazing his flesh. Again their lips met, tore away, and met again. And still the tide roared, deliriously sweet, receding, flowing again. His hands lifted her and she willed her body to accept his ever more deeply, caressing him inside and out. At last came the moment in which she cried out his name, heard her own echoed in response. The moon seemed to have disappeared, replaced by dazzling, brilliant light. But of course that dazzling flash of heat came only in her mind with the shuddering quakes of her body's fulfillment; they receded again and there were moments of delightful, languid peace as she slowly drifted down from the clouds.

Andrew was smiling at her. "I thought, sometimes," he said huskily, "that I had only dreamed all that you were. I didn't."

She touched his cheek, smiling in return. "You're not going to hop out of bed?"

"No, not until we hop out together."

Lorna started to smile, but gasped instead when something very cold touched the bottom of her foot. Then something huge and hairy landed on her bed.

"What the—" she began, but Andrew was quicker.

"George!" His voice was a burst of fury. "Get off the bed! What kind of a police dog are you?"

George whined and wagged his tail. Andrew sat up and pushed the dog, grunting. "George!"

169

"George!" Lorna snapped, "You're getting hairs all over my bed. Oh, my God! Does he have fleas?"

"Fleas? Of course not. It has nothing to do with fleas or dog hairs—it has to do with moment. George, get down!"

At last the shepherd whined and jumped to the floor. But then the phone started ringing.

"Don't answer it." Andrew groaned. "It will stop."

"But what if it's something important?"

"This isn't important?"

"Andrew . . ."

Lorna was right, he knew. It might well be something important. He reached over her sweetly damp body and grabbed the receiver from the nightstand. "Hello? What do you want?" he practically shouted.

"Andrew?" There was a slight pause. "It's Luke."

"Luke," Andrew murmured. "Hi."

There was another pause, then his brother started laughing.

"I didn't wake you, did I?"

"No, you didn't wake me." To his annoyance, he heard Luke talking to Donna. "We didn't wake them, but I think we're even. Sounds like we interrupted something."

Donna was laughing delightedly in the background.

Andrew took a deep breath. He glanced at Lorna and found her watching him with wide—and still very sensuous—eyes. He touched her cheek, then drew an idle line along her belly.

"Luke," he said into the phone, "did you want something?"

"Yes. I was worried. Is everything all right?"

A little chill touched Andrew's spine; Luke's senses were uncanny.

"We had a little bit of trouble this morning." He paused. "You were right, Luke, the house *was* safe. We

170

had a prowler outside, but everything's fine now. Better than it was, as a matter of fact. Can I explain later?"

There was a silence, then his brother chuckled again. "Sure. Just as long everything's all right. We'll be seeing you soon."

"Day after tomorrow," Andrew agreed. "I didn't intend to be your source of amusement for the evening, but I appreciate your concern."

Luke was still laughing.

"Good night, brother," Andrew muttered. He hung up without waiting for a reply.

He grimaced at Lorna. "I think Luke and Donna are aware of how we're spending the evening. Does it bother you?"

Lorna smiled. "No."

He grinned in return, sliding his hand along her rib cage to her hip.

"Want to go downstairs and sit before the fire?"

"Dressed or undressed?"

"We'll wear the comforters."

"Mmm. And then I can seduce you after we nibble on crackers."

"And each other, of course," he whispered into her ear.

"I get to lean against your chest and watch the fire crackle?"

"I'm not enough 'crackling fire' for you, eh?"

"Oh, you are—just a different variety."

"Only if I get to sip blackberry brandy out of your navel."

"What about the Jack Black?"

"Blackberry brandy is better for navel sipping. More romantic, sweet."

Her eyes were very brilliant, like sunlight and a

171

clear blue sky. "Whatever you desire," she told him softly.

He sprang to his feet with a burst of energy, lifting Lorna, a pillow, and the comforter into his arms all in one.

"I can walk, you know," Lorna told him.

"I know. But this is kind of like the blackberry brandy. Infinitely more romantic."

"Ah, Lieutenant! Romance does lurk in your hard-bitten soul!"

"My hard-bitten soul? I resent that."

Do you? Lorna wondered. But she said nothing. She rested her head against his shoulder. They had been honest about their feelings, their needs and desires.

All she had asked was that he hold her and not turn away. She was receiving far more than that. And for tonight, she would not question him—or herself.

When they reached the bottom of the staircase his eyes met hers, and Lorna smiled. They were totally engrossed in one another.

Andrew set her down carefully before the fire. He grabbed the throw pillows from the couch and the second comforter, then poured their drinks. Lorna watched him, appreciating the glow of the firelight on his body. He was comfortable walking around naked with her.

Far different from New York . . .

He sensed her watching him and raised a brow curiously. "Am I being graded?" he asked with a laugh, handing her a refilled snifter of brandy and sitting down beside her.

"I was thinking that you have a nice body," she replied honestly, then hesitated, touching the scar on his chest. "Only slightly marred," she murmured.

Andrew adjusted a pillow behind his head, slipped an arm around her, and pulled her close. He rested his chin on her head and she felt the movement of his throat when he sipped his drink.

He pulled the comforter up over her shoulder, then idly stroked her arm. "I have a scar on my left toe too," he told her. "I fell off a dock in Connecticut once when Luke and I were fishing and sliced myself on a tin can."

Lorna ran a finger over the thumb that held his glass. "Meaning?" she inquired.

"That police work isn't the only way to get hurt."

"I thought you were about to say that." She couldn't see his eyes, and it bothered her. She knew his reactions only by his touch, and she wondered if she didn't feel him tense somewhat.

"Well, it's true," he told her.

"It's also true that policemen put their lives on the line every day."

"Most people in Manhattan put their lives on the line every day. The driving is crazy, the subways alone could provide enough information for a study on unusual human behavior, and there's always the possibility of being trampled to death."

"Andrew. You're reaching for excuses."

He did stiffen. His fingers no longer moved along her arm. He took another sip of his drink and she heard the slight sound as he swallowed.

"I'm not reaching for excuses. I don't need an excuse. I'm a cop. I like being a cop."

Lorna wondered why she was pushing the point. She had sworn that she was going to leave moot points moot for the night. It was nice to lean against him, feeling the hairs on his chest tickle her cheeks and inhaling the scent of him, but she didn't seem to be able to shut up. "Psychologists always have a hey-day with cops, you know."

"Oh?"

"The power thing, and all that."

He sighed. "I don't need to feel powerful, Lorna. I don't get my kicks from running around clobbering people on the head. But I do get something out of it, Lorna. I get a real intense satisfaction when I know I've nailed a dope peddler who has been making junkies out of grade-school kids. And when we've pulled in a murderer, I feel good about all the people who will live because a psychotic is off the streets. It hurts when we don't get them in time to save a life. Some of what I see go down hurts like a razor twisting in my gut, but it still hurts less to know that you're doing your damnedest to do something about it."

Lorna felt her throat constrict and her fingers tighten around the stem of her brandy snifter. "And what happens, Andrew, on the day that you don't get the dope peddler? When that murderer is just a little bit faster than you are?"

"Lorna, there's always danger. But, damn, give me some credit for training! I've done a lot more than go to target practice.

"I know that, Andrew, but still—"

"You're forgetting something, aren't you?"

"What's that?"

"It's your life on the line right now, not mine."

She shivered. Andrew immediately regretted his words.

"I'm sorry, Lorna," he murmured.

"So am I," she returned softly, making him wonder just what it was that she was sorry for.

They were silent for several moments. The fire glowed with warmth, and he realized that they were both tacitly allowing the conversation to drop. But when she spoke, she surprised him again.

"Andrew, can you teach me to shoot?"

"To shoot?" He frowned.

174

"Yes—as in a gun."

"You want to walk around armed? Lorna, guns can be dangerous."

"Yes, I know," she said impatiently. "I've never owned a gun and I've never wanted one in the house. But I do now. I'm aware that they're very dangerous; that's why I want to know how to handle one properly."

"I'm here to protect you—" he began.

"Andrew, I'm totally against any form of violence, but I also refuse to be a victim. I can't expect you to be glued to my side forever. I'd like to know a little bit about self-defense."

He was silent for a long time. Then she felt him shrug. "In the mountains, I'll teach you how to shoot."

He twisted around to set his glass on the coffee table and stared straight into George's brown eyes. The shepherd was behind him, panting and ready to dip his tongue into the bourbon.

"Get out of my drink, George. You've got water in the kitchen."

George gave a funny little woof, as if he were sniffing indignantly. But he obediently ambled toward the kitchen.

Lorna lifted her head and laughed. "Didn't you tell me that he was extremely well trained?"

"He is, when it matters most," Andrew said. "George caught our culprit this morning, not me."

"George did?" Lorna was surprised.

"Yep."

"Then I'll be as nice to George as I can," Lorna murmured. Bless George! she thought. She had been so horribly frightened when she saw Andrew racing into the pines, but George had gone before him as a

175

front-line squad. She made a mental note never to yell at George about his dog hairs again.

"It's his job," Andrew said lightly. He pulled her snifter from her hand and pressed her down on the pillow against the floor. The conversation kept steering into dangerous channels. He couldn't give up being a cop; she couldn't accept the violence involved. Their differences were cut and dried, short and sweet —simple.

But not tonight. He lifted the brandy glass with a devilish smile.

"Andrew!" She laughed as he started to tip the glass. "What are you doing?"

"I told you, blackberry brandy served a la navel."

"You're going to spill it all over the place."

"Nope, just on you."

She gasped as the first drops fell on the smooth flesh of her stomach, twisting instinctively.

"Hey, lie still or it *will* spill all over everything."

"Andrew." She kept wiggling, the glass kept tipping. She had brandy on her stomach and her breasts, and she still couldn't stop laughing. She finally managed to twist the glass from his fingers, then emptied the remainder over his shoulders.

"Lorna, you're spilling it all over the place!"

"Am I?"

Suddenly she shrugged, tossing the empty glass into the fireplace. "I've always wanted to do that," she told him.

He gripped her shoulders and pushed her back to the pillow. His mouth found hers and he engaged her in a passionate kiss. Then his lips roamed feverishly over her breasts to her ribs, his tongue tracing the blackberry trail. She rose against him, kissing his shoulders, whispering her lips over his chest.

He held her, trembling as her kisses continued.

176

"We have made a mess," he told her huskily.

Her eyes rose to his briefly, alive with firelight and mischief.

"Even fanatics have off nights," she told him.

"I don't think . . . oh, Lorna, I don't think this is an . . . off night at all. . . ."

CHAPTER EIGHT

When Lorna awoke, she did so with a smile. Andrew was still beside her, still holding her.

They had moved back upstairs after finishing off all the crackers, cheese, and pepperoni—and a good portion of blackberry brandy. Of course, after some of the brandy had wound up on them, they decided on a long bath, and Andrew had announced that some of her quirks weren't so bad since two people could comfortably sit in the huge, claw-foot bathtub.

And George . . . well, he had learned to stay off of the bed, but had chosen his own spot at its foot and was not to be moved.

It feels almost like a family, Lorna thought, ridiculously like a family.

She tried to shift from Andrew's side without waking him, but when she twisted, she found that his eyes were open. He was looking at her curiously, and yet by the morning light, his eyes seemed to be guarded, somehow remote.

Yes, he was still lying at her side, but was he really with her?

He touched her hair and smiled, but that puzzling shield remained over his eyes.

"Know what time it is?" he asked her.

Lorna gazed at the bedside clock. "It's just after seven."

Andrew swung his legs over the side of the bed. "Then we'd better get moving."

"Andrew, we're only an hour and a half from Boston and the auction isn't until three."

He was already in the bathroom and closed the door without replying. Puzzled, Lorna stared up at the ceiling, clutching the sheet and comforter to her chest.

What now? she wondered. Was he afraid that he was committing himself to her? You needn't worry, Trudeau, she thought bitterly. I'll never hold you to anything.

He emerged from the bathroom, one of her massive towels wrapped around his hips. "My clothes are all in the den," he said a bit sheepishly. "I'll get the coffee started before I dress, so take your time."

"Fine," Lorna murmured.

She watched him leave the room, still puzzled by his behavior. With a sigh she crawled from bed herself. The hell with him! she decided.

Fifteen minutes later she was dressed as faddishly as she had been the day before in a short, black corduroy skirt, matching vest, and gray cavalry shirt. Staring at herself in the mirror and playing with her new ash-brown bangs, Lorna was momentarily glad that she had the same weaknesses for clothing that she had for antiques. She didn't particularly care for the outfit she was wearing, but had bought it on a whim. It didn't look like Lorna at all, but it did look like the young woman with the frothy bangs.

She grimaced, remembering Andrew's mention of her height. Well, if she wore flat boots, she should blend in with shorter women wearing heeled boots. It sounded logical enough. And, she thought with a shrug, this was her own safety precaution. If it helped a little, it helped a little. Besides, Andrew said he thought they had a handle on the Massachusetts connection, so things were looking pretty good.

Or they should be looking good. She had enjoyed their night together as she had enjoyed few moments in her life. The memory of the passion they shared was still a physical thing, filling her with heated tremors and a wonderful, tingling sensation. But it had been more than the physical expression of love; it had been the laughter, the ease of being together, the comfort, and the honesty.

Comfort and honesty that seemed to be gone this morning, she thought bitterly. "Ah, well!" she told the mirror, "I guess we all must wear our daytime masks!"

"Lorna!"

She hurried out to the landing and gripped the bannister as she stared down at him. He was smiling, but it just wasn't a comfortable smile.

"Get your bags packed while you're up there, okay? I'm ready at this end."

"Sure thing."

Lorna retreated to her bedroom, dug under her bed to pull out her suitcase, and hastily filled it. "Time to be efficient rather than fanatic," she murmured to herself.

She was proud to see that it took her less than five minutes to pack. But, Mr. Trudeau, she silently charged, it's possible to be efficient because I *am* a fanatic—and I know exactly where everything is.

Lorna picked out a low-brimmed hat, angled it over her forehead, and gathered her purse, an old trench coat, and the suitcase. Then she hurried downstairs and set her bag at the landing before going into the kitchen.

Andrew was standing by the sink with his coffee. He assessed her with that same distant smile.

"You do look different."

"Good. Do I have time for coffee? Why the rush?"

"Because we're not heading straight for Boston. We're not taking the highway, we're taking the back roads."

"Why?"

"I just want to make sure we're not followed."

Lorna started to protest, then decided not to bother. She poured herself a cup of coffee. Andrew didn't stay in the kitchen. She heard the front door open and close, and when she looked out the front window, she saw him putting their suitcases in the trunk of his rented Mustang. A few minutes later he was back in the kitchen. "Ready?"

"Sure," she murmured.

He held her arms as they left the house. He was drawn, very serious this morning, and she knew that his attention was on their surroundings. But George, who followed along behind them, seemed to sense nothing, and Andrew appeared to relax a little.

Twenty minutes later she knew why it was going to take them so long to get to Boston. They drove to a parking lot at the Rutland State Park. Andrew pointed to a fairly new Cutlass and told her that they were switching cars.

"Switching? Andrew, you can't just take someone's car like that."

"Lorna, it isn't someone's car. I had it brought here. Please, just do as I say."

Sighing, she gathered her things and moved to the Cutlass. George, wagging his tail, followed behind her. Andrew quickly moved the luggage from trunk to trunk, and they were on the road again.

Andrew didn't seem to be in a talkative mood as they drove, so Lorna made no effort at conversation. She turned on the radio and leaned back in the seat, closing her eyes.

Was he so tense, she wondered, because they were going out in the open today? Or was it something else? He hadn't crawled out of bed right after they'd made love. He'd slept with her, held her through the night, but . . . she'd expected something this morning! The slightest reference, one real, warm smile, just one little comment. Something like "What a wonderful night."

They stopped in Framingham and changed cars again. Now they were driving a Fuego.

"I'm sorry," Andrew said, glancing her way as he started onto the road again. "I should have asked if you wanted something to eat. I guess I'm just anxious to get into Boston."

Lorna glanced at him. "It's all right. I can wait until we get there to eat."

He took his right hand off the wheel, found hers, and squeezed it. Lorna tried to smile, but her effort felt as false as his, and so she stared out the windshield.

What are you afraid of, Andrew? she wondered. I'm not the clinging type, I'll never stake a claim on you. I know that your work is your life, that you can't live without those city streets of yours.

"Tell me, Andrew," Lorna said, breaking the silence as casually as she could, "how's Tricia doing?"

He cast her a glance, frowning, as she mentioned his old partner's name. "Tricia's fine. Why?"

"I was just asking. She's a nice woman, I like her." Lorna had only met Tricia twice. Once when she had come to the New York apartment, and again on the day Lorna left New York.

"She's doing all right," Andrew repeated.

"She's such a pretty woman," Lorna murmured. "It seems strange that she's a detective."

"Why?"

"Oh, I don't know."

"We have a number of attractive policewomen."

"Aren't you two still working together?"

"No, we're not. With my promotion to lieutenant, I lost out on having a partner. She's been assigned to another case."

"Oh. I wonder if her work is hard on her personal life."

Andrew gave her another suspicious glance. "Don't you want to ask me if I've ever slept with her?"

"No, not particularly."

"You don't?" His eyes remained on the road, but he arched a brow, and she saw a rueful smile wrest its way into his lips. Small, but real.

"It isn't any of my business, is it? But she is very attractive—I wouldn't be surprised if you had slept with her."

Andrew's smile faded. "She was my partner. I never slept with her. I don't make a habit of sleeping with women just because they're attractive."

Lorna laughed—a little bit dryly. "I wonder if I should take that as a compliment or not."

"What are you getting at, Lorna?"

"Absolutely nothing. I'm just making conversation." She shifted on the seat as Andrew pulled out a cigarette, pressing in the lighter for him.

"I know what I was thinking! That Tricia would probably make the perfect wife for another cop. Think of it, a relationship made in heaven: two people who understood the death thing and all that brotherhood that seems to go around."

She heard a long, impatient sigh. He pulled out the glowing lighter and lit the cigarette without taking his eyes from the road.

"Lorna, I don't think many policemen run around with death wishes. And there is no secret fraternity to any of it. As for Tricia, she dates an attorney." He scowled slightly, piquing Lorna's curiosity further.

"You don't like the attorney, I take it?"

"I don't dislike him."

"It sounds as if you wonder if his attentions are honorable."

"Maybe I do."

"Ah, the perfect big brother. But I wouldn't be too overprotective, if I were you."

"Oh? Why?"

She smiled sweetly. "Men always seem to assume that women are determined to cling to them until the subject of marriage comes up, and that's such a fallacy. Most of the single women I know are enjoying their lives; they don't need marriage for security. In fact, they like their independence, and they don't want to be married. From what I've seen, men tend to be more possessive."

"Do you think so?" he asked politely.

"Nine out of ten, yes."

"Well, I'm glad you left some room for that tenth man."

"Such as yourself?"

"Maybe."

They drove in silence for a time, nearing the outskirts of Boston. Lorna gazed out without seeing the old Victorian houses that lined the small hills by the road.

"I've always taken it, Lorna, that you're one of those women who's very fond of independence. In fact, I get the feeling that you were independent when you were married."

He looked at her, then back to the road.

"Maybe," she replied.

Boston's tall buildings were coming into view. "Well, I don't want to rattle any of your beliefs in independence," Andrew said dryly, "but when we

check into the hotel, your name is Mrs. John Montgomery for the day."

"You made reservations for us as a married couple?" Surprise made Lorna's tone sharp.

"Don't worry, we have two adjoining rooms."

She was going to tell him that she hadn't been worried, but then decided not to. She suddenly felt weary,
as if none of it meant anything.

"Mrs. John Montgomery. Great. Do I have a first
name?"

"Jane."

"Fine."

They didn't speak again until they reached the hotel. George—to his credit—behaved admirably. He
padded quietly along at Andrew's side after they left
the car at the curb and entered the lobby. Lorna was
at Andrew's other side, her elbow held tightly in his
hand.

The check-in went smoothly. The clerk didn't bat
an eye at George, and George continued to be a model
of deportment.

They were on the tenth floor. Neither spoke as the
bellman accompanied them up. Lorna assumed,
though, that the bellman must be finding them a
strange couple; two separate rooms and they hadn't a
word to say to one another!

Lorna wandered around the room as Andrew tipped
the bellman. George followed behind her, as if he were
aware of a tension in the air and was afraid to find a
place to lie down.

As soon as they were alone, Andrew glanced at his
watch. "What time did you say your auction was?"

"Three."

"Well, we did make it early. Check the room service
menu and we'll have lunch brought up."

"All right."

While Lorna pretended to study the menu, she watched as Andrew brought her suitcase into the second bedroom.

"The door in that room stays bolted at all times," he told her firmly when he returned.

Lorna shrugged. "Whatever you want. You're the cop."

"You like to keep reminding me."

"Do I? Maybe I can't help it."

"I don't think you can. What do you want to eat?"

"The steak sandwich, I think."

George barked. Andrew glanced at the dog. "Sorry, George, it's still Alpo for you."

He called for room service as Lorna wandered to the window. She loved Boston with all the old churches, the streets where Paul Revere had made his famous ride, and the historic cemetery where he was buried. She'd known the city all her life and she still loved it. There was an ambiance there like nowhere else in the world. Snow would be frosting the Common, she knew, and it would be beautiful.

And there she was, stuck in a room with a man she had slept and played with all through the night, a man who now seemed like the most reserved stranger she had ever met.

"I don't like you standing by windows, Lorna."

She whirled around. "Oh, come on, Andrew! We're on the tenth floor. Besides, you told me that the Massachusetts connection or whatever it is had been broken!"

"I said I *thought* it had been broken."

"This is absolutely absurd—oh, never mind!" Lorna snatched a copy of one of the magazines off the television stand and sat in a chair to read.

Andrew turned on the television, pulled a pillow from beneath the spread, and lay down on the bed.

George wagged his tail, looked at them both, and sat down on the floor an equal distance between them.

Words swam before Lorna's eyes as she felt the tension that they were both ignoring grow. She was so wound up that, when a knock came on the door, she jumped. Room service, of course. She rose to answer the door.

"Get back," Andrew snapped.

"Andrew—oh, hell!" she muttered, turning around and walking into the adjoining room before his warning stare.

"Room service!"

Andrew still opened the door with discreet care.

The trays were carried in and set upon the small, round hotel table. Lorna smiled from the doorway. The waiter accepted Andrew's tip and left them. Andrew locked the door and pulled the table in from the window before allowing Lorna to sit.

"This is getting ridiculous," she told him.

"Staying alive is ridiculous?" he asked sarcastically.

"Haven't you ever heard of quality of life?"

He didn't answer her. He bit into the sandwich he had ordered.

Lorna did the same. All she could hear was the two of them chewing, and George's occasional movement as he scratched or shifted.

Suddenly she threw down her fork. Startled, Andrew looked up at her.

"I can't stand it!" she grated. "I can't stand sitting here like this another minute. It's almost time for the auction. Couldn't we go now, please?"

"Lorna—"

"Please, Andrew! This is Boston. We took such precautions getting here, and I do look different! It's not far, just over by the Prudential. I'll stick by your side like glue if we walk, I swear it."

"Can I finish eating?" he asked her.

"Yes, yes! But please, let me feel normal, just for today."

He glanced at her—uneasily, she thought—and took another bite of his sandwich. But a few minutes later he was through.

"Hey, George," he called to the shepherd.

"Wait a minute, Andrew," Lorna protested. "I can't, I really can't, take a dog to an auction. A single vase there could be worth thousands. You can't bring a dog to an auction. Believe me, they won't let him in."

"I'm not so sure this was such a hot idea," Andrew muttered, not glancing at her. He patted the shepherd on the head. "Okay, George, I guess you're going to have to hold down the home fort." He glared at Lorna. "You'll have to wait a few minutes. George needs out worse than you do."

He gathered George's leash and attached it to his collar. Before he left the room, though, he reached into his jacket and set his gun down in front of Lorna. She immediately felt her mouth go dry.

"I wouldn't know what to do with it, Andrew. That's why I was asking you to teach me to shoot."

"If anyone comes after you, pick it up and pull the trigger," he said briefly. "The safety's off."

Lorna knew she wouldn't be moving the entire time he was gone. She would be staring at the gun and praying that it didn't have a life of its own.

Andrew left with the dog. He wasn't gone long but, as she had expected, she hadn't moved a hair.

"We can go now," Andrew told her, putting his gun back into his shoulder holster.

When George barked, Lorna looked down at him a little guiltily.

"Shouldn't we leave him some food and water or something?" she asked Andrew.

He shook his head regretfully. "We don't dare; we might end up paying the hotel's cleaning bill and wind up sleeping with a very unpleasant odor. We won't be gone that long, anyway, and he had a drink right before I took him out."

"Sorry, George," Lorna murmured. The dog seemed to be looking at her very reproachfully.

Andrew opened the door for Lorna. "George, no unnecessary barking, okay, fella?"

George whined. Andrew and Lorna left.

She was so excited with the feel of the city that it was hard for Lorna to remain at Andrew's side. But he had no intention of letting her go; his arm was firmly about her waist.

"Where are we going?" Andrew demanded.

"Beacon Hill," Lorna said. The air was cold and wonderful, fresh and clear as it hit her face. People were all around them. Bostonians smiled a lot and Lorna smiled in return. She felt like skipping.

Andrew was not smiling. He didn't seem at all happy with the situation.

"Have you been to Boston often?" Lorna asked him. She wasn't about to let his scowl ruin her day.

"Once or twice," he replied curtly.

Lorna was undaunted. "What kind of an American are you?" she teased. "We're in the 'Hub of the Universe,' the Cradle of the Revolution, the Birthplace of our Nation!"

"I thought that was Philadelphia."

"Yes, well, it really started here. Come on." She tugged the hand at her waist. "We'll stop at the Old North Church, then the Granary. I'll give you a history lesson."

"Lorna."

189

"Come on, Andrew! Being careful is one thing—being paranoid is another."

She led him to the Old North Church where she gave him a fiery lecture on the lanterns hanging in the steeple that signaled the British march toward Concord. Andrew listened in silence. Lorna insisted that they move on to the Granary Burying Ground, where she pointed out a number of the important tombstones. Andrew didn't like being at the Granary because they were in the open, surrounded by buildings. He didn't like being cornered. With a sigh, Lorna at last agreed to be dragged away.

Andrew didn't like the auction either. He stared blankly at the auctioneer who spoke with an incredibly fast sing-song that only seasoned bidders could follow.

Lorna, however, was pleased. She made a number of purchases, which she considered wonderful bargains.

When the bidding was over, she wrote checks for her purchases and arranged for delivery.

Andrew stood stiffly behind her. She ignored him and was very polite to the clerk. But before she could say good-bye, he was gripping her arm and leading her away.

"I want to get back to the hotel," he told her curtly.

Lorna was in a very rebellious mood. So much so that his attitude irritated her, and she was cringing at the thought of returning to the hotel.

It wasn't like New York, but only because they were still together. He was so stiff and distant that she might as well have been alone. And it hurt because she didn't understand. How could they share so much together and then wind up like this?

"I'd rather stay out," she told him.

"No."

"Andrew, you go straight back if you want. I'm not."

190

"Listen, airhead—"

"No, you listen! I'm not an airhead. Tomorrow we're going to go lock ourselves away in a godforsaken mountain resort. One hour, Andrew, I just want one more hour."

Andrew had an urge to strangle her right on the street. "You are an airhead," he told her through clenched teeth.

"One hour, Andrew."

They started walking down Beacon Hill, then turned right, in the general direction of the hotel. His arm was firmly around her and Lorna felt the tension in his hold. No affection whatsoever in that touch, she thought bitterly.

She stopped to look in the window of a boutique. It was a custom shop, filled with handmade articles, knits and embroideries, clothing and small household items.

"Oh, look at those dishtowels, Andrew!" Lorna exclaimed suddenly. It was a lovely set of four linen towels and an apron, all with the letter "T" embroidered on them in a copper color. "They'd be a perfect gift for Donna," she mused.

"I don't want to look at any damn towels," Andrew grated back.

"Well, don't look at them then. I'm going to buy them."

"You might as well. You've bought everything else in sight today."

"I went to the auction to buy."

He wasn't touching her any longer, she was between him and the window and his hands were shoved deeply into the pockets of his coat. His jaw had a thrust to it that did more than hint of deep aggravation and simmering anger.

"Just don't ever cry poverty to me again."

"I never did any such thing."

"You did so. Oh, your poor business! Closing it up again would be such a problem! Well, lady, you just spent enough money to feed half the orphans in the city."

"I did not!" Lorna protested, returning his heated stare. She knew exactly why she had given way to the temptation to clobber him on that first day; there was just something about him . . .

"Andrew, what I do or do not spend is none of your damn business. This is my life and my income. Don't give me any of your moral righteousness. The Trudeaus are hardly living on Skid Row—except for you, perhaps, and that's entirely by choice."

"It's my job, just as you are my job."

"And you're taking your damn job way too seriously. You're driving me crazy, Andrew, absolutely crazy. Let's cut this thing right at the quick before it gets any more out of hand. I don't want it; I don't want to be smothered, I don't want to be called an airhead by the man I spent a wonderful night with, and I sure as hell don't want him turning into some absurd moralist the next day. I don't know just what your problem is, Trudeau, but I can't take your behavior. Don't touch me again. I mean it. Not for protection and certainly not because you've decided that a lapse into an affair with the woman you're guarding is okay for a moment here and there."

"Lorna!" He moved toward her, almost pinning her to the glass. He started to take her elbow but she wrenched away and moved past him.

"I mean it, Andrew. Keep your hands off me until you decide what it is you really want and that you can quit acting like a cold fish. I've had it! And I'm going in that store to buy those towels without you hanging on to me like a second skin."

She went into the store. Andrew stared through the window, a rush of heat boiling so hotly inside of him that he felt his face darken with a flush.

Damn her! Couldn't she begin to understand that he was continually sick with fear for her?

No, oh no! She was too busy with her petty fears about her freedom and her grand independence. It all seemed to be a damn lark to her. She didn't like cops, she said so often enough. Cops were violent and Mrs. Doria was above singeing her pristine hands with anything so base.

He ground his teeth together as he watched her gathering the towels, laughing and talking with the saleswoman.

She caught his eyes through the window. Hers held a little blaze of defiance and hostility. Then they left his as she turned back to the shopkeeper.

Andrew groaned aloud when he saw that Lorna was walking around the store with the saleswoman. She was inspecting every single item just to annoy him, just to prove that she was going to do whatever she so chose to do.

"Airhead!" he grated out furiously between his clenched teeth.

He scanned the store. Lorna was the only customer at the moment. He shuffled his feet impatiently, then started pacing up and down the sidewalk.

He lit a cigarette. It was a cold day, but he didn't mind the cold. He didn't even feel the cold. He felt as if he were burning up with anger.

I'm warning you, sweetheart, he thought, inhaling deeply and trying to get a grip on his emotions, you buy your towels and get out of there fast, or I'll come in and drag you out and you'll get a *real* idea of what its like to be hounded by a second skin.

He glanced back into the shop, inhaled, and exhaled. Lorna was at the counter, apparently paying for her purchases.

Cool down, cool down, he warned himself. You don't have any ties on her. Legally, she can do what she chooses.

He gazed up and down the street. It was already dark. Just a few minutes ago it had been light. Winter had stolen any semblance of dusk or twilight. Night had come like a blanket being tossed over the city.

He walked to the end of the store, then passed back to the other end. He took one last drag on his cigarette, then crushed it out beneath his foot.

He walked back to the end of the store again and looked into the window of the next shop. It was some kind of a computer store, nothing to hold his interest.

Nothing would have held his interest at that time.

All right, Lorna, he decided, walking toward the other end of the store and feeling so tense he wished he could crush something with his hands, you now have two seconds to get your sweet rear out here—then I'm coming in.

The street was filling with rush-hour traffic now. The cars were backing up, brought to a dead stop. A few horns blared.

The stupid shop should be closing.

Andrew turned around to stare into the boutique window. His heart did a double-take.

She wasn't there.

He charged into the store. The middle-aged saleslady was closing up the register.

"Where is she?" Andrew shouted.

The woman started with a little gasp and stared at him, her eyes betraying total fear as if she was certain that she was being accosted by a madman.

She swallowed and stuttered when she spoke. "Where is who, sir?"

"The woman who was just in here buying towels."

"She walked out just a moment ago."

"No, she didn't."

"Yes, she did, sir. I'd swear it to you on—"

Andrew didn't wait for her to finish. Cursing himself for not paying attention, he raced back out the door. Traffic was still rushing by. People were hurrying along the sidewalks, all wearing that drained look from a day of work, yet moving briskly, determined to keep up an energy level until they could get home.

People . . . everywhere. But no Lorna.

And then he saw her. She was standing in front of the computer store. He rushed up to her, furious with her because he was so furious with himself.

"Oh, Andrew, there you are—" she began.

"Damn you, Lorna!" he swore, rudely interrupting her. "Damn you! You're aging me ten years a minute out here!"

"What are you talking about?" she retorted with annoyance. "I went into the store, I bought the towels, just as I told you I was going to do. I came outside, and *you* were gone. I—" She broke off suddenly, staring past his shoulder.

"What's the matter?" Andrew demanded heatedly. Damn, but he was in bad shape! His nerves were worn ragged. She had been right in front of his eyes and he had missed her. The job was wearing him to pieces; he was unnerved by his sudden lack of competence. He just cared about her too much.

"I, nothing, maybe," she murmured.

"Don't tell me 'nothing!' " he grated out furiously. *"What?"*

She swallowed, and he knew she was frightened because she wasn't shouting back.

"Andrew, there's a car on the curb. It's just been sitting there. I saw it when I came out of the store. It's a black Lincoln, I think. I'm not sure, but I have this sense of being watched. And I think—I think that it might be after us."

He turned around. There was a black Lincoln on the curb. A rich car and, at the moment, a stealthy-looking car. Maybe his nerves were overstretched. He just couldn't accept anything at face value.

The chauffeur's door started to open.

"Start walking!" Andrew whispered the command to Lorna. He gripped her elbow fiercely and her low boots clattered against the pavement as they rushed along.

Andrew cast a glance back over his shoulder.

The chauffeur's door had closed again. Andrew heard the engine being started.

It wasn't any overreaction on his part. The black Lincoln pulled into the street. It was definitely following them.

He gripped her arm more tightly. "Keep moving, Lorna! Please, just keep moving and do what I say!"

He quickened his footsteps until he was almost running. When he looked back again the Lincoln had increased its speed and was closing in on them.

CHAPTER NINE

It was rush hour; there were people everywhere and cars lining the streets. But somehow the black Lincoln was managing to keep up with them.

Lorna was breathless, her feet were killing her, and her ankle twisted as she tried to keep pace with Andrew.

"Andrew!" She cried out at the wrenching pain. "I can't—I can't run any more!"

She didn't even know where she was, she realized. How far had they gone? In what direction? She clung to his shoulder, trying to keep moving, trying to get her bearings. They were almost back to the Granary, she realized with a bit of shock.

Andrew gazed down at her tensely. He hadn't wanted to run into a building and endanger others, but now it looked as if he had no choice. She couldn't go much further.

He saw the door to a hat shop. "Here, get in here!"

Lorna grasped frantically at the door. "It's locked!" she cried out.

Of course it was locked, everything was going to be locked. It was cold and dark and Boston was closing down for the night. They were going to have to reach a hotel or a restaurant.

"Come on, Lorna," he urged her, "we've got to get somewhere. You understand?"

"Yes," she whispered. But then she glanced back and screamed. "Andrew! The car has stopped. Men are getting out of it!"

He whirled around and saw that two men in coats and hats as black as the car were coming after them now on foot.

"Down the alley, Lorna, now!"

She could barely see any more; pain was shooting through her ankle, she felt dazed, and a light snow was starting to fall. Blindly she leaned against Andrew, allowing him to lead her.

He paused suddenly before a wooden door, pulled at it, then wrenched it open. He shoved her in front of him, and she spun into complete darkness. Andrew followed her, closing the door behind him.

"Andrew—"

"Shush, Lorna!"

She realized that he was looking out a crack in the door. She fumbled to touch him, and instead came in contact with the icy steel of his gun. She started to scream but he clamped his hand hard over her mouth. "Lorna, for your life, be quiet!"

She nodded; he released her.

After a few minutes she was ready to run out the door no matter what happened. The horror of the darkness was sweeping all around her. She heard . . . things, tiny squeaks, shuffling noises. There were creatures all around her, she realized, near hysteria, probably rats and roaches.

"Andrew, please?" she whispered in ardent beseechment. "What's happening? I can't stand this. I—I've got to see."

He closed the wood door very carefully, leaning against it. "They're walking around outside," he told her, and in the darkness, his quiet voice sounded something like a death toll.

"Oh, God," she whispered.

A second later there was a sudden spurt of light, a small flame. Andrew had flicked his lighter to survey their surroundings.

It appeared to be some kind of abandoned warehouse. Boxes, covered with dust and spiderwebs, were everywhere. The lighter went out. Lorna shivered violently.

Andrew's arms came around her. "Lorna," he said gently. "We've got to sit it out for a while."

She swallowed fiercely. "I—I know."

"It's not that bad, love. They don't know where we went. I'd been hoping for a phone or something, some way to get help. But there's nothing here. We've just got to wait until they give up."

"I . . ." She couldn't think of anything to say. It had all been her fault, hadn't it? She just had to come to Boston.

"You're all right, you're all right," Andrew whispered to her.

No, she wasn't. She wasn't all right in the least. She was terrified, but he was with her, and he wasn't telling her that it was all her fault. He was just holding her.

"Oh, Andrew, I'm so sorry!" she whispered miserably.

He hugged her, and his hushed return brushed her forehead with a reassuring warmth. "For what? We've both been tense, that's all." He hesitated. "Want to sit awhile? You can lean on me. Nothing will get you here by the door."

She nodded and they sank down to the floor together. He tried to talk to her, whispering things that she didn't really hear. It didn't matter; as long as she heard his voice she was okay. Cold, filthy, frightened, and miserable, but okay.

At last he ran out of things to say. He shifted to look out the crack in the door again, wondering why they weren't searching the buildings. Who were they?

"Damn!" he muttered.

"What?" Lorna almost sobbed.

"They're just standing out there!" He was silent, holding her. "Lorna"—he cleared his throat—"try to rest, okay?"

"Rest?" she whispered incredulously.

"We'll, uh, probably be here a long while."

A long while. Just seconds later it seemed like a long while. But it seemed that there was little choice other than to stay. Minutes passed. She grew colder, more cramped. The night seemed endless, and eventually she realized that hours had passed. Even Andrew had given up trying to keep her spirits going.

At last he shifted again, only to fall beside her once more. "The guys are across the street, just beyond that old cemetery."

"The Granary?" she asked.

"Yeah." He fell back against the door. More interminable time passed before he moved again. Lorna heard a clock chiming midnight.

Andrew twisted again, cracking the door. His heart started with a wild thud. Beyond the men, and beyond the Lincoln on the far side of the street, just visible beyond the alley, was a police car. He turned to Lorna. "Listen, there are some cops out there. I'm going to run—"

"No!"

"Lorna, quiet down."

"No, no, no! You aren't leaving without me."

"Lorna, I think those guys are still out there. I've got a gun, honey, but one could be shooting at you while I was shooting at the other."

"Andrew, the cops are out there! You said so!"

"But—"

"You won't leave without me! Don't you dare leave me alone!"

He hesitated. She was right. It would be better to have her with him; his body and his gun would have to be protection enough. He didn't dare leave her alone. He took a breath and checked the alley. It seemed clear.

He rose, drawing her to her feet. "You okay?"

"Ah, yes."

"So help me God, Lorna, stay behind me."

"I will."

They crept into the alley and headed toward the street. Andrew saw the black Lincoln and the police car ahead of it. "We're going to make a run across the street, understand?"

She nodded. Andrew had his gun in one hand. With the other, he kept a tight grip on Lorna, pressing her behind him.

Someone yelled when Andrew and Lorna reached the opposite side of the street, directly in front of the cemetery.

Lorna saw the fence and the centuries-old graves covered in a soft blanket of snow. Then she found herself being lifted, almost thrown over the barrier. Andrew caught hold of the fence and smoothly vaulted over it behind her. There was a flurry of footsteps behind them.

"I've got to know that it's the cops!" he whispered vehemently. He was as tense as coiled wire. Except for the ragged sound of their breathing around her, Lorna felt a tangible stillness, like being in a forest right before a storm. Andrew had her hand. His fingers clenched more and more tightly until she wanted to scream in protest.

They started running into the cemetery.

"Hey!" someone called out.

Lorna screamed suddenly as she tripped on a headstone, almost falling into the snow.

Andrew caught her and dragged her back up. "Who am I dealing with here? Lot's wife? Don't look back, or you might get us both turned to salt."

He wrenched her back to her feet and they were running again, dodging the old broken stones. They reached one of the mausoleums near the back of the cemetery. Andrew ducked behind it and drew her beside him. The snow soaked through her stockings and clothing.

"What are we doing?" she asked in a beseeching whisper. She was more frightened than ever. Then, suddenly, lights were shining all around them, illuminating the snow and the weathered tombstones.

"Waiting," he whispered. He tapped the tomb and tried to smile. "Who's in here?"

"What? Oh! I don't know."

"You don't? I thought you knew this place like a native."

"Andrew!" she wailed.

He peeked around the tomb again, then fell against it. "Thank God—it *is* the cops." He started to stand, and Lorna tried to follow him. He pushed her back down. "Wait, stay here."

"You just said it was the police. Andrew, I'm fond of history and this particular cemetery is steeped in it, but I'm not fond enough of Paul, Sam, and John to want to spend the night with them." She was trying to joke because she was still so frightened.

But Andrew's sudden, sharp intake of breath brought her to a pained silence again.

"What the hell?" he murmured. "My God, they've got that guy with him."

Lorna went still. Andrew stood in tense silence.

202

Then suddenly, incredibly, he began to laugh. Laugh so hard, doubling over, that there were tears in his eyes.

"It's Flaherty!" he exclaimed. "Oh, my God! I've been running us ragged, losing years of my life, and it's Flaherty."

Lorna didn't feel at all like laughing. She hadn't the faintest idea who Flaherty was.

But Andrew must have. He was stepping past the tombstones, striding toward the man who was leading the police into the cemetery, and offering his hand to him.

Lorna, dazed and stunned, watched the scene with incredulous disbelief. Then Andrew, with a rueful grin, was coming back to her. He took her in his arms, hugging her tightly, and started to laugh again.

"Who—what—"

"Oh, Lorna! The guy in the black coat is William Flaherty! Don't you recognize the name?"

Then she did. It was synonymous with Vanderbilt or Rockefeller. The man was one of the wealthiest moguls in the country, possibly in the world.

"William Flaherty?" she repeated.

He nodded. "He's sorry as hell that he frightened us, but once he lost us, he was frightened himself and didn't want anyone to get hurt—that's why he didn't search the buildings in the alley."

"You know William Flaherty?" she asked, unaware for the moment that she was freezing. *"How?"*

He laughed again. "I met him in New York. His daughter, Penny, was one of the mugging victims. I met him at police headquarters. Thankfully, Penny came out of it all okay. We didn't really know at the time that it was connected with Simson and this whole thing. He does, of course, have an interest in the case, although he just told me he doesn't know much of

203

what has been happening lately. He wants to know what's going on. And he wants to help us."

"Help us?" Lorna repeated.

"Yes!"

"But why? I don't get this, Andrew. One of the most wealthy men I've ever heard of chases us around and scares us half to death because he wants to help us? Why should he care? Why should he do such a thing?"

"Because he knows what it was like for his daughter to be a victim of crime—our particular criminal, we think, although we can't prove it. Being rich doesn't make him an uncaring human being, Lorna. It wasn't you he was watching from the car, it was me. He was surprised to see me. When we bolted, he called my precinct and found out that I was guarding you. He stuck with us because he didn't want us terrified and because he was so determined to help. Hell, Lorna, I don't know! He told me once that he was a great mystery fan. Reads Travis McGee novels and Agatha Christie in his spare time. I don't have to understand all his motives. If the man wants to help us, we've just got to let him!"

"You think that he *can* help us?"

"Anything's possible."

"How?"

"I don't know, but come on over and meet him."

She followed Andrew across the snow and he introduced her to a middle-aged man, tall and broad and fit for his age. His hair had once been black, but now it was streaked with white. His nose was long, his brows were thick, and his features were gaunt, but his jaw was firmly squared.

William Flaherty smiled at her, and she saw that it was a nice face, if a stern one. "Mrs. Doria, I'm so very sorry for frightening you. All I ever intended to do was help."

She nodded, at a total loss for words.

She'd been what she would term fairly affluent all her life, but she realized then that she'd never met a multimillionaire before; for all she knew, Flaherty might even be a billionaire.

His smile deepened and she flushed. She wasn't accustomed to being gauche either. Her present lifestyle, she decided wryly, was wearing her thin.

"Mrs. Doria, are you all right?"

"Oh, yes, I'm sorry! Oh, Lord, Mr. Flaherty, may I start over? I'm terribly sorry, Andrew says that you want to help, and I'm extremely grateful."

"Mrs. Doria, please don't apologize, I'm the one who owes the apologies. I've given you a miserable night. Let me make it up to you. I'd like to talk to you both. Tonight, if you're up to it. If you'll be my guests, I'll see to it that you're provided with anything you might need."

"Lorna," Andrew said firmly, "please, answer the man. Mr. Flaherty thinks he can help us."

Lorna smiled. She had been so terrified, but now everything really was all right. Better than all right. She had been chased by a multimillionare, but only because he wanted to help her.

"By all means then, Mr. Flaherty, we accept your invitation with the greatest pleasure," Lorna said, finding her voice at last, and finding it with enthusiasm.

Flaherty smiled. "Shall we go?"

William Flaherty's chauffeur-driven Lincoln took them back through the streets to a beautiful apartment building near Beacon Hill. A night guard opened the door to a stupendous lobby of marble and oak with a magnificent crystal chandelier, and then they were rid-ing an old-fashioned elevator to the penthouse where the Flahertys' lived in elegant splendor. The balcony looked out over the lights of the city; Boston had never appeared more beautiful.

Flaherty led the way back to a massive and airy sitting room. "Not to insinuate that you're anything but charming company, but I'm assuming you'd like to bathe after I forced you to spend hours creeping around dirty alleys. Lieutenant Trudeau, the room down the hall to your left is my son's. You'll find everything you might need. Mrs. Doria, I hope you won't mind borrowing one of my daughter's robes."

Lorna smiled uncertainly. "Not if you're sure your daughter wouldn't mind."

"I assure you that she would be honored. I'm prejudiced, of course, but my daughter is a lovely and generous woman. She and my son are in Vermont with their mother right now, but I know Penny would be pleased to offer you anything you needed."

"Thank you," Lorna murmured, a little over-whelmed.

Andrew was looking at her, grinning. It had begun as a horrendous evening, but this was fun, and with the future looming before them, it was delightful to enjoy the fun.

But even as Andrew grinned at her, Lorna stared back with a slow-dawning horror.

"What is it, Lorna?"

"George! Oh, my God, Andrew, we forgot all about George. It's been hours!"

Andrew's face was draining of color. "We've got to get him right—"

"Lieutenant," William Flaherty interrupted indignantly. "One does not maintain and increase a fortune such as mine by not checking into all the facts. I'm assuming that George is a very large German shepherd."

"Yes," Andrew replied meekly, staring at Flaherty with an even greater respect.

Flaherty kept smiling. "I called your precinct when I realized that I had frightened you to death and I didn't know where you were. Someone told me right away about the dog; I offered to see to him, but they sent out a Sergeant Wilkes. If I understood things correctly, George and Sergeant Wilkes are on their way to one of the Carolinas."

"Thank God," Lorna murmured. How could she have forgotten George? Steadfast, loyal George—whose dog hairs she didn't even mind anymore!

"Please, make yourselves comfortable," William Flaherty said. "I'll arrange to have some food ready as soon as you're out."

Andrew and Lorna gazed at one another, smiling a little foolishly like a pair of kids. Andrew shrugged. They both murmured their thanks again and departed to their separate rooms.

Lorna wasn't accustomed to being dazzled. After all, old, beautiful, and elegant things were her business and, to an extent, her life-style. But Penny Flaherty's room was breathcatching. Splendid in its simplicity, the room had to encompass a good six hundred feet. A cream-hued Persian rug covered the hardwood floors and the draperies were a matching color, their layers rustling from the heat coming out of air vents in the floor near the windows. The wallpaper appeared to be fashioned of golden embroidery, and the bed was set on a raised dais along with Oriental cabinets and dressers.

A step down brought Lorna to a small sitting room, complete with a built-in television and stereo system and glass-encased bookshelves. Lorna gazed at the titles and determined that Penny's major interest was chemistry.

Lorna suddenly felt a bit like an intruder. But when she turned around again, she saw the door to Penny Flaherty's closet ajar and she couldn't resist the temptation to see her clothing.

It was fun. Penny's closet was the size of Lorna's bedroom, and her clothing ran from a wall full of plush and elegant furs to a wire rack of well-worn jeans. Lorna mused that she would probably like this girl with a myriad of tastes and a penchant for chemistry.

But again, she felt that she was intruding. And she was a mess. For a fanatic, she was filthy. She hurried to the bathroom door and was again dazzled by the size of the room.

Penny didn't have an old clawfoot. Her bathtub was a sunken marble affair with a built-in whirlpool. There was a skylight above it that afforded a glimpse of the velvety heavens, dotted this night with a multitude of stars.

Just a shower! Lorna told herself. But she knew she wasn't going to settle for a shower. The tub was much too inviting.

And someone, some invisible entity working for William Flaherty, had set out soft towels in a muted violet, a terry robe in the same lovely shade, and even shampoo and a hairdryer. Opulence, built to order for her this evening, and she intended to take full advantage of it.

Lorna stripped off her clothing. The outfit, she decided, was going in the garbage as soon as possible. The snow had ruined it and it really wasn't her style. And once she washed her hair, the brown rinse would be gone too. It was just as well, she decided. Tomorrow she and Andrew would be headed for South Carolina. What she looked like then wouldn't matter. She would be as safe as it was possible to be.

Lorna played with the spigots and came up with just the right temperature for the water and just the right pulse for the whirlpool. Then she leaned back against the tub and just lay there for a while. Finally, with a burst of energy, she scrubbed her hair and herself, and when she was satisfied that she had washed away all vestiges of the night, she lay back against the marble tub again.

She started as she heard a knock at the door. Andrew? Her heart began to race. This tub was even larger than her own, the warmth and the jets of water were almost ridiculously sensual. It would be lovely to have him here. . . .

But her fantasy died a quick death. Andrew was—although she was sure he'd be shocked by the description—very upright and moral. He simply wouldn't appear at her bathroom door when they were guests in another man's house.

"Yes?" she murmured, puzzled.

The door opened a crack. An older woman in a black and white maid's uniform appeared. "Mr. Flaherty thought you might enjoy a glass of wine in the bath, mum."

"Well, Mr. Flaherty is an absolute doll." Lorna laughed. "Thank you very much."

The wine was served to her in crystal on a silver tray. Lorna sipped it delightedly.

"I'm Jenny, mum. If you wish anything else, you've only to touch the little red button by the light switches."

"Thank you, Jenny, I can't think of another thing I could possibly need."

"Will the robe suffice, mum?"

"Beautifully, Jenny, thank you."

209

The woman smiled, bobbed a curtsy, and left. Lorna smiled like the Cheshire cat, sipped her wine, and settled back. There were things to think about, and always things to worry about, but for the moment she could only delight in absolute sensation. All she would need to know the zenith of delight would be Andrew.

Her smile paled, but then returned. Time was on her side. She would still have Andrew for days and weeks to come. And with Andrew, it would never matter where they were, or under what circumstances. He *was* the zenith of delight to her, even if it could only be borrowed delight.

Lorna realized, when she at last rose from the tub, dried herself, and belted the violet robe, that she had left Andrew and Flaherty at least an hour ago. Feeling guilty, she hurried down the long hallway to the sitting room.

Andrew's white terry robe was a shorter version of hers, revealing his legs from the kneecaps down. Nice. She hid a smile. The white was perfect on him, emphasizing his dark coloring, enhancing the golden tone of his body. And his legs . . . she delightedly took in his long, muscular calves with their thick profusion of short, curling hair. Then her eyes were drawn to the vee of the robe and the hair on his chest.

Lorna swallowed a little guiltily. There was something about the relief to be living that made her terribly . . . thoughtful about Andrew. Yes, thoughtful was the word.

He was holding a bottle of imported beer, sitting in one of the hardbacked chairs that was angled around a glass-covered oak coffee table. He was the one talking, so he didn't notice her at first. He was telling Mr. Flaherty all about George, things Lorna hadn't known herself.

"George is a product of a completely new form of

was saying. "He belongs to a national
police, as does the program. Once the
that you're a friend, he's as safe as a
still in the experimental stages, of
think that George is sound proof that the
methods are going well."

Flaherty had noticed Lorna standing at the entrance
to the room. "Come in, come in, my dear." He swept
an arm in a broad circle that encompassed the coffee
table. Lorna looked at the array of food spread before
her and realized that she was famished. And Mr.
Flaherty's offerings were mouth-watering. There were
plates of fresh vegetables and fruits, clams on the half
shell, jumbo shrimp tempura, and what looked like
baked scallops.

"A feast," Andrew said aloud, rising and smiling at
her. Again she had that feeling that they were two kids
set loose in Santa's playland.

"Fix yourselves plates," Mr. Flaherty said. "I'll refill your wine, Mrs. Doria, and then the two of you can
fill me in completely on everything that's happened."

Neither of them were shy as they heaped their
plates with food. Andrew began the explanation with
the very first robbery and the death of Luke's first
wife. He stared at his plate while he was speaking
then.

"My God," Flaherty interrupted. "I never knew the
girl who died was your sister-in-law, Lieutenant. But
then, I guess that you didn't really have the connection when Penny was mugged, did you?"

"No," Andrew said. As he continued, he looked
straight at William Flaherty, his emotions concealed
again. "You see, sir, this is hard to explain, but we
finally knew because the robberies were just too pat,
too well planned for too little gain. We began to sus-
pect that there was a deeper motive involved. Then

211

when Mrs. Simson was killed and Lorna gave our
ist what was almost an exact likeness of her grandso
it all fell into place." He paused again, chewing a scal
lop thoughtfully. "Then a sniper took a shot at Lorna,
and it was obvious that we were in serious trouble.
The D.A. said we still hadn't the evidence to take a
man as powerful as Simson to trial. We had to have
more evidence, and we had to keep Lorna safe."

"I know that part of it," Mr. Flaherty said. "Tell me
about Mrs. Doria's connection."

Lorna plunged in, trying to explain her own role,
and Donna's, giving Andrew a chance to eat. She woefully admitted that she had drawn her friend into danger with a letter she should never have written.

Mr. Flaherty lifted his hands. "Don't blame yourself, we all do things like that with no idea of the scope
of the consequences."

"Well, yes, but Donna's in the same position I'm in
now. Simson doesn't want either one of us appearing
in court."

Andrew took a sip of his beer and cleared his throat.
"You see, Mr. Flaherty, Donna was taken to Simson
by a pair of his goons; he intended to find Lorna
through her. At any rate, she has a mile-long statement to go into court with now too."

"But Simson is out of jail?"

Andrew sighed and explained about the hearing and
the indictment, and that Simson had still been entitled
to pay bail until the trial.

"They're getting this trial going in record time,"
Andrew said, "especially when you consider the work-
load in New York City courts."

William Flaherty kept nodding throughout the explanation. At last Lorna had nothing else to say, and
neither did Andrew. They glanced at one another uneasily and then at Flaherty.

Flaherty was smiling. "I do think I can help you."

"How?" Lorna asked softly, baffled.

"What can outbuy wealth, my dear?"

Lorna shook her head. Flaherty's pleasant smile deepened. "Greater wealth. And power can be bested by—"

"Greater power?" Andrew supplied, frowning.

"Precisely."

Lorna shook her head. "I'm still lost."

"Ah, elementary, my dear Mrs. Doria. Well, fairly elementary. I can't give you particulars yet, but it's very possible that I can get a few of my own rumors going that will subdue Mr. Simson. And, well, let's just say that if things work out the way I plan, you'll be safe for the rest of your life."

Andrew looked uncomfortable. "What do you plan to do, sir?"

Lorna knew he was thinking that Flaherty might just be planning an execution of his own.

Mr. Flaherty spoke softly. "Don't worry, young man. I'm not a murderer." He leaned forward. "But you see, Simson isn't either. Well, he is, but not in the physical sense. The man is probably a horrible coward, hiding behind a tide of green. Strip away that money, and he no longer has control or strength."

"You think you can break him financially?" Andrew asked.

"Well, I believe the courts would do it eventually, anyway," Flaherty said. "But yes, I intend to break him financially. Do you have any objections, Lieutenant?"

"Not one," Andrew said, then paused. "But how can you do it?"

Flaherty smiled grimly. "I've been watching the man and his company for a while now, since I heard

213

he was arrested. Do you understand anything about stock, young man?"

"Very little," Andrew admitted.

"Well, it can work different ways. But usually, when someone wants to start up a company, they have to sell shares for the capital to get it started. They keep the largest amount of stock for themselves."

"Right," Andrew murmured.

"Now, that doesn't always mean that you'd keep fifty percent, because what's being bought is diversified. Someone here has three shares, someone else has five, and so on. All you'd have to do is hold the majority of shares. That's a little simplified, but it's the basic idea."

"I understand that much," Andrew replied.

Flaherty smiled. "Well, I'm going to try to get my hands on every stitch of Simson's stock that I can. He's been selling quite a bit lately, which makes sense. Hit men are expensive. Once I gain enough stock, I also gain control of the company. I can devaluate what he owns and I can break him. Follow me?"

"Perfectly," Andrew replied. "I think."

Flaherty chuckled. "It's almost dawn. I think I should let you people get some sleep."

Just as she had realized that she was hungry, Lorna suddenly realized she was also exhausted. She smiled, still puzzled and overwhelmed, and stood. "I think I will go to sleep," she said, walking over to Flaherty. "Thank you so much again. For everything. For tonight, for your help, for your hospitality."

"And again I tell you, my dear, it has been my privilege."

Lorna couldn't help looking back at Andrew, but he wasn't looking at her. He was studying his nails. She smiled once more at Flaherty and went down the hallway to Penny Flaherty's room. She closed the door but didn't bother with the light. She walked straight to the bed, pulled down the soft covers, and crashed into it. Within minutes she was asleep.

Her dreams were as sweet and fragrant as the patterned sheets on the bed. Her dreams were of Andrew, and they were good.

She saw his eyes, deep green and sparkling as they did when he laughed, the crooked twist to his mouth when he smiled ruefully. In a distant drumroll she seemed to hear his laughter, the husky cadence of his voice when he spoke. She saw him as they had sat before her fire, and she smiled as she slept, remembering his touch.

His touch . . .

She wasn't dreaming. Someone was beside her.

A scream rose in Lorna's throat, but faded to gasp of surprise as a hand—one she knew well—gently covered her mouth.

"Shh! It's me! Flaherty will think he's harboring a rapist!"

Lorna smiled and pulled his hand from her mouth. "Well," she whispered huskily, "if you're not here to ravish or be ravished, I'll thank you to let me sleep."

She rolled toward him. It was very dark in the room, but she saw his eyes, the eyes she had so recently dreamed about. The same crooked, sheepish smile was on his lips as well.

"I needed to be with you," he said softly.

She embraced him and pulled him to her. Their lips met, a soft, tender touch at first. But then Andrew's arms enveloped her, and his mouth blazoned against hers with a deep, searching hunger. Tongues met and clashed, and the kiss became both sweetly consuming and igniting. Lorna was breathless and quivering.

He rolled to her side. His lips touched her throat, his hands tore at the belt of her robe. She brought her

215

fingers to his chest, to revel in the feel of the coarse hair there, to his shoulders and on down his back.

"You haven't got a thing on!" she whispered.

"Of course not. I have enough sense to take my clothes off before I get into bed. All decent ravishers take their clothes off—didn't you know?"

"Makes sense," Lorna murmured. She shimmied the violet robe from her shoulders, and when she was freed of it, she held his face between her palms, kissing him again. And as she kissed him, she covered his body with her own. She felt his fingertips against her bare back, caressing her, loving her. It was so good to be with him. His scent was that of clean male, an aphrodisiac as stimulating as the calloused touch of his fingers and the taste of his lips when she kissed him.

She continued to kiss him, his throat, his chest, his hips, touching him, bringing her body against his all the while and luxuriating in the joy she experienced. His fingers tangled in her hair, his whispers encouraged her to ever greater intimacy. He did not mind that she was the aggressor, nor did she care when he took that role from her, lifting her, cradling her. He took her slowly, fully, completely . . . and then with a whirlwind passion that could never cease to amaze and fulfill her, leaving her both exhausted and absurdly smug with contentment.

They lay quietly for a long time, fingers laced together, legs still entwined.

She should have dropped back to sleep, but she didn't. She moved to curl against him, laying her head on his chest.

"You know, I'm in love with you, Andrew," she said softly.

He rubbed his palm lightly over her back. "I love

you," he murmured, and then his fingers gently tugged at her hair, bringing her head up so her eyes met his.

"What are we going to do about it?" he asked.

"I don't know," she murmured, lowering her eyes. "Andrew, do you . . . mean it?"

"Yes. And I was afraid of it."

"So was I."

"I'm still a cop."

"I know. And I'm still not happy with it." She paused. "But, Andrew . . ."

"Yes?"

"It's so good to say it. To know it, to hold you now, no matter what happens in the future."

His arms went around her very firmly. He held her, and she could feel the beating of his heart and the warmth of his body.

"I do love you . . . oh, yes," he murmured passionately, "I do love you."

"We have time together."

"Yes."

"To see."

"Yes."

For a long while he held her, stroking her shoulders and the silky flesh of her back.

"Lorna?"

"Yes?"

"Are you tired?"

"Yes, of course."

"Too tired?"

She smiled, and when he rolled her to her back, she met his eyes with laughter and tenderness.

"I'll never be too tired," she vowed, and set about to prove it.

CHAPTER TEN

By late afternoon the following day, Lorna and Andrew were aboard a small jet that would take them to a private landing strip in northwestern South Carolina. The jet, too, was private. Bill—as Lorna had been asked to call William Flaherty—had insisted on arranging their transportation.

The plane was like a lounge. Comfortable swivel chairs were arranged around a chrome table that was generally used for business purposes, Lorna assumed. She and Andrew played cards while sipping the steward's specialty, cocoa rum coladas.

Andrew kept winning at gin, so Lorna decided to change the game. She taught him how to play honeymoon bridge, and was pleased to see her luck take a swing toward good. They kept their conversation light aboard the plane, but it was a comfortable lightness, different from what it had ever been before. Lorna didn't feel at all distant from Andrew. The future—the distant future that could only come after Simson's trial —was still a problem that caused her to ponder and worry. It was there, and so she couldn't help it, even though she had promised herself that all she wanted was to be close to Andrew for the time that they were together.

And they were close. Last night had done that for them. Maybe it all had to do with innate defense mechanisms. It was frightening to love someone when that someone might think you were a fool for doing so. Maybe all people need reassurance, Lorna thought, and once the reassurance was there, they were free from the shields of their defenses. Lorna didn't really know. All she did know was what she felt, and when Andrew looked at her, when he touched her, when he laughed, it was with an intimacy that denied nothing. She was certain that she had changed too. Life was, after all, a series of actions and reactions.

She had a feeling that Andrew was perfect for her. Not in the obvious sense—they were too different for that—but in that strange way she had sensed the first time she had seen him, as if she had waited a lifetime for him. And now he was there. But that thought always brought her to the future.

They lived in different states. She liked her home; he liked his. And she liked what she did for a living; her bric-a-brac and furniture were a way of life, just as Andrew's job was a way of life for him. Andrew's job . . .

That, of course, was really the sore spot. Ordinary patrolmen put their lives on the line all the time, but Andrew was more than an ordinary patrolman. It was one thing when the cop was guarding her, but that wouldn't always be his job. Andrew would go back to the streets, seeking danger with an instinct for a criminal's trail.

He didn't want to give that up. He had told her so. Lorna didn't believe in forcing choices, anyway, it was just not her style. If he were to give up his job for her, he would no longer be the same man. Without his self-respect, he wouldn't care much for himself, and then he would never be able to love her.

Lorna knew that things weren't even that simple. She was well aware that there was no real point of compromise for them. If the matter of a lifetime commitment ever came up, she would have to be the one willing to accept his life. But she knew, too, that it might never come to that. Andrew was independent, and there was a big difference between loving a woman and living with her. Then, too, just as she knew that she loved Andrew, she didn't know if she could ever live with him.

He seemed as pensive as she when they folded up their cards for a dinner of veal marsala prepared with gourmet touches miles off the ground. Lorna watched him curiously. His brows were knit together in a frown, his eyes lowered as he scattered ground pepper over his meat.

She touched his hand. His eyes flew to hers.

"A penny for them?"

He grimaced. "I was thinking that sometimes it just all seems so senseless; the fear and worry and the aggravation. All this because you happened to be on a street at the wrong time. And because of April, of course," he added softly.

"It has to be the roughest on Luke, don't you think?"

He frowned again. "Yeah, but you really had a knack for just walking into it all."

Lorna sat back in her chair with a little sigh. "I know," she murmured, glad, at least, that the conversation had slipped past the still painful topic of his brother's deceased wife. "I do seem to have an incredible streak of bad luck going, don't I?"

Andrew shrugged. "Incredible goes both ways," he told her. "It was incredibly bad luck—or fate, or whatever you care to call it—to become involved with a man like Simson." He grinned. "But then, it's incredibly good luck to wind up with a devoted friend like William Flaherty. Unusual and incredible. You understand what I'm saying?"

"I suppose."

Andrew laughed. "I guess it doesn't really make sense. Or else it makes perfect sense. There's always the good with the bad. In your case, they just happen to come in extremes."

Suddenly he pulled her out of her chair, around the table, and into his lap. "You," he murmured, "were incredibly good luck for me."

"Andrew!" Lorna laughed. "There's a steward on this plane."

He kissed her. "I'm not doing anything improper."

"You're supposed to be eating dinner."

"I'm going to. But I was just thinking . . . for now, it really is a vacation. I'm looking forward to the mountains. To spending time with Luke and Donna. And you."

"I want that time too," Lorna replied softly. Andrew smiled, then set her on her feet so that she could return to her own chair.

When Andrew looked up again, he noticed that she was frowning. "What's that for?" he asked.

"I was just wondering what this place is going to be like."

"It's a house on two acres, I believe, with an electric fence around it."

Lorna flushed. "That's not exactly what I meant."

Andrew arched a brow. "You're thinking it might be a little awkward?"

"Not awkward. Just . . ."

"Awkward," Andrew supplied with a laugh. "I think," he added, pausing to chew a piece of carrot in butter sauce, "that Luke and Donna are aware of our relationship. And don't you dare tell me that bit about a 'lack-of-relationship.' "

221

"I wasn't going to," Lorna retorted primly. "But someone knowing and someone seeing are—"

"Seeing? I wasn't planning on making love on the living-room floor, Lorna."

"That's not what I mean and you know it. Your brother is a priest."

Andrew grinned. "Somehow I can't see my brother following you around to threaten you with damnation for your illicit and immoral life-style."

"Andrew—"

"Oh, Lorna, come on. You know Luke. How could you possibly be uncomfortable around him?"

"I don't know. We'll have to see. Anyway, they're our hosts, of sorts, so we'll follow their lead."

"Meaning?"

"If we're chastely separated, that's how we'll remain!"

Andrew chuckled. "Are you threatening me?"

"No, I'm worrying myself!"

Andrew cut into his veal again. "We'll be there soon enough," he replied serenely.

At the airfield they were met by an employee of Flaherty's who gave them the key to a maroon sedan. The drive to their retreat, as Andrew was calling it, took about twenty minutes through curved and winding roads. It still seemed to be fall there. Snow capped the tall mountain peaks, but along the roads and in the valleys the landscape was colorfully beautiful. Shades of gold and orange were still abundantly visible.

The road took them around a little curve and Lorna saw a pair of simple frame houses. Beyond them was a dirt road, and beyond the dirt road was an exquisite place that resembled a Swiss chateau. It was cast against the panorama of a rising mountain peak and, standing there before them in the soft dusk, it looked enchanting. The coming darkness shadowed the six-foot fencing around the place, enough so that Lorna could ignore it, or at least press its reminder of constant danger to the back of her mind.

The door to the left frame house opened and an armed man walked out and approached the car. Andrew rolled the window down and produced his identification.

The armed man introduced himself as Kevin Parker, told them that he had been expecting them and was glad to meet them. He waved toward a window in the small house and the gates to the "retreat" swung open.

Another drive, one that seemed to stretch for a mile, brought them to a circular driveway that swept by the front door. Andrew stopped the car just as the front door swung open and a streak of movement came rushing toward them.

Lorna smiled. It wasn't a streak of movement. It was Donna, eagerly racing out of the house.

"Lorna!"

She had barely managed to exit the car and stand beside it before Donna was hurtling against her, hugging her and talking away a mile a minute.

"Oh, you've made it. I'm so glad. We heard all about Boston from that nice Mr. Flaherty—Lorna, you've got to tell me all about *him*. I'm so glad I didn't know about it until it was all over. This whole thing is just so awful, isn't it? But I feel so much better that you're here. It will be nice, it really will, the house is just beautiful, wait until you see—"

"Donna, if you stop for air and let her walk, she will be able to see it."

Lorna laughed as she gave Donna a tight squeeze, then stepped back to look over her friend's head as Luke approached her more decorously from the door. Luke stretched out a hand and Lorna accepted it, leaning over to give him a kiss on the cheek. "Luke, how are you?"

"Fine." He had a crooked smile that was very much like Andrew's. He was perhaps an inch taller and ten pounds heavier than his brother. His hair was almost black, and his eyes were a gold-studded hazel rather than green, but there was no denying that they were brothers.

"We're awfully glad that you're here," he said quietly, slipping an arm around his wife's shoulders. Lorna sensed an undercurrent in his voice, but she didn't question him then, because he was looking past her to Andrew.

"Drew! You made it!"

"Yeah." Andrew was coming around the rear of the car with their suitcases. They both grinned as they shook hands. Luke took one of the suitcases from Andrew and they started for the house.

Donna and Lorna followed them.

"Did something happen?" Lorna asked Donna.

Donna glanced at her uneasily. "Why do you ask?"

"Just something about the way Luke spoke."

Donna lowered her head and, since Lorna was so much taller, all she could see was a thick wealth of her friend's sable hair.

"Let's get in the house, shall we? Then we can talk about everything."

They caught up with Luke and Andrew. Luke, with a sparkle to his eyes that made him look more like the handsome devil than the priest, was ribbing Andrew.

"Hope you don't mind going through the door rather than the window. The windows are all wired."

"Actually," Andrew replied blithely, "I'm quite fond of doors. Yours is the only window I'm accustomed to going through."

"Lucky me," Luke murmured.

"Luke, get in the house so that I can come in too, please." Donna rolled her huge blue eyes at Lorna with an affectionate insinuation that the two of them were going to be in trouble if they were locked away with the brothers Trudeau for any great length of time. She hurried past Lorna and caught the door, holding it as the men entered with the suitcases.

When Lorna passed Donna, she saw that the house looked like a ski lodge inside. There was a huge hearth and an open balcony above the stairs that created a huge, cathedral ceiling in the living room. Everything was done in light wood, comfortable and welcoming. But Lorna had barely stepped inside before she heard a joyous bark, and then she was welcomed in truth as George came running unabashedly up to her.

"George!" Lorna cried delightedly. The "well-trained" shepherd jumped up and licked her face with such enthusiasm that she buckled to her knees. It didn't matter, though, she hugged him and scratched his back with fervor. "Oh, George! I actually missed you, you mutt! I had forgotten all about you, and then I went through the worst guilt! Let me see you, George. Oh, you don't look at all the worse for wear!"

Andrew dropped his suitcase and hunched down to the balls of his feet beside her, also scratching George and pulling his black snout up to take a good look at him. "George, you look good."

George whined and wagged his tail. Luke laughed. "I feel like I'm interrupting a family reunion. Of course he looks good. Sergeant Wilkes brought him down yesterday and taught us all about caring for him. I thought we were excellent adoptive parents. Didn't you, Donna?"

"The best," Donna agreed. "Hey, guys, are you hungry?"

"No, thanks, Donna," Andrew said, rising and

helping Lorna up from her knees. "We had dinner on the plane."

"How about hot chocolate?"

"That sounds good," Lorna said.

"Mmm," Luke agreed, "but watch out for her hot chocolate. She spikes it with Khalua."

"Sounds even better," Andrew said.

"Drew, why don't we take your suitcases upstairs," Luke suggested.

"Lorna, want to give me a hand in the kitchen?"

As Andrew followed Luke upstairs, Lorna followed Donna into the big, eat-in kitchen. It was bright, with sunny yellow curtains softened by powder-white daisies.

Donna didn't really need any help. She turned on the kettle and pulled mugs from the cabinet, asking Lorna questions about her brothers and Theresa. Finally Lorna interrupted her.

"Donna, something happened, didn't it?"

Donna hesitated, ripping open a serving of powdered chocolate, dropping it into one mug, then winding her long hair into a knot at her nape. "Yes and no."

"Come on. You were talking a mile a minute, and all of a sudden you're being evasive. What did—or didn't—happen?"

Donna shrugged. "The rangers caught a guy with a rifle out by the fence yesterday. He didn't do anything, but he was there, and he didn't have a permit for the rifle."

"Oh."

Donna shrugged and ripped open another cocoa sack. "I feel good about it in a way; George barked his head off, and the rangers were right there. The guy never got anywhere near us, so, you see, it made me realize just how safe this place is. What bothers me is

226

that he was there. I just wonder how long all of this can go on. It's hardly begun, and I'm sick of it already. Oh, Lorna, I'm sorry. You've been going through much worse. I just start to wonder sometimes if . . ."

"If what?" Lorna prompted.

"I shouldn't even say this. It's so un-American. And I've never breathed a word to Luke because of April, you know. . . ."

Donna's voice trailed away, and Lorna frowned. She knew that Donna and Luke had been married before he had told Donna that his first wife had been a victim of Simson's plot, but as far as Lorna knew, there had never been contention between the two because of it.

"Donna, I don't understand. What are you saying?"

Donna sighed. "I don't know. Just that life might be more simple—might continue, in fact—if we both refused to testify against the man."

Lorna was silent for several minutes. "I'm sorry, Donna," she said at last, "really sorry. It's all my fault that you're involved at all."

Donna shook her head vehemently. "No. If you hadn't gotten me involved, I would never have had Luke, and Luke is worth everything. I'm just rambling, I think."

Lorna hopped off the stool and started ripping open a cocoa packet too.

"Donna, it wouldn't do any good to refuse to testify. Andrew told me that the State of New York can legally insist we do."

Donna gazed at her and smiled. "I think I was just talking because I had to say it to someone. Don't you see? I could never really refuse to testify, no matter what the State of New York had to say. Luke's first wife was killed, Lorna. I love Luke. I know that he

227

loves me, but I don't think he'd ever feel right if her murderer went unpunished. Do you see what I mean?"

"Yes, I guess I do," Lorna replied quietly. The kettle whistled and Donna went for the water.

"Where's the Khalua?" Lorna asked. "I think I want a lot in mine!"

"Top cabinet," Donna answered.

Lorna added the liqueur to the mugs. "You know, Donna, things might be looking up," she said.

"Oh? How?" Donna was busy filling a tray with an assortment of cookies.

"Mr. Flaherty."

Donna glanced at her skeptically. "He's going to get a contract killer after Simson?"

Lorna shook her head. "No. He thinks Simson can be broken financially."

"I don't know." Donna's voice was bleak. "Sometimes I wonder if anything can break Simson. My God, the man was caught red-handed and he still thinks he can get out of it. And, with all this talk about admissible evidence and his word against ours, he just might."

"No, I don't think so," Lorna replied after a moment of thought. "I think Simson is frightened. As frightened as we are. If he wasn't, why would he try so hard to get us?"

"You've got a point," Donna agreed.

"Yes, I definitely have a point."

"Okay, then we've got to get into a party mood and learn to think vacation. Of course, it is hard, because Luke yells at me every time I go near a door."

"Luke yells? I don't believe it."

"Believe it. Luke yells." Donna laughed. She handed Lorna the cookies and picked up the tray of mugs, her lashes sweeping over her eyes. "I wonder who's more temperamental, Luke or Andrew?"

"Andrew. I guarantee it."

"Don't go that far." Donna laughed. "I think Luke is worse. I'll admit that Andrew has more quirks, like entering the house through the window, and I never know if I'm going to see him in tattered jeans or a tux, but I like his temper."

"Mmm," Lorna said noncommittally.

Donna started to walk through the doorway, but she turned around so quickly that Lorna had to hop back to keep the cocoa tray from connecting with her stomach.

"Sorry," Donna murmured, but her eyes were sparkling and her smile was broad. "Just how are you and Andrew getting along?"

"Fine," Lorna replied sweetly.

"Does that mean just fine, or *fine?*"

"We're not throwing things at each other, if that's what you mean," Lorna answered innocently.

Donna laughed. "Let's get serious here, please, because Luke is giving me an awfully hard time about butting in. Okay, I'll get to the knitty gritty. I *know* that you two were messing around because, well, just because. What I need to know is, are you still . . . ?"

"Messing around?" Lorna asked wryly.

"Yes!" Donna laughed. "You see, I have to ask, because you are the craziest people. I mean, I thought something was going on in New York, but then, on the day you were going home, Andrew appeared at our place. Then you appeared, and Andrew had disappeared—through the window, of course. And, well, I didn't want to force you two in one room here, just in case you didn't want to be together. But if all you two needed was a little nudge, I wanted to make sure you were easily accessible to one another, so I gave you the master bedroom, which has a little side room that must have been planned as a nursery."

Lorna was watching Donna as she listened to her explanation. She burst into laughter. "Donna, if I'm crazy, you have to be too."

"Only a little. But please tell me that you two are still messing around, because if I've done something wrong, Luke is going to kill me."

Lorna flushed. "You haven't done anything wrong. But I am glad you kept up a little bit of a facade of respectability. You *are* married to a priest."

"Oh, that," Donna said lightly. "If you were stealing from the poorhouse, he would definitely nail you. But sleeping with his brother . . . Luke considers that to be your own business." She grinned. "He has a penchant for reminding me that it's none of *my* business. But, oh, Lorna, you two are just so right for each other!"

Lorna's smile faded a bit. "Don't go planning a wedding, Donna. We care about each other, but that doesn't change life."

"What does that mean?" Donna demanded.

"Just that we do have differences."

"Oh, come on, Lorna. Everyone has differences."

"Great differences," Lorna said.

"You do not." They had been telling each other their secrets since they were toddlers; Donna was as close as a sister, and Lorna knew that she wouldn't back down easily.

"Donna," Lorna explained, "Andrew is a New York City cop. He doesn't want to change that, and I'm not at all sure I want to move to New York, give up my business, or spend my life like that. As for Andrew, he doesn't know if he would want a wife—any wife. Please, Donna, I'm not ready to push any of this."

"All right," Donna said amiably, but she was still watching Lorna.

Lorna smiled again. "Okay, Donna, you want to say something. Say it."

Donna shrugged. "I was only going to state the obvious. But if you don't want to hear . . ."

"I want to hear it, Donna, really I do."

Her friend smiled sweetly. "Marriage is supposed to be a fifty-fifty proposition, right?"

"I suppose," Lorna murmured suspiciously.

"Well, sometimes it can be, and sometimes it can't be. If you—don't get excited, I'm being hypothetical—if you marry Andrew, you would have to give the first percentile, and it would be a big one. His job is in New York, but you could run an antique store anywhere. You'd be giving another huge percentile because you'd have to accustom yourself to living with a cop. So far, it's Lorna one hundred, Andrew zero. But somewhere along the way, Lorna, the tide would turn. On something else that was important. Andrew might well be the one to give the whole hundred. Do you understand what I'm saying?"

"Yes."

"Well?"

"I just don't know yet." Lorna laughed. "Is that it, Mom? Or have you got any more lectures for the day?"

"No, that one needs to sink in. And the drinks are getting cold. Let's go join the brothers, 'temperament' and 'quirk.' "

"Let's do it," Lorna agreed.

Donna started talking in a new vein as they left the kitchen behind. "You should see everything that we've got here. Monopoly, Tripoli, Trivial Pursuit, cards, movies on video cassettes, all kinds of things to keep from going crazy." Donna chuckled. "Of course, my father decided to help out by giving me half his business books to transfer onto a new computer system. Drew and Luke's mother bought us all the games and one of the other priests at St. Philip's found a supply of reading material at a secondhand store you just wouldn't believe. You'll love some of them, they're right up your alley: *The History of the Duncan Phyfe Sofa.*"

Luke and Andrew were still upstairs, so Lorna and Donna took seats in the living room before the huge granite hearth. George curled up by Lorna's feet. Donna glanced over her shoulder, and Lorna knew that she was being very careful not to give away the extent of her fears and frustrations to her husband.

Donna demanded to know all the details about William Flaherty's penthouse apartment. Lorna responded, but she was thinking about other things even as she spoke.

It would be nice—more than nice—if she and Andrew could plan a lifetime together. It would be so perfect, so much fun. Her best friend was married to his brother, and it was important to have friends to share things with, danger, bad times—and good times too. Yes, the good was there too, right along with love and comfort.

Upstairs, Andrew was leaning against a dresser smoking a cigarette and Luke was sitting on the bed. Their conversation was similar to the one that had recently gone on in the kitchen.

I'm telling you, Drew, I honestly start to wonder what this is all worth sometimes," Luke was saying. He had already told Andrew about the man at the fence with the rifle. "I can't forget April; I can't forget that she was so young, that she died randomly as part of a greater plot. And I don't want it happening again.

Donna . . . or Lorna. My God, Drew! It still makes me shake when I think of the night they took Donna. I wanted to strangle Simson that night. And it's still going on." He looked at his brother. "I wasn't supposed to tell you this yet, Donna wanted to surprise you together, but she's pregnant."

"Pregnant?" Andrew repeated.

Luke grinned. "As in expecting a child."

Andrew laughed. "I know what it means! Congratulations, that's wonderful. And quick."

It was Luke's turn to laugh. "Donna wanted to have a baby before she turned thirty. She said she wanted to be young while the baby was young. And I'll be thirty-seven next year. We both wanted children, and we decided we wanted them as soon as possible."

"That really is wonderful, Luke," Andrew said. "I'll be an uncle."

"I guess that's why I'm just so . . . thoughtful lately."

"Frightened, you mean."

"Yeah, frightened. We've got a long way to go to that trial. And then what?"

Andrew felt his throat constrict. Yes, it was easy to be frightened, terrified even. Moments like this made him feel as if a boa were squeezing the breath from him.

Something of his feelings must have shown in his eyes. Luke stood up, walked over to Andrew, and took the cigarettes from his shirt pocket. Andrew reflexively flicked his lighter for his brother. Luke wandered over to the window, then turned back to Andrew, grimacing.

"Sorry, Drew, I was just sounding off. Showing my nerves a bit, I guess."

"Don't be sorry, Luke."

"And don't let me make you frightened. Most of the

233

time I'm just determined to see that man behind bars. I get furious that I'm frightened and fighting mad because I'm sick of it. Then"—he grinned—"I do have my moments of optimum faith. I don't believe in bargaining with God, I just don't believe God would let Simson get away with this."

Andrew exhaled and smiled. "Let's hear it for faith!"

"Remember you're addressing your priest, son!" Luke rebuked him with a laugh.

"I'll try to keep that in mind." Andrew's eyes roamed from the large room where they stood to the door that connected it with a smaller room. There was another door in that room, one that connected it with the hallway. The set-up could be one massive room or two separate ones. He smiled and glanced at Luke, raising a brow.

"Don't look at me. Talk to my wife if you've got any complaints or objections."

"I don't have any complaints. Or objections." He laughed. "But the set-up comes free, without any lectures?"

"If I had anything to say about your sex life, I probably would have said it by now."

"No advice on the sanctity of marriage?"

"That's between the two of you, isn't it?"

Andrew's smile wavered, then was gone. "I'm a cop, Luke."

"And I'm a priest. Donna is a bookkeeper, and Lorna runs an antique store. What has that got to do with anything?"

"A lot, and you know it."

"I know that it only matters if you let it."

"I can't change what I do, Luke."

"Maybe you could—a little."

"Meaning?"

234

"You're a lieutenant now, Andrew. Most lieutenants run things from a desk and go out only when the level of the problem reaches them. They still go out, but not as much."

"I don't think I'm the right man for marriage, Luke."

"You weren't going to get a lecture, but now you've asked for one. You've been half in love with Lorna since you met her. I think you've fallen over the edge by now. Let her go, Andrew, let some misguided sense of isolationism break you apart, and you'll be sorry for the rest of your life."

Andrew shrugged. "It's just not me, Luke."

"Maybe it is." Luke started walking toward the door, then paused and glanced back at Andrew. "Come on. I want to hear everything that happened in Boston. And"—he chuckled—"Donna has decided to be the social director for the upcoming weeks. I'm sure she has something planned for the evening."

They spent an hour just talking and catching each other up on everything that had been happening. They talked about their families, about New York, New England, and South Carolina. Donna made her announcement about the baby, and Andrew watched as Lorna hugged her friend and showered her with enthusiasm and congratulations. Something touched him about Lorna at that moment; her eyes were alight with warmth and caring and when she laughed at something that Donna said, Andrew felt a little tug at his heart. It was clear to him in that moment just how beautiful she really was.

He felt another little tug—of jealousy—when Lorna hugged and kissed Luke. Not really jealousy—he couldn't be jealous of his own brother, especially when that brother was very happily married. Maybe it was a touch of longing to share the emotion.

Andrew shrugged away his feelings. Donna was pulling out the Trivial Pursuit game and trying to assure them that it would, of course, be hard to be confined, but between the books and the house and everything else, they shouldn't die of boredom or claustrophobia.

"I'm not going to be bored at all," Lorna said, and her eyes connected across the table with Andrew's. "I'm going to learn to shoot."

He started. She was very serious, and there was a grain of strength to her voice that surprised him.

"You really want to do that?" he asked.

"I would think that learning to be a decent marksman, or woman, wouldn't hurt anyone," Luke said casually.

"Guns can be dangerous," Andrew said uncomfortably.

"When you don't know how to use them," Luke agreed. "Oh, good, Donna just landed on sports. There's no way she's going to get her little wedgy."

"Don't be so smart, Father Trudeau," his wife retorted. "Give me the question." It was on the Boston Bruins, and Donna got it right.

They stayed up until midnight, then Donna yawned and said she was going to start picking up. Luke was immediately on his feet. "Don't pick up tonight, let's just go up to bed if you're tired."

Andrew laughed. "Donna, you've been away from Lorna too long. Go to bed. Lorna and I can pick up. You know she won't sleep until the last chair is back in place."

"Andrew!" Lorna protested with a laugh.

"I said 'we'd' pick up."

"Yeah, I guess you did."

Andrew noticed that both Donna and Luke glanced at him and Lorna, then at each other, and grinned. He didn't know whether to laugh or tell the two of them to keep their smug little grins to themselves.

"Are you sure you don't mind, Lorna?" Donna asked.

"Go to bed!" Lorna returned.

"Good night, then."

Donna and Luke disappeared up the stairs. Lorna looked at Andrew, smiled, and started collecting cups. Andrew gathered the pieces and then returned the game to the shelf. Picking up the ashtrays, he joined Lorna in the kitchen. She was cleaning the last cup. He put the ashtrays on the counter and slipped his arms around her.

"Ready?"

"Just the ashtrays, Andrew. And I really should sweep the floor."

Andrew firmly set her aside. He emptied the ashtrays and rinsed them quickly while she watched.

"That's it."

"The floor—"

"Will wait."

She tried not to, but she laughed. And she was still laughing when she saw the room arrangement upstairs.

"Donna was really covering all her bases, wasn't she?"

"Yes, I guess she was." Andrew kicked off his shoes and fell onto the bed, lacing his fingers behind his head and grinning at her. "What base am I getting to?"

Lorna smiled, picked up his shoes, and put them in the closet. "Well, one way or another, I'll be close to you."

"How close?"

She slipped off her shoes and put them beside his in the closet. She walked slowly to the bed, undoing her cuffs and then the buttons to her blouse. She moved

237

fluidly, shedding the blouse and then her skirt. They fell to the floor and, to Andrew, it was like a butterfly —a beautiful process of metamorphosis.

When she came to him at last, climbing onto the bed and leaning on an elbow beside him, she was naked.

He reached over and pulled her on top of him, kissing her, cupping her breasts tenderly in his hands. He glanced into her eyes and saw that she was frowning. "What's the matter?"

She shook her head.

"You're worried about Donna and my brother?"

"No, well, maybe just a little. Andrew, he *is* a priest."

Andrew grinned. "Want him to come bless the bed?"

"Andrew! That's irreverent! Luke is a priest."

"He's also my brother and that's always been first in my book. And—" He paused, frowning slightly.

"And what?"

"I think he knows that I love you," Andrew said seriously and softly.

Lorna smiled and began working at the buttons on his shirt. He gazed at her, the frown gone, a lazy grin in its place. "You've decided you want to be close."

"Mmm."

Andrew rose from the bed, too impatient to be free of his clothes to have her help him undress. Then, as naked as she, he got back into the bed, sliding beside her and holding her to him. His chest was hard against her breast, his hips pressed against hers, his desire for her evident with a pulsing heat and warmth. Their legs entwined when he touched his lips to hers, then raised them to stroke her cheek and whispered, "Is this close enough?"

"You're getting there," Lorna returned huskily.

"Well, then," he murmured, pausing to tease a breast with his tongue, "well, then . . ." He moved his face to the shadowed valley between her breasts and attended lovingly to the one that had been neglected. "Let me get even closer."

He met her eyes, slipped his hands around her waist, and drew her over him. She cradled his hips with her thighs. He lifted her and shuddered as she came to him.

"Close . . . enough," Lorna murmured.

"Beautifully close," Andrew agreed. But then his words were gone as her lips touched his, and he lost all coherent thought.

CHAPTER ELEVEN

Bang!

The retort of the gun sent Lorna staggering back, but she was smiling. Following the explosion, the clear bottle with the red label shattered into a thousand pieces.

She didn't even fall! The first time she had squeezed the trigger, she'd landed royally on her rear. A week. It had taken her a week, but now she was actually hitting things!

"I did it!" she shouted to Andrew.

He shrugged with a motion that gave her only a certain and slightly grudging admiration.

"Okay. So you're not such an airhead after all." He laughed. He walked over to the strip of fencing he had built to accommodate the bottles and picked up the pieces to throw in a garbage box. "Try it again."

"Which should I go for—the soda or the bourbon?"

"Get them both."

"Sure."

Grinning, Andrew walked back to her and retrieved his gun. He took quick aim and held his hand steady as he squeezed the trigger. The sound was deafening, but as Lorna instinctively put her hands over her ears, both bottles exploded.

"Showoff."

240

"Yeah," he agreed. "Now you can go for the milk bottle."

"Okay."

It was a large bottle. She took little time to aim, but did so carefully. A second later the milk bottle shattered.

"I hit it!"

"Of course you did." Andrew ruffled her hair. She saw that he was looking beyond the lawn, down the slight hill that rolled to the fence and the slope that started rising again. He was never comfortable outside. She knew he was about to tell her that it was time to go back in.

She was right. "George!" he called out. "Hey, George, let's go in."

The shepherd came bounding around the side of the house. He ran to Andrew, wagged his tail and panted as Andrew gave him a scratch on his head, then turned to Lorna, hopping up on his hind legs.

"George, you're going to knock me down again!" Lorna laughed. "And you're getting my sweater all muddy. Get down, you mutt!" George jumped back to the ground, but he kept wagging his tail.

"He's got your number," Andrew warned Lorna. "He knows you're all bark and no bite."

"Oh, he does, does he?"

"Yep." Andrew cleaned up the last of the glass, walked back to Lorna, and slipped his arm around her shoulder. "George knows you're just a sweet little pussy cat inside."

"And that's what you think too, huh, Trudeau?"

"That's what I know, Mrs. Doria."

"Pretty certain of yourself, aren't you?" Lorna was teasing, but she noticed that Andrew took a long time to reply, and when he did, his voice was a bit edgy.

"Shouldn't I be?" But before Lorna could worry

241

over his tone, it changed and he continued lightly, "There isn't a wide variety of men to choose from here, is there? You've got me, or a married priest. So, my little pussy cat—" He stopped suddenly, pulling her dramatically and playfully into his arms and dipping her back, "I'm as sure of myself as a man can be."

Lorna laughed, but sobered quickly. She reached out a hand and touched his hair. "You should be sure of yourself, because you know that I love you," she said softly.

"How much?" he challenged her suddenly.

"How much?" she repeated, then smiled and gave him a child's answer. "To the moon and back."

"But is that enough?" Andrew murmured as he straightened her up and opened the back door to usher her in. After calling George in, he carefully locked up. He walked over to the stove. "Want coffee?"

"Sure."

Andrew filled a pot with water. "It's so quiet. I wonder what Luke and Donna are up to."

"Luke was studying one of his law books, and Donna was fooling around with the new computer."

Lorna pulled off her jacket and scarf and sat at the kitchen table. There was a magazine sitting there, and she idly began to turn the pages. Andrew finished measuring coffee into the drip machine, then joined her. "She's not knitting booties yet?"

Lorna glanced up at him. "She's not that pregnant yet."

"What is 'that pregnant'? You either are or you're not." He sounded angry.

Lorna frowned. "She's not that far along yet. She won't have the baby until July. And, as far as I know, Donna doesn't knit."

"You mean it's not a prerequisite?"

242

Andrew was smiling then, and Lorna shrugged. "I guess not." She turned her attention back to the magazine, then shut it. "Andrew, I feel . . . so excited."

"We could go upstairs."

"That's not what I meant!" Lorna protested with a laugh. "I mean, I feel as if I've accomplished something. I hope I never use a gun against anything living, but I am beginning to learn how to use it. Aiming and then hitting what you're aiming at gives you a little thrill. I think I'd enjoy getting into skeet shooting or something like that."

"Maybe. It can be a sport like anything else."

He stood up and waited by the coffeepot for the last of the water to drip through, then poured them each a cup. He set the cups down and lit a cigarette. Lorna gazed at pictures of a diamond mine in South Africa. She heard the click of Andrew's lighter, then looked up slowly as she realized that he was also drumming his fingers against the table.

He wasn't watching her, he was staring into space. His fingers continued to tap against the table.

"Bored?" she asked him quietly.

"What?" His eyes met hers and he flushed a little. "Oh. No."

"Yes, you are."

"No, I'm not. Really." He stood and idly paced around the kitchen. "It would be nice to ride around here. Get some horses and spend the day just enjoying the scenery."

"Yes, it would."

"Maybe some day," he murmured. He sat down opposite her again, and in a second he was drumming his fingers.

Lorna closed the magazine. "Well, I've thought of a project for the next few days."

"What's that?"

243

"Christmas is coming. We can have one of the rangers find us a huge tree to decorate and we can make popcorn strings and all sorts of things."

"You sound like you're trying to amuse a child," Andrew said with a sheepish grin.

"Maybe I am. You're just like a restless little boy."

"I'm sorry. I'm just accustomed to being more useful."

"Active," Lorna corrected him. She stretched her hand across the table and entwined her fingers with his.

"You know," she murmured in a soft drawl, "a lot of men wouldn't think it was such a terrible thing to be holed up—your words, not mine—with a pussy cat."

Andrew burst into laughter, clasped a hand around her neck, and found her mouth for a lingering kiss. "The nights are magic, the mornings are terrific, and when I can catch you up there in the afternoon, it's sheer delight. I've enjoyed teaching you to shoot, and there's no other couple in the world I'd rather be shut away with than Donna and Luke. But when we're outside, I'm nervous."

"And when we're inside you're restless."

"I'm sorry. I'm going to make an effort not to be so restless. Donna brought a bunch of suspense novels for me. I'm going to pick one out and learn how to enjoy sitting around reading."

Lorna nodded. "Want to start now? I'm in the middle of a great horror novel. We can take turns in one another's laps."

"Deal. Just let me refill my coffee."

A few minutes later they were comfortably situated on the sofa. A fire was blazing from the hearth, and they both had their books out. Lorna was able to get through a hundred pages with her legs stretched out

on the coffee table and Andrew's head on her thigh.
Then Andrew rose, stretched out his legs, and pulled
her head to his lap. He lit a cigarette and remained
silent a few minutes, then started talking again.

"What do you think I should get Luke and Donna
for Christmas?"

Lorna set her book down. "You know your brother
better than I do."

"I know, but I was trying to think of something for
them as a couple. I thought about a crib or one of
those old wooden cradles, but that wouldn't really be
for them, would it?"

"I think it's a great idea. I even know where to find
the exact cradle you're talking about. I could make a
phone call and get it delivered here, if you want."

"Great."

He picked up his book again. She felt his fingers
playing lightly over her forehead. "Lorna?"

"What?"

"Why didn't you and your husband ever have children?"

"We weren't ready," she replied, turning a page.
Then she gazed up at him and met his eyes, reversing
the personal challenge. "Why didn't you ever get married?"

He started to say something, then closed his mouth.
He lit another cigarette, started to talk again, then
laughed. "I don't really know. I was going to say my
job, but that isn't really it. I guess I just wasn't ready
myself."

Lorna nodded, then turned her attention back to
her book.

His fingers continued to play over her forehead and
she realized that he wasn't reading at all. He was smiling down at her. "You know, pussy cat, you might not
be so hard to live with on a permanent basis."

245

"That's a left-handed compliment if I've ever heard one," Lorna replied. "And I'm not so sure it's even true. You're so restless you can't sit still, and one minute you're calling me an airhead, the next I'm a pussy cat."

"Ah, but you are a pussy cat—when you're not being an airhead. If we were really off on a romantic tryst, we'd be doing all sorts of things. Maybe we'd be on a beach, swimming a little, relaxing a little, boating, fishing, out dancing at night. We'd be alone an awful lot too, of course. Making love by waterfalls and all that sort of thing."

Lorna laughed. "Sounds nice. Be sure to call me sometime when you're on vacation." She turned her attention quickly back to her pages, her breath catching in her throat. She suddenly felt more like crying than laughing. For all that passed between them, there were still those things that didn't, and sometimes she felt a little lost.

"Let's make a date to do it," he told her huskily.

"When?"

"When this is over."

She didn't answer him. He plucked the book from her fingers and leaned over to kiss her. "Are you really into that book?" he asked her huskily.

"I was."

"I am suffering a terrible case of restlessness. I'm sure it could be cured with a little vigorous activity."

"Is that a proposition?"

"Yes. I'll make it worth your while."

She couldn't help but laugh. "Andrew, it's the middle of the day."

"No one's around!" he whispered.

Lorna shrugged. "You'd better not be restless for the rest of the afternoon."

He pulled her to her feet. "I don't plan on being

downstairs for the rest of the afternoon," he replied with a laugh.

They didn't go back downstairs. They made love, fell into a doze, made love again, and dozed again. Finally Lorna noticed that it was getting dark. She started to stretch and rise, not wanting Donna to be working in the kitchen alone.

Andrew stopped her, barring her with an arm braced over her waist.

She glanced at him to see that his features seemed dark and stern in the shadows, his eyes were a dusky green.

"I love you," he told her.

She smiled and kissed him. She knew that he watched her while she dressed.

William Flaherty called while they were laughing over a bridge tournament that night.

Andrew remained on the phone with him for a long time. When he returned to the group, they were silent and expectant.

Andrew took his seat again. He picked up his cards, then, when he realized that everyone was looking at him, he set them back down.

"Bill has managed to do just what he planned. He bought up all available stock and even went after some of the unavailable too. Anyway, he's become the majority holder in the company. It was uncanny, how smoothly it all went. Simson is after a lot of cash, so Flaherty was actually able to buy some of the stock from Simson. He's gotten rid of a number of the board members who were in Simson's pocket and he plans on splitting the stock—that means doubling the shares and halving their value. Presumably—or hopefully—Simson will start selling more, counting on the value to rise again. But it won't because Bill will keep tight controls on it until Simson has nothing left."

"And?" Donna asked quietly.

Andrew smiled at her. "Broke people can't hire contract killers. Especially when they're behind cell bars."

"God bless that man," Donna murmured.

"I'll say amen to that," Andrew told Luke.

Luke smiled. "Two no trump. Donna, listen to my bidding. Two no trump."

"I'm listening!" Donna retorted. "I just don't have a damn thing to go with your two no trump!"

The game continued. George curled up at Lorna's feet, and Luke and Andrew decided to pop corn.

By the end of their second week in the house, Lorna could aim at a dime and hit it. Things were going much the same, so much so that Lorna couldn't imagine living without Andrew. They still had occasional arguments, but Luke and Donna did too. Arguing now and then didn't alter the depth of their love at all.

The rangers brought the Christmas tree that Lorna had asked for, and they spent one night decorating it. They played Christmas carols on the stereo, made eggnog, and then settled back as couples to watch the display of blinking lights. It was a lazy grouping that night, comfortable, and intimate.

Lorna mused that, though she would be hidden away, she couldn't remember a holiday season that had meant more to her. Soon it would be Christmas. The cradle Andrew had wanted for Luke and Donna had arrived and was waiting down in one of the ranger's houses. Lorna had ordered an embroidered infant set to go along with it, and between them they had decided to buy a few other things to go with them, earrings for Donna and a jacket for Luke.

The phone rang while they were sitting quietly. Andrew took the call in the kitchen.

"Flaherty," he said when he returned. He picked up his drink and sat beside Lorna, putting an arm around her shoulder.

"He said he'll own Simson's company by the first of the year."

"That's great!" Donna exclaimed. Andrew was silent. "Andrew," she persisted, "isn't that great?"

Andrew sipped his bourbon thoughtfully. He felt Lorna's eyes on him. "It is great, yes. But Bill suggested we take extra precautions until then."

"I don't understand," Donna murmured.

"If Simson knows he's going down, he'll make every last-ditch stand against us that he can," Luke explained.

Andrew stood up and tossed another log on the fire. "Good," he said flatly, "at least it will be over with." He met his brother's eyes and knew that this had been one of those times when Luke had known the subject matter of his conversation before he had been told. He needed to talk to Luke alone.

If he had any streak of psychic awareness, it was in knowing when his brother did.

Donna and Lorna were talked into going up to bed first. Luke and Andrew smiled as they watched them go. The brothers walked into the kitchen, and as soon as they were there, Luke turned around and gripped Andrew's shoulders.

"Don't take her out shooting again until after Christmas."

Andrew swallowed. "What's up?"

"I think Flaherty is right. I don't know when or what, but I get pictures of the yard. Something happening."

Andrew sat down at the table and raked his fingers

249

through his hair. "Maybe you were all right. Maybe we should call in a magazine and get someone to do an article stating that neither Donna nor Lorna have anything to say that could possibly hold up in court. Maybe we should do something to end it before—"

"No, Andrew."

"I guess not," Andrew said with a sigh.

"All we have to do is make the two of them be careful."

Andrew sat back, gazing at his brother. "Luke, you could be a target too."

"Drew, I've spent almost as much time on the streets as you have. I know what I'm doing."

Andrew laughed. "I'm not always sure that I do."

"You'd be the better target, brother. You were the investigating police officer. But . . ."

"But what?"

"I'm really not worried about either of us."

"Donna and Lorna?"

"Yes. We have to keep them in the house and away from the windows."

Andrew twisted uneasily. "Lorna's big on those shooting lessons. And she's stubborn. Of course, Donna is too. How have you managed to keep her inside all this time?"

Luke grinned. "It's easy. I just remind her about the baby."

"Oh." Andrew drummed his fingers on the table. "Well, that one's out for me."

"For life?" Luke raised a brow and Andrew saw that he was laughing.

"Is this the proper time for a discussion on my life? If it would save her life, I'd do anything. I'd tie her to a tree and make love to her ten times a day. But it's too late, and it wouldn't—what kind of a priest are you, anyway?"

250

"Your brother. Of course, in such a situation, I would suggest the sanctity of marriage."

"Great." Andrew groaned. "But for now, you've just got to help me convince her that she shouldn't go outside for any reason."

"Lorna isn't stupid, Andrew. She'll understand."

"Yeah, I guess so."

Luke and Andrew parted for the night, going to their respective rooms.

Lorna had been half asleep, but Andrew woke her. He made love to her with a tender ferocity she couldn't begin to understand.

He wasn't terribly sure that he understood himself.

Lorna stared at him a little blankly the next morning when Andrew explained that they shouldn't go outside the house at all.

"There has to be at least an acre between the house and the fence," she told him, frowning.

They were sitting around the kitchen table eating breakfast. Luke smiled at Lorna. "There's no cover once you're outside, Lorna. And if someone should breech the fence, or even if they didn't, and they had the right weaponry . . . well, it isn't for that much longer. When Flaherty called Drew, he said the next weeks might be the desperate ones. We have to think the same way."

Lorna nodded. She turned to Donna and asked her if she wanted help with the accounting books. Donna said she'd be grateful for any help.

They left the kitchen together and Andrew stared at Luke.

"What's the secret? How come she listens to you without a word?"

Luke shrugged. "Maybe it's because I'm a priest. Or

251

maybe I just have a more charming way of saying things. You know, low tone, friendly smile."

Andrew laughed. "Sure, you just reek charm."

"To tell you the truth, she's a bright woman and she would have listened to either of us. I just happened to offer the explanation first," Luke replied.

Tension mounted in the days that followed. Lorna wondered how it could be so close to Christmas and things could be so miserable among all of them at the same time. She and Andrew were snapping at each other, Luke and Donna were ready to hop down one another's throats, and they were all ready to mix and match their arguments.

Lorna decided that there was only one "person" in the house she was really getting along with, and that wasn't a person at all; it was George. He was always at her feet, except for those times when he got to go outside and chase rabbits. She shook her head sadly at the turn of events. She would never have believed that she could be envious of a German shepherd, but she was envious of George for having the liberty to chase rabbits in the fresh air and sunshine.

Two days after the phone call from Flaherty, one of the rangers called to tell them they had arrested another drifter with a rifle near the fence. During the same afternoon Tricia called Andrew. He was going to have to return to New York the first week of January to prepare for the trial. Luke, Donna, and Lorna didn't have to be there until the twentieth.

The four carried on a subdued discussion and decided they would all return to Luke's house. For some reason, after that conversation, things started going a little better again.

Lorna and Andrew sat before the fire for a long time that night, talking about the upcoming trial. His arm was around her as they watched the flames, and Lorna voiced her fear that it would never end.

"Suppose the jury does find him guilty on two counts of murder. They'll put him away, but he'll eventually be eligible for parole. Does that mean we have to worry about him all over again? Or even before then? As long as he's still alive, he can have visitors. Maybe he'll even keep people coming after us."

Andrew squeezed her shoulder. "It's not that bad, Lorna, really it isn't. Just because a man is eligible for parole doesn't mean that he's going to get it. Besides, if Flaherty succeeds with his plans, Simson will be broke—and broken."

"*If* Flaherty succeeds," Lorna murmured. But she smiled because Andrew was trying so hard and because she loved him whether they argued or not. "We should do something for Bill, Andrew. But what does one do for a man who really, truly has everything?"

Andrew shook his head. "I don't know, but you're right. We owe William Flaherty." He snapped his fingers. "Dinner! We'll invite him and his family for dinner."

"Dinner? Andrew, he could go to any restaurant in the world."

"Ah, but there's still nothing like a home-cooked meal prepared with love."

"Think so, huh?"

"I know so."

Lorna was quiet for a minute. "Are we having him to dinner in Paxton or New York?"

"New York? Luke's house?" he suggested. Lorna was quiet. His arm tightened around her. "You don't like New York, do you?"

Lorna looked into his eyes. "You're wrong. I love New York."

" 'To visit, not to live in,' " Andrew quoted dryly.

253

Lorna shrugged. "I don't know . . ." Her voice trailed away, then she started as George began to bark furiously.

Andrew was instantly on his feet. "What is it, boy, what's up?"

George kept barking while he bounded past them for the kitchen door. Andrew, who had been walking around in his socks, grabbed his shoes and the gun that was always discreetly near.

Lorna, too, hopped to her feet. "Andrew, what are you doing?"

He glanced her way quickly. "I'm going out with George."

"Andrew, no."

Luke Trudeau was coming down the stairs. "What's going on?"

"I don't know. George seems to think that something is up," Andrew replied.

Luke nodded. "I'm coming with you."

Donna was right behind him. "No, Luke, that's foolish. Both of you are always so worried, and you want to leave us both behind? Call the rangers—"

"Good idea," Andrew interrupted her. "Lorna, call the rangers." He and Luke were already headed for the front door.

"Wait!" Lorna called out. "This doesn't make—"

"Here." Luke stopped by her side and stuffed something cold and metallic in her hand. It was a gun, smaller than Andrew's. She gazed at Luke in surprise; she'd never thought of him owning a gun. She knew that he could be a tough man, but she also knew that he was a man of God in the deepest sense.

He was also protecting his wife and their unborn child.

"It works just like Andrew's," he said. "You aim

and squeeze the trigger. If someone comes after you, don't hesitate."

Andrew opened the door. George, barking furiously, bounded out into the night.

Lorna turned around. Donna was already on the phone at the foot of the staircase, trying to call the rangers. Luke and Andrew were gone.

"Oh, my God!" Donna gasped.

"What?" Lorna demanded.

"There's something wrong. The phone doesn't work."

"What do you mean, it doesn't work?" Lorna ran to Donna and wrenched the receiver from her hands. There was nothing, just a dead silence.

"The wires must have been cut," Donna murmured.

The two of them sank to the bottom step. "We have to tell them somehow," Lorna muttered.

"They're gone."

A Bing Crosby recording was playing Christmas carols on the stereo. Nothing had ever seemed so incongruous to Lorna in her life.

Lorna sighed nervously. "I guess we don't go out. We might only put them in greater danger."

"We don't go out," Donna echoed. "What do we do?"

"Uh, let's go make coffee," Lorna said. She stood, suddenly very decisive. "Yes, we make coffee. And the kitchen will be the best place to be. We can watch the living-room entrance and the back door at the same time. Come on."

Donna, clutching her robe tightly, followed Lorna into the kitchen. She sat at the table, facing the living room, as Lorna put Luke's gun on the counter and started fiddling with the coffeepot. She spilled coffee all over the counter.

She and Donna didn't try to talk. Their friendship

was too close for the need of meaningless conversation. The coffee began to perk.

"I hear George barking," Donna finally murmured.

Lorna frowned. The barking seemed very close to the house.

"Maybe Luke and Andrew are on their way back," she said.

The coffee finished dripping. Lorna started to pour two cups, but suddenly there was a shattering noise at the back door. Lorna dropped the coffeepot. The glass cracked and split on the counter, spilling coffee everywhere.

She didn't even notice. The bolt on the rear door had been broken by a gunshot. A small dark man was standing on the threshold, raising the gun he had just used to smash the lock. The house alarm was shrilling and Lorna knew that the alarms in the ranger station and the nearest police headquarters would be going off as well.

But none of those alarms would help her and Donna, because the man was there and his arm was moving.

Lorna screamed and scrambled for Luke's gun. She knew that the stranger could squeeze his trigger long before she could squeeze hers, but she kept screaming as she moved, her heart pounding furiously as she denied the death she was facing. . . .

She cringed, expecting the explosion, but there was none. She had her gun in her hand and someone was screaming, but it wasn't her. There was a blur of motion at the door, a furious growl, and the man was down in the doorway. George!

The man's gun went off. Lorna heard her own gun explode and then the man screamed.

And there was chaos at the door. She stared at her

gun in horror. She stared at the door. Luke was there, and Andrew, and two rangers.

She had nicked the man's arm. He was gripping it and rolling in the doorway, screaming out his pain. One of the rangers was calling for help on a walkie-talkie.

She dropped the gun.

Luke was rushing into the room, sweeping Donna into his arms, holding her. Lorna kept staring at the door. Andrew's eyes caught hers, but he didn't come to her, not right away. He was bending down. She couldn't see what he was doing.

One of the rangers had pulled the small dark man to his feet. Despite the wound, they were leading him away. Andrew stood, a taut and strained look on his features as he approached her.

"Lorna." He started to take her into his arms, but as she fell into them, she saw past his shoulder.

She broke away from him, understanding his look.

George was lying in the doorway, a dark-red stain spreading over his shoulder.

Lorna started to scream again as she raced to the dog and fell to her knees beside him.

"George! George, George . . ."

But George didn't move. Lorna put her arms around him gently, lightly resting her head against his furry neck. Sobs shook her, wracking her from head to toe. She wasn't thinking then, not logically. She couldn't be grateful that the dog had died to save their lives. All she knew at that moment was that the shepherd's life and blood were draining away on the floor. The great heart that had loved her, protected her to the last call of loyalty, would beat no more.

For Lorna, it was the breaking point. Her sobs rose and rose.

Andrew came to her. He tried to pull her away from

the dog, tried to tell her that it would be all over now, that they were all safe and well.

"Lorna—"

"No!" She screamed. "No! He's dead, he's dead. None of this was his doing, or his fault. Just leave me alone! Leave me alone!" She wrenched herself from his hold, tore from the kitchen, and raced up the stairs to throw herself on the bed where she continued to cry in terrible, hysterical gulps.

In the kitchen, Andrew stared at the door, his features strained and twisted with his misery. He clenched his fists and unclenched them, wondering with a sick heart whether to go after her or not. Tears stung his eyes. He walked to the door, turned around, walked back again.

Luke gripped his arm.

"Andrew, let me talk to her for a minute."

Andrew gazed at Luke as if he didn't see him.

"Andrew," Luke persisted. At last Andrew swallowed and nodded. Luke glanced at Donna. She, too, nodded imperceptibly, then Luke started for the stairs.

Donna walked to Andrew and gave him a little hug. "She'll be okay, Andrew."

Andrew nodded.

"I think I'm going to fix us all a brandy," Donna murmured. Mechanically, Andrew nodded again. Donna slipped away from him. He heard her opening the cabinet doors.

"Lieutenant, you're going to have to come to the police station with us." There was still a ranger standing discreetly in the door.

Andrew turned around. "Yes," he murmured. "But we're going to have to get the door fixed, and I'm going to want men right at the house, both doors covered."

258

"It's already being taken care of, Lieutenant," the young ranger told him.

"Thanks," Andrew murmured. He walked jerkily to the door, but he didn't follow the ranger.

He knelt down by the dog and put his hand against the blood-stained fur. "You were the best, George. The absolute best."

He frowned, sensing something. It seemed as if the fur rose a little. A brown eye opened, then closed. "George?"

Andrew no longer felt the slight movement, and yet . . . the dog had opened an eye.

"Donna, get me a blanket, quick!" Andrew gazed at the ranger. "I need a vet, or a hospital. Hell, I don't care which—we've got to get him somewhere."

Donna brought the afghan from the living-room couch. "Andrew," she said softly. "Andrew, look at the blood. He can't possibly make it."

Andrew stared up into her eyes. "I've got to try, Donna."

She gripped his hand, smiled sympathetically, and nodded.

"Help me," he told the ranger. The young man stooped beside him and together they lifted the shepherd.

He was very, very heavy. Like dead weight, Andrew thought sickly. But George had opened an eye, and Andrew could still hear Lorna's echoing cries in his mind.

How much could anyone take, even a strong woman like Lorna? The dog just might mean everything now. And hadn't Luke always told him that miracles could only occur to those who believed in them?

CHAPTER TWELVE

By the time Luke reached Lorna, she was lying on the bed, staring silently up at the ceiling. She heard the soft knock at the door but didn't feel capable of reacting. A few seconds later she heard the door open. She knew that it was Luke. She was aware, but just couldn't really care when he came in to the room and sat at the foot of the bed.

"Lorna." Her name seemed to hang in the air for a long time. He moved closer to her and took her hand. "Talk to me, Lorna. Are you all right?"

She started to nod, but when she nodded, she burst into tears again. Then she found that she was in his arms, shaking and crying, and that he was whispering soothing words. And then she realized that she was crying over a dog when Luke had once lost a wife to the whim of the same killer.

"Oh, Luke, I'm sorry, I've no right . . ."

He held her from him and smiled. " 'All creatures great and small,' " he quoted. "George was loyal and loving, the very best of many things. It wouldn't be right if you didn't mourn him."

"But April . . ." Lorna began miserably. She had never seen Luke lose control; he never brought his personal tragedy to others.

"April would have felt the same, Lorna. When we were first married, April's mother warned me that she was soft-hearted. When she was a child, she used to cry when the Christmas tree died. It got so bad they had to buy a fake tree. She brought home strays and nursed them. Even in New York, she'd find pigeons with broken wings and I frequently opened a drawer to find she'd made it into a bed for an orphaned kitten."

Lorna watched Luke curiously. She'd never heard him speak about the wife he had lost.

"How do you stand it?" she whispered.

Luke shrugged, offering her a half smile that was heart-wrenchingly like his brother's. "I'm a priest, Lorna. I couldn't preach about faith if I didn't have any. Of course, I am human. I had my nights of torment, and at times I was ready to turn against God. It happens to everyone at some point in life. But . . . I do believe, you see, so I was able to know that April was in a finer place, loved by her Maker." His gentle smile grew. "And then there was Donna. But you must know that yourself. You've lost a husband who was young."

Lorna nodded slowly, then admitted, "But I wonder if it was the same. I loved Jerry very much, but I just don't believe that we ever had the closeness that you're talking about. This sounds terrible, but there was something different when . . ."

She allowed her voice to trail away. This was Andrew's brother she was talking to!

Luke chuckled softly, wiping a tear from her cheek. "There was something different about Andrew, I take it? Love is different, Lorna. One never replaces the other, but each has its separate beauties. You're very much in love with him, aren't you?"

Lorna hesitated, then nodded.

Luke lowered his head for a minute. When he raised it, she saw a golden sparkle in his eyes. "Remember that I'm a priest, Lorna. The secrets of the confessional are safe with me."

Lorna managed a smile in return. "Episcopal priests don't go to the confessional."

"Sure they do, those who choose to."

"All right, you want a confession, Father? From the first time I saw Andrew, I had the strangest feeling. I felt as if I had waited my entire life to meet him. Does that sound crazy?"

"Not to me." Luke grinned.

"But I keep wondering if there's any future in it."

"There's always a future, if you choose it to be so."

Lorna shook her head, afraid she was going to start crying again. "I don't know, Luke. I don't know if there's a future at all. Everything is so . . . wrong. I met him because of a murder, and we're together now because of attempted murder, and George is—but George made us a family, somehow. I just feel so horrible about everything, and tonight I feel that it can never be better."

"But, Lorna, it is better tonight. It's over."

Lorna's eyes widened. "How can you say that, Luke? We've still got the trial to go through."

"Lorna—" Luke hesitated, then smiled. "You have faith in me, don't you?"

She smiled. "Yes."

"Then trust me. Intuition. It's over. This was Simson's last, desperate attempt. It failed and it's over."

"I hope you're right, Luke. I pray you're right."

"I am right. I'm so sure that—that I intend to go back to New York tomorrow." He grinned. "I'm an Episcopalian priest and it's almost Christmas, my hottest season of the year! And here I am with two Roman Catholic beauties."

"Flattery!" Lorna accused him, and she was able to laugh.

"Well, the flattery is true, but so is the problem. I want to go home. And I feel so strongly that it's all right that I'm going to."

Lorna hesitated. "What do you think Andrew will say?"

"I think he'll agree with me. But you'll do what he says, won't you?"

"I—yes, I guess I will."

"Why don't you marry him, Lorna?"

She stared down at her hands. "He hasn't asked me, Luke."

"Maybe he needs a little prodding. And maybe—well, maybe he's a little afraid of you and your answer. You know, he had some strange reactions to you too. I think he's always put you on a little cloud, perhaps a shade higher than mortals. And it was hard for him because he wasn't accustomed to worrying about rejection."

"But—"

"Lorna, you are very lovely and very elegant. And independent. You have your own life and you're well established in a different state. I don't think that he could give up what he is, and maybe he feels that he should—for you."

"But I wouldn't ask that!"

Luke grinned. "Tell him. Let him know."

Lorna smiled. "Maybe I will, Luke." She took a deep breath. "I'm okay now. Really, I am. And you've got a wife downstairs who is all alone. Go back to Donna, Luke."

"We can all go downstairs, Lorna, and wait for Andrew to get back. There's no reason for you to be alone."

"I want to be alone right now." She impulsively set her hands on his shoulders and kissed his cheek. "Thank you, Luke. You've—you've always been around when I needed someone. But I am okay. I want you to go to your Donna, okay?"

"Okay. But if you do need anyone, just yell."

"I will."

"Good night, then."

"Good night, Luke."

When Luke left, Lorna stared at the ceiling a while longer. She no longer felt hysterical, but there was a dull pain in her heart, a void in the spot that had held her love for the loyal German shepherd. After talking to Luke, she knew that it was right; she would miss George for a long, long time.

Finally she rolled from the bed. She took a long, hot shower, slipped into a flannel gown, and climbed back into bed. But she didn't sleep. She waited.

The hands on the bedside clock had climbed around to four A.M. before the door to the bedroom at last opened and Andrew came in.

The room was dark but he didn't turn on the light. He closed the door quietly and, just as quietly, began to take off his clothes. He crawled into the bed beside Lorna, trying not to waken her. She felt an incredibly light stroke against her hair, then his arm settled tenderly around her.

She shifted, meeting his eyes in the darkness. "I'm awake, Andrew."

His knuckles brushed her cheek. "Are you all right, Lorna? I'm sorry, so very sorry."

Lorna caught his hand and kissed the knuckles that had brushed her cheek. "I'm all right, Andrew. Really, I am."

His arm came around her and he cradled her close. She laid her head against his chest. If she stroked him, she knew that she would find strength. If she touched his face, she would find the character there, sometimes rough and sometimes tender, but each was a part of the man she loved. She felt his fingers smoothing over her hair, and she knew that his eyes were open to the night.

"Luke wants to go back to New York tomorrow," Lorna said.

"I know."

"You do?"

"He and Donna were downstairs. They waited for me, just in case you did need company."

"Oh," Lorna murmured. Tears stung her eyes, and she didn't really know why, except that it was nice to have friends who cared so dearly.

"And?"

He shifted slightly beneath her. She felt the rise and fall of his breath, and the warmth of his flesh.

"I think it might be best. Luke says that it's over. I still want to be careful, but I do have lots of friends in New York, lots of protection." His arms tightened a little convulsively around her, then relaxed again, as if he had made the firm effort for them to do so. "I want you to stay at Luke's, though. I think we should be together to make it all easier. I—Lorna . . . do you think that you could possibly live with me . . . after the trial?"

She smiled and moved her lips to press a kiss against his chest. The hair tickled her cheek, and she rubbed it against him. She knew that her heart was pounding like his.

"Andrew, I know that ours has been an unusual affair."

"Meaning?" She heard the huskiness of his tone, the catch in his throat.

At last she rose from his chest, planting her hand upon it to raise above him and challenge his eyes. "Andrew, I don't want to 'live' with you."

His eyes began to darken and narrow; in a minute she knew he would turn away.

Lorna moved her hands to his shoulders and shook him. Or tried to shake him, he was a little too solid to really shake.

"Andrew! Damn it, when are you going to ask me to marry you?" she demanded in whispered frustration.

A green sparkle seemed to glitter from his eyes. His breath seemed to—to stop.

"Would you do that, Lorna? Would you leave your home behind and . . . come to be with me, as my wife?"

"Yes."

"Are you sure?"

"Yes."

"Lorna, do you really know what you're saying?"

"Yes, Andrew."

"Oh, my God . . ." His arms encircled her tightly. He kissed her forehead and then he rolled with her, kissing her cheeks, pressing his head to her breasts, kissing her forehead again, then her cheeks and at last her lips. There was nothing fevered to that kiss, it was slow and gentle and beautifully fulfilling.

His eyes met hers. "Do you really mean it?"

"Yes."

"I'm the one asking you to give everything up."

"A hundred percent," Lorna agreed with a smile.

"What?"

She shook her head. "Just something Donna said. It's my turn to give you the hundred percent. Of course, you'll have to watch out, because somewhere along the line you'll have to give a hundred percent."

"You've got a hundred percent," he whispered, brushing her lips with his. "A hundred percent of my love, my loyalty, everything I can ever give you."

Lorna pressed a finger to his lips. "Andrew, it's my choice to do this. I want to be your wife, and I don't ever want to make you choose between me and your career. It wouldn't be right."

"Lorna, I'll spend more time in the precinct on desk work. I want to."

"Thank you," she murmured softly, then she smiled. "I'm just glad that you also want a wife!"

"I didn't know that I did until I realized I would be empty without you. And then I was afraid. I mean, we were always honest, and you honestly didn't want a cop."

Lorna laughed. "Well, I don't want a cop. I want you, and you just happen to be a cop. And I do love you for all that you are, Andrew. I think that's what I've realized."

"I love you, Lorna. I'll be fanatically neat, I promise."

"You don't have to be. I'm fanatically neat enough for both of us."

"We'll find a place for you. New York can really be a wonderful place for an antique store. And I'll be glad to go on your buying trips. We'll see a lot of the country together."

"You don't have to."

"With your penchant for trouble? I'll never let you go off by yourself!"

"Never?"

"Never, not even when you're an old, old lady!"

Lorna curled her fingers tightly into his hair and pulled him to her. She kissed each corner of his mouth. "We'll work things out, Andrew. Because we want to."

"Yes." He smiled and scooped his arms around her again, holding her to him. "Look at Luke and Donna. Every Sunday he goes to church to preach and she goes to mass at a different church. And they're perfectly happy. She goes to all his functions, and though they're not the same, they're as close as one. Lorna, the secret is in caring and in respecting. To the hundredth percentile, I promise that I'll always care."

She ran her fingers over his chest. "Do you think it's possible that we could find a place with a little yard?"

"Sure, grass does grow in New York."

"It does? You'll have to show me."

"Wise guy. I will."

Lorna was still for a minute. "You know, I wanted to keep George. I knew that he was a police dog, but I was going to ask you if there was any way . . . I guess the yard doesn't matter so much now. I just kept thinking that you needed a bit of a yard for a German shepherd."

Andrew was silent, but she felt his hands running along her back, tender and warm and intimate, despite the flannel of her gown.

"We'll be happy, Lorna," he promised.

"Can I have a wedding just like Donna's?" she asked. "A silver-gray gown, I think, and your brother and a Catholic priest to officiate. I want your family, and I want the Miros, and I want a guitarist to play, and a flutist and—"

"And you can have anything that you want. I'll be there early. When?"

Lorna hesitated. "After the trial."

"That long?"

"I just think it would be best. I want to start off married life with everything bad behind us."

"Whatever you want," he told her again. He continued to hold her, lovingly, quietly, tenderly.

Lorna raised herself and smiled at him. "Andrew?"

"What?"

"You're not very good at hints."

"Hints?"

"I want to make love."

He laughed. "I was trying to be gentle and reasonable. It's been such a bad night."

"That's why I need you," Lorna told him.

Her words were all he needed. He cupped her face between his hands and kissed her deeply. Then she felt his fingers coursing along her thighs, lifting her gown from her.

His warmth became a blazing heat; his tenderness turned to passion. As his mouth found her breasts and grazed them with liquid kisses, the tips of his fingers raked along her inner thighs. Lorna reached out for him, touching him, goading him, freely whispering of her love and desire. His mouth continued to rake her body with fiery ecstacy and a delicious fever consumed her. She could never get enough of him, his scent, his taste, the delicious ripple of muscle beneath the touch of her hands and lips.

Then at last he came to her, lifting her above him, guiding her hips and kneading her buttocks until the fever mounted. They twisted together, entwining ardently with all their love and need.

And through it all she knew the greatest thrill and wonder; she was going to be his wife.

Passion, tenderness, laughter, and tears . . . moments of ecstacy, moments of peace . . . for a lifetime.

She had always known it was meant to be. She just hadn't known how right it was to trust her own heart. And his.

It was Christmas Eve morning and they were all at Luke's house in New York City. Lorna awoke with a smile. She had insisted that she and Andrew keep separate rooms—Luke was, after all, a priest. No one had really argued, and Lorna knew that the propriety was right.

But Andrew still slipped into her room at night like a sweet dream that came with darkness and disappeared with the morning light. Lorna knew he just left her; his side of the bed was still warm.

She jumped out of bed and hurried to the window. New York had received a snowfall during the night and Luke's small lawn was covered with white. Beyond the lawn she saw two men, blowing warmth into their gloved hands as they walked back and forth.

Policemen, she knew, keeping watch. Andrew's friends.

As Luke had prophesized, things were very quiet. But by order and by choice, policemen were guarding the Trudeau household.

Christmas Eve. She felt wonderful. The trial was still before them but, as she never had before, Lorna felt a complete faith that things were going to work out.

She dressed hurriedly in a long wool skirt and sweater; they had all promised to help Luke out at St. Philip's. She and Donna had decided to attend midnight mass at Luke's church, then attend Catholic services in the morning. Lorna had always wanted to go to St. Patrick's Cathedral for a service and Donna had thought it a wonderful idea. Luke had even arranged for Father Pat to officiate at the eleven o'clock service so that he could accompany his wife.

Giving, Lorna thought, really learning how to give was the mystery that those two had deciphered.

She brushed her hair and hurried down the hall to the kitchen. Luke's housekeeper, Mary, was there, helping Donna with breakfast.

Andrew was on the phone and Luke was standing beside him, listening.

270

Andrew saw Lorna and beckoned to her as he listened. Curious, she went to him. He slipped an arm around her, thanked whoever he was talking to, and hung up. Then he laughed and kissed her soundly.

"Andrew!" Luke said with exasperation. "What did he say?"

"What did who say?" Lorna demanded.

Donna looked over her shoulder from her place at the oven. "It was William Flaherty, Lorna. Andrew, come on, what did he say?"

Andrew kept laughing and he swept Lorna in a circle before answering.

"He said . . ."

"Andrew!" Lorna pleaded.

"He said that he did some debt maneuvering, and he now owns Simson's company and Simson is very close to destitute. He's spent an awful lot of money on attorney fees and trying to get us. In fact, he went so far with his expenditures that he couldn't bail out when Bill Flaherty started his financial attack. Hal Simson is going to be lucky to retain his attorneys for the trial."

"Hallelujah!" Donna cried.

"What a Christmas present!" Luke murmured.

"Amen," Lorna agreed. "Oh, Andrew!"

Andrew turned to the others. "Donna, have we got a few minutes before breakfast? We should be helping, but—"

"Go talk to Lorna. You two can help Mary with dinner."

Andrew smiled and pulled Lorna down the hall and into Luke's den. He drew a small box from his pocket and handed it to her, stuffing his hands back into his pockets after he had done so.

"I know it's early," he told her, "but I've got another present on the way, and I thought this one might pale beside it, so I wanted you to see this first."

"Pale?" Lorna murmured. She began to tear at the wrappings to reveal a small jeweler's case. Opening it, she found a small diamond surrounded by delicate gold sculpture and tiny sapphire chips. She gazed at Andrew, her breath stopping along with the beat of her heart. Then her breath came in gulps along with a hammering thunder from her heart.

"Andrew, it's the most beautiful ring I've ever seen. No gift could make this pale. It's my engagement ring and it means I'm about to be your wife, and what on earth could be more wonderful?" She went into his arms and kissed him soundly.

"I'm glad you like it," he told her huskily. "Donna gave me the size, so I hope it's right."

"Try it."

He slipped the ring on her finger. It dazzled beautifully in the morning sunlight filtering through the windows.

"Oh, Andrew!" She threw her arms around him again and kissed him. She heard a chiming sound. Did you really hear bells when you were this much in love? she wondered.

Andrew unwound her arms from his neck. She couldn't understand why.

"Bells," she murmured.

"The doorbell, airhead," he murmured affectionately.

"Airhead," she began to protest.

He laughed. "Don't yell at me until we get the door. It should be a couple of old friends."

Lorna frowned, then followed him as he stepped back into the hall and walked to the front door. Andrew opened it and she saw Tricia, his old partner. Tricia kissed Andrew's cheek with a "Merry Christmas," then greeted Lorna with "Lorna! Merry Christmas, and the very best to you both!"

Lorna accepted the woman's hug with only slight misgivings of jealousy. Tricia was very, very pretty. And she and Andrew were friends. Good friends. But Andrew was capable of friendship and love. Lorna knew that she had his love.

"Merry Christmas, and thanks so much," she told Tricia.

Tricia smiled, as if she were aware it was natural that Lorna would be wondering at her appearance. "I've brought one of your presents," she explained. "Sergeant Wilkes and I, that is."

"Sergeant Wilkes?" Lorna murmured, and then she saw that Wilkes was walking toward the door carrying a huge bundle of fur. The fur whined.

"Where can I put him, Lieutenant?" Wilkes was asking Andrew. "He's still got to be kept quiet."

Lorna cried out with incredulous joy, searching Andrew's eyes for reassurance that she wasn't dreaming.

"In the den, please," Andrew told Sergeant Wilkes. He found Lorna's gaze on him and smiled. "It *is* George, Lorna. There was a vet in South Carolina who was a miracle worker. I couldn't tell you that night because we didn't know if George would survive the surgery. He'll never be completely well again. He's always going to have a limp and he'd never be up to police duty again, but . . . he is George, Lorna. He is the same dog."

She looked at Sergeant Wilkes, who was carrying the massive shepherd down the hall. She looked at Andrew, raced to him and kissed him feverishly, then followed Sergeant Wilkes.

"Oh, thank you!" she cried, bending down to the bed of blankets on the floor where the sergeant set George. George woofed and licked her full in the face.

273

She embraced his neck carefully. "George, oh, George, it's so good to have you back."

She felt a presence beside her. Andrew. She kissed the man and hugged the dog at the same time.

"I told you a diamond would pale in comparison," Andrew said lightly. Tears were streaming down Lorna's cheeks, and she was laughing.

"It didn't pale, not in the least. But, George! Oh, Andrew."

Sergeant Wilkes cleared his throat. "Excuse me, ma'am. George is going to need lots of care for a while."

"He'll get it, Sergeant," Lorna vowed. "He'll get it." She smiled at Andrew, then hugged the dog again.

"You've got hairs all over your sweater," Andrew teased her.

"They're George's hair," Lorna retorted, "and he can shed on my sweaters any time he wants."

She heard the soft sound of Donna's laughter in the room. "You know, I was thinking lately how wonderful it was going to be because our children will be cousins. But it seems like I'm going to get to be the aunt of a bundle of fur called George."

Lorna grinned at Andrew. "Oh, we'll give you and Luke some regular nieces and nephews somewhere along the line. But for now, George, say hello to Auntie Donna."

"I asked for that one!" Donna laughed. "Well, coffee and fresh doughnuts in the kitchen, guys." She hesitated. Luke was behind her with his arms around her waist. "What do you think they mean by somewhere along the line?"

Andrew was watching Lorna as she hugged the dog. He raised a brow and smiled. "Whenever Lorna chooses, Donna." He lowered his voice. "A hundred percent—when she chooses."

Lorna smiled. "Tell your sister-in-law, umm, not before a year and a half, not later than three. But only if that makes you happy too."

"It makes me happy." Andrew looked at Donna. "Not before a year and a half—"

"I heard her!" Donna groaned. "Tricia, would you mind helping me with the coffee?"

"Not at all. I think we should leave the happy couple alone with your nephew."

The others left the room. George kept thumping his tail as Lorna and Andrew shared another kiss.

They'd all known it was coming. Christmas and the New Year were locked in happiness, but afterward it was time to begin the preparations for the trial.

By the time the first day arrived, the newspapers had been carrying the story for weeks. The networks had been scrambling for the rights to a film and they had all been rejected.

It was expected that the trial would go on for weeks, possibly months. And then, of course, if the jury found Simson guilty and he decided to appeal the decision, the case might linger on for years.

Lorna wasn't with Andrew in the courtroom. He was with Tricia and a number of other officers who had worked on the case. She was sitting with Donna and Luke. Their testimony probably wouldn't come for several days.

But they weren't alone. The courtroom was filled with curiosity seekers, law students, and the like. But it was also filled with friends. Three rows of seats were filled with Episcopal clergymen showing their support for Luke. Worcester police had been called in to support the conspiracy charge, rangers had come in from South Carolina, and William Flaherty was there.

He had seen Lorna from the courtroom door, waved

to her, and then threaded his way through the crowd to be with her. He held her hand when the judge entered and they rose, then sat again, and listened as the proceedings began.

"You've been a good friend," she told him, "the best."

"It's been my pleasure. But I had a vested interest since Penny was one of his victims. I'm just glad I could be of help."

They smiled at one another, then fell silent. The attorneys were giving their opening statements, long speeches, but at last they finished and Andrew was called to the stand.

Lorna was very proud of him as he spoke. He never faltered; he was always certain. His memory of all the events in the investigation was detailed and flawless, and she knew that he was making quite an impression on the jury.

As she watched him, she felt a strange wave of coldness, an uneasiness sweep over her. She turned her head slightly and discovered that Hal Simson was staring at her from his place at the defendant's table. The cold fear that hit her was a terrible thing. He was just staring emotionlessly, and for a time she couldn't tear her eyes away.

He said something to his attorney, and not even then could Lorna turn away.

"I wonder what's happening," Flaherty murmured.

"What?"

"Counsel is approaching the bench," Flaherty replied.

A few minutes later court was recessed. Lorna rose with Luke, Donna, and Bill, and they filed out of the courtroom.

She felt that horrible cold again and turned around. Simson was right behind her.

"Mrs. Doria, I'd like a word with you."

Her throat seemed to lock, and her blood congealed. It was Simson talking to her. There was a guard on either side of him, and still she was terrified beyond reason. Luke, a few steps ahead, had seen the interaction and was trying to get to her. But Lorna couldn't move away. She just stood there, listening as Simson began to talk.

"You've all won, it seems," Simson said. His eyes were still on her in that strange fashion; he neither smiled nor frowned. "I just wanted you to know that it was never personal."

The guards led him away. Lorna still hadn't moved. Bill was beside her, then Donna was there, and Luke, putting an arm around her shaking shoulders.

"What did he say to you?" Luke demanded.

"I—I don't think I really understood him. He said it wasn't personal."

"Lorna! Lorna!"

Lorna turned around. The halls were full of people, with police, reporters and cameras. Through them all, she saw Andrew, grinning broadly, trying to weave his broad shoulders through the milling people to reach them.

Finally he did. He lifted Lorna off her feet and into his arms. "It's over! Oh, my God, it's really, truly, over!"

"What?" Lorna was still up in the air, bracing herself against his shoulders and staring down into his eyes in confusion.

"What?" Luke tugged his brother around. Andrew slowly lowered Lorna, keeping an arm tightly around her.

"Simson has opted to confess! A full confession. His attorneys told him it was the best move he could make at this point. If he wanted to live to make any kind of parole, which probably won't happen, anyway. Don't you understand? He's confessed! It's all over, except for the sentencing."

There were several moments of incredulous silence. Then Luke began to laugh, relief sweeping the burden of pain and determination from his shoulders. He grabbed Donna and hugged her. Then he grabbed Flaherty and hugged him and Bill started to laugh too.

Lorna discovered that Andrew's eyes were on her again. She met them, feeling as dizzy with relief as Luke.

"Oh, Andrew, really? Can it really be over? Just like that?"

"Really," he said tenderly. "We do have a lifetime, Lorna. No more terror. It's finished."

They kept staring at one another until Luke tugged Andrew's arm. "Come on. Let's get out of here before the reporters get around to us."

"Right!" Andrew grabbed Lorna's arm. "Come on!"

"I'm coming!" Lorna agreed. "Oh, Andrew, I want to go to Central Park. I want to run around in the sunshine. I want to go out to dinner, and I want to see a play. And I want to start looking for a new home with grass and trees—we have George to worry about, you know. I want—"

They left the court and the sunshine greeted them outside. Andrew pulled Lorna to a halt and stopped her flow of speech with a long kiss.

"I want to plan a wedding," he told her. "Hey, Luke!"

Luke and Donna, several steps ahead of them with Bill Flaherty, stopped and looked back.

"Luke," Andrew repeated, "think we could have the church for a Saturday wedding in two weeks?"

"For you, Andrew?" Luke retorted. "Definitely. I'll be rolling out the red carpet!"

Andrew grinned and his lips brushed Lorna's once again.

"Think we need a red carpet?"

Lorna gazed at him, and then at the clear, blue sky. She was very much aware of life all around her, and she was very much aware of Andrew, of his smile, his touch, and all the love he had.

"I don't think I need anything that I haven't got already," she told him. "But if Luke wants to give us a red carpet—"

"We'll take a red carpet."

"Exactly. But for now—"

"Let's go run around Central Park."

"Exactly."

He led her down the steps and into the future.

EPILOGUE

The strangest thing was that she knew it was a dream. She always knew that she was dreaming when she saw them.

She saw it all as one might see an old photograph. The center was clear, but the edges were blurred, framed by a gray mist.

She knew exactly what was going to happen, and in her sleep, she would begin to smile, reliving the sense of beauty, of wonder.

The church would be decked in flowers, full of color, a touch of spring against the winter cold. There would be music, a harmony of organ, flutes, and guitars. When she came down the aisle, faces would turn to her. Smiling faces, those of people she trusted and loved.

It was a dream that never entered a nightmare world; everything about it was soft and lovely.

She could see herself. The gown was made of a silvery gray silk and lace. There was a short veil, studded with pearls. She would never forget the veil, because Andrew had so much trouble with it when he had raised it to kiss her, and they had both laughed. Luke had laughed too, and even Donna, who had been crying sentimental tears, had laughed.

She could see so many things in the dream! The separate petals of a certain lily, the red carpet stretched down the aisle. And people. Bill Flaherty, who had come with his family, Theresa, Joe, and Tony, Andrew's parents and family, his friends, some in their police blues, Tricia and Sergeant Wilkes.

But mostly she could see Andrew. Very tall and broad-shouldered in a gray tuxedo, clean-shaven, his hair, as always, just a little long. His eyes were very, very green, dazzling as they met hers. His smile was just a little crooked, a little nervous . . .

Lorna could hear Luke's voice, strong and sure as he read the words to unite them for life. She could hear Andrew's responses. Low and husky, but unfaltering. From the sweet netherland of memory, she could remember his touch, his hands as he fit a simple band of gold over her finger.

His touch was strong and sure, as unfaltering as his voice, and as promising as the day.

A beautiful, beautiful dream, misted in memory, relived with the greatest feeling of peace and contentment. Fading now, but it would come again . . .

Lorna awoke with a little start, not at all sure why she had awakened. Then she smiled, because Andrew had twisted in his sleep and pulled her along with him.

His head was resting against hers and she could feel the silent whisper of his breath against the lobe of her ear. His arm was around her, his hand lay against her waist, pulling her to him even as he slept. His warmth was all around her.

Lorna closed her eyes again, her smile deepening. Dreams . . .

It was possible to live a nightmare; it was equally possible to know the realization of the sweetest dreams. Somewhere near the fire a German shepherd who ran with a noticeable limp was dozing. Outside, beyond the windows and frost, was a patch of land where green grass would grow in the spring.

And beside her . . .

Beside her lay Andrew. Her husband. Husband. The word was still so delicious to her that she could think it over and over again, and still marvel at the wonder of it. So much so that she turned with enthusiasm, leaned against him, and kissed him passionately.

He awoke, eyes only half open, curious, bemused, and yet touched with a dazzle of laughter. "Lorna?"

"Shhh," she whispered, "it's all part of a dream."

"A dream?" He still sounded confused, but then he shrugged and wrapped his arms around her. He kissed the corners of her lips, then her mouth in full.

"Ah. Well, then, let's get on with this dream, shall we?"

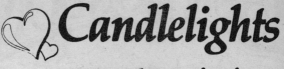

Catch up with any Candlelights you're missing.

Here are the Ecstasies published this past September.

ECSTASY SUPREMES $2.75 each

- [ ] **89 MORE THAN SHE BARGAINED FOR,** Lori Copeland . 15820-6-15
- [ ] **90 MAN OF THE HOUR,** Tate McKenna 15457-X-15
- [ ] **91 BENDING THE RULES,** Kathy Alerding 10755-5-15
- [ ] **92 JUST FOR THE ASKING,** Eleanor Woods 14405-1-52

ECSTASY ROMANCES $2.25 each

- [ ] **362 TOMORROW AND ALWAYS,** Nona Gamel 18987-X-26
- [ ] **363 STAND-IN LOVER,** Barbara Andrews 18276-X-34
- [ ] **364 TENDER GUARDIAN,** Cathie Linz 18645-5-38
- [ ] **365 THE TEMPTRESS TOUCH,** Lori Herter 18568-8-15
- [ ] **366 FOREST OF DREAMS,** Melanie Catley 12630-4-12
- [ ] **367 PERFECT ILLUSIONS,** Paula Hamilton 16907-0-27
- [ ] **368 BIRDS OF A FEATHER,** Linda Randall Wisdom . . 10558-7-22
- [ ] **369 LOST IN LOVE,** Alison Tyler 14983-5-11

At your local bookstore or use this handy coupon for ordering:

DELL READERS SERVICE—DEPT. BR811D
P.O. BOX 1000, PINE BROOK, N.J. 07058

Please send me the above title(s). I am enclosing $_____ (please add 75¢ per copy to cover postage and handling). Send check or money order—no cash or CODs. Please allow 3-4 weeks for shipment.
<u>CANADIAN ORDERS:</u> please submit in U.S. dollars.

Ms./Mrs./Mr._____

Address_____

City/State_____ Zip _____